MURDER FOR HEALTH AND FITNESS

NICK LENNON-BARRETT

FUNNY BOOK PRESS

I dedicate this book to my grandmothers Phyllis, and Marion, who taught me that life wasn't about sitting quietly in the corner

PROLOGUE

Slam!

Giselle lost her balance and knew it was over. *I'm going to die, and with shit hair!*

Why couldn't this have happened tomorrow after she'd had Maxine sort her out? The police were going to assume she was a whore - and a whore she was not... anymore, well not really. It depended what your definition of whore was.

She wouldn't cry out. It would give them a satisfaction they didn't deserve. There would be no pleading. Was she paying the ultimate price for being a complete bitch? She knew what people thought of her. That was who she was. She'd had to erect this defensive shield around her so the hurt would stop; she had done that for so long, she was incapable of feeling any form of human emotion. Happiness, sadness and even anger were not things that she allowed to occupy her mind. Now, she was feeling something she hadn't for years – fear. She knew she should not feel guilty about being afraid, yet she did; it was a sign of weakness. The blows were too severe for her to even contemplate fighting back and perhaps in the end they were doing her a favour. What sort of life had she had so far? What was there to look forward to? Just more of the same vicious cycle of being crapped on.

Now she was feeling anger. It wasn't because someone was killing her, she'd been told by enough people that it was her probable destiny, given the life she had chosen. What angered her the most was *who* was killing her. She hadn't seen this coming and she believed she could read people; this was someone she thought she could trust.

She glanced round and was reminded that this would be the place she was found. There would be nobody to mourn her. Her mother was long gone, and any siblings had been lost in the system years ago. Nobody had taken her away. The social worker had stated that some people simply can't be saved. She was *some people*. The damage had already been done.

This grotty alley would be her end. The kind of place where people urinate, vomit, screw or meet their drug dealer. Her nose twitched with a smell combining piss and blood – her blood. Perhaps she'd get moved to a nice field, like what happened on TV. She didn't want to be found by some tramp taking a piss; a man walking his dog was far more respectable. Why was it always men walking the dog? Didn't women ever walk the dog?

She looked into the eyes of her attacker and knew she must have shown her fear as they looked back at her with excitement. The eyes were wild, almost savage with blood lust. One final glance up was enough to ensure the last thing she ever saw was the brick and a glint of triumph in those feral eyes.

CHAPTER ONE

Ryan looked round his gym – proud of everything he had accomplished. It wasn't part of a gym chain; the kind which lock you into a ten-year contract, and still try to tap you for more money every time you visit, by claiming that what you were looking for was only part of their *premier service*. It was also not one of those no-frills gyms which were popping up everywhere. Some were now so basic that you needed to take your own toilet paper. No, this place was different – special. He'd named it Ryan's Retreat and plumped for Covent Garden as its location which guaranteed an eclectic mix of clientele, which Ryan loved. As the place was so special, Ryan considered the one hundred pounds a month membership fee to be a worthwhile investment.

His vision had been to create a space where people could get everything under one roof and get real results. He'd realised his dream after what felt like years in the industry. He was already twenty-eight and knew there were younger studs with quicker metabolisms branching out into the saturated health and fitness market. It was a jungle out there, and he meant that literally as his gym was covered in murals of trees and wild foliage. The thinking behind it was to demonstrate to people that you could conquer the most difficult demon in the world here – your inner saboteur. Yet it highlighted that this was no walk in the park as there was no open green space on the walls. If you wanted real change then you had to work for it. The metaphor often needed explaining, however people really bought in to it once they knew why the gym was decorated in such a way. It was off-set by equipment which used pastel shades of primary colours, an idea he'd stole from his friend Karen – with her permission of course. Nobody fucked with Miss Karen!

When Ryan had first started working in the fitness industry, he'd noticed that people would join a gym and be dedicated for about three weeks and then never come again; yet they keep paying their membership. He didn't have contracts here. It was a hundred pounds a month with no minimum term. For that you got a session with a personal trainer every week, a weekly nutrition plan and free access to all his classes, so he believed this was a great deal for people. The price tag also meant that his clientele was more likely to be dedicated to a healthier lifestyle, ensuring the sweaty, smelly types stuck to their pay as you pump gym and stayed clear. Despite his perfect business model, a few gremlins always crept in as members. There was little Ryan could do about it; nowadays you can't refuse service to a tramp without them claiming some form of discrimination. They didn't last long though, even someone completely lacking in self-awareness would eventually come to the realisation that they simply didn't fit.

Another thing Ryan noticed was that despite the eclectic clientele there was one thing they all had in common: tattoos. It appeared to be the latest fad; if you had the mere hint of some muscular definition then you must scar it for life. That and beards – what was with the beard thing? First the gays and now the straight guys; the women would be getting in on it soon. Ryan looked down at his own muscular frame – free from any ink and stroked his baby smooth chin. It would all remain that way. On some of the guys and girls the tattoos looked hot, yet on others they really had gone too far and a few of the more extreme ink lovers just terrified the life out of him. One client, who was one of those types who lack self-awareness, had tattoos on every visible piece of her skin besides the face – thankfully! What was with tattoos on the face? Did people just want to make themselves unemployable? This client had multiple piercings as well – and those were just the visible ones. Shudder! The only machine she ever seemed to use was the resistance weight that worked the inner thigh. She would inhale and exhale deeply, her eyes locked and focussed on the same thing every time – the pole dancing class. Every now and then Ryan liked to move things around the gym to keep it looking fresh and to accommodate new equipment. He had learnt, after a very frightening incident, to leave the thigh mistress, as he called it, in the same place – forever!

He walked round the gym observing his clientele. It was just after seven in the morning and the gym was already busy with the pre-work crowd. The weight area was dominated by built men with slutty low-cut vests who all insisted on doing their chest on the same day of the week. This then caused carnage and queenie tantrums when people took too long to get through their sets, and that was the hetero guys. The cardio area was popular with the drag queens, and he had no idea why. In fact, his gym had a large drag queen clientele, who would work out in full drag, so usually only did so at night. Maybe the jungle theme spoke to them. Still, Ryan wasn't fussed as they paid each month, despite his rule implementation of no heels on the treadmill. After the fourth one had been wrecked, he'd had to draw the line. As a compromise he had allowed them to wear stilettos on the cross trainer, which was quite some sight to behold.

One of Ryan's personal trainers approached – Becky. She was a goddess. Ryan was besotted with her. He hadn't felt this way in a long time. He had a rule about fraternising with the staff – stupid rules. He let them screw each other silly. There was little point in implementing a rule that was never going to be followed. It would just cause too much turnover and paperwork. He employed young and fit people, and they were horny with lots of energy. The rule was for him, so he could maintain an air of professionalism, although several of his staff had been former bed mates in a past life. However, to Ryan that was how most of his friendships had developed. He would meet someone, there would be an attraction, so you'd have sex to get it out of the way and then get on with the friendship, and this would mean there was no tension bubbling away. It was the grown-up way to deal with such feelings. Becky was different though. She had beautiful dark skin, wild untamed jet-black hair and her dark eyes looked so kind, and yet so lonely. Everyone liked Becky, except Becky herself. She had once said she wasn't worthy of anyone's love, which had made Ryan feel so desperately sad and was the trigger for him developing the feelings he harboured today. He wanted more with her. This wouldn't be a quick fumble in the sauna after hours like he'd had with some of his male clients in a moment of weakness, Becky was special. Yes, there was no other way to describe her – she was special.

"Becky, I thought you had a client?" Ryan asked.

"I did, but she hasn't shown up."

"That's not like Giselle, have you called her."

"Three times, straight to voicemail."

"That's unusual for her, so don't let her lose the session. Find some time to reschedule her later in the week. I'm sure she'll get in touch later today. Something probably just came up."

"I heard she walked out on Karen the day before yesterday."

"Ah – that's probably why. She'll be keeping a low profile. It's not like her to not to call and cancel."

"That's what I thought. I'll keep trying her."

"Any sign of Tony yet?"

"No, his phone isn't switched on either," concern clearly in her voice.

Such a wonderful person Ryan thought, so caring. Tony was probably being whipped and beaten in some grotty dungeon somewhere and loving every second of it.

"We've got Paul on holiday as well," Ryan noted aloud, wondering how everything was going to be covered.

"Your diary is free for the circuit training class. I can give you a hand setting up," Becky remarked.

She could just read him so easily. It was clear they were meant to be together. Maybe he should say something? It was only his rule. Although if she said no, she would probably leave to stop it being awkward for him and he wouldn't see her each day. No, he'd keep his mouth shut, hoping it was a crush and it would pass, or that she would realise he was everything she had ever dreamed of and fall into his arms. Whatever, he wasn't fussed!

They started to put barbells, dumbbells, medicine balls and mats around the room to make up the circuit stations for the class. Ryan didn't need to tell her what exercises he was planning, or where to put anything as she just got it. Becky was another former worker from Karen's Klub, although she had genuinely put that all behind her. Circuit training was a great class to run; you could really push people to their limits and beyond. Ryan regarded a circuit training class a success when all the participants hobbled out in a way which made you think that customs officers couldn't find what they were looking for.

"In fact, do you want me to take the class, Ryan?" she asked.

"Would you mind? I need to get that paperwork done and I might need to take his Spin class at lunchtime if he continues to be a no show. I'd better sort out a playlist for that just in case."

"Not at all. They can help me set the rest up," she pointed to the door where clients were entering in preparation for the class.

"Thanks, Becky. I owe you one."

"You owe me plenty, but go and get your stuff done," she smiled.

That breathtaking smile which caused his heart to stammer, stomach to lurch and groin to twitch – he was still a man after all. Ryan smiled at her and went off towards his office – what a girl.

He got to his office and sat down thinking about whether he could say anything to her as he created a playlist for the Spin class. He looked at the schedule on the wall and it was one of the express classes which were only thirty minutes, so it needed to be very intense. He would use the class to get some of his own calorie burn for the day. Could he really say something to Becky about how he felt? He had thrown her a lifeline and couldn't bear to see her go running back to Karen, who would take her back in a flash. Everyone knew how special Becky was, including Karen. Could she ever go for someone like Ryan?

He looked at himself in the mirror, he knew he struck quite an impression owing to his physique. He was under six foot yet still tall enough to not look stocky. He had the typical Irish look with the dark brown hair and emerald green eyes, yet he had never set foot in Ireland his entire life. He'd been born and raised in East London, although he was one of the few genuine cockneys who had never developed the accent. At school he'd been constantly mocked as being a *posh boy*; he'd hated it and hoped one day he'd sound like the cast of EastEnders. Thankfully, that had never happened, and he was grateful for it now. Sounding like you were from the home counties had given him a wider reach in terms of clients in the early days. It was those early days when he had first developed his dream, but it had been his best friend who had helped that dream to become a reality. It had been too long since they'd seen each other, but that was what had been agreed, along with Karen. It was their pact and despite his feelings of nostalgia, Ryan knew that it was unlikely the three of them would ever be together again. It was the only way to guarantee their safety.

CHAPTER TWO

"Where is that fucking bitch?" screamed Karen Kowalski, as she stalked around her club. "I will kill her with my bare hands. Nobody fucks with Miss Karen."

Karen was pacing up and down in front of three of her girls – Harriet, Aerial and Sandra. It had been a good night at the club; they had only just kicked out their last customer. The girls had done some great business, but there had been many requests for Giselle, and she was still nowhere to be found. Karen had hoped the girl would have cooled off by now and come to her senses. She was destined for this life, so she may as well be working for Karen; there was nobody better.

"She said she wasn't doing it anymore, maybe she really meant it," replied Aerial, with her vulgar Essex accent.

Karen couldn't stand the woman, but she had big tits and the customer is always right.

"Who the fuck you think you are talking to?" Karen retorted slapping Aerial hard across the face. "Do you think I came all the way from Poland, busted my ass to make this club what it is, to be back chatted by a cheap little tart? Know your place you stupid little bitch."

Aerial held a hand to her face and said no more – *sensible girl.*

"Anyone else got anything to say? Well, have you?"

Silence – *they are learning.*

"That Giselle does not set foot in this club again. To disappear for twenty-four hours is taking the piss, but after two days and nothing she has fucked me over for the last time. You hear me? Sid get in here," she screamed.

"I was just getting the crates Miss Karen, ready for tonight," said Sid, as he came from the back of the club.

"Don't you fucking backchat me as well, you should know better. Now, you listen to me. That Giselle whore is not to step foot in this club again. She comes anywhere near it and you kick her up the fucking arse and tell her to piss off. If I see her then I will not be held responsible from my actions and it will be all your fault. You hear me."

"Yes, Miss Karen."

"Good, you carry on. Good boy."

Sid disappeared into the back again. Such a loyal boy. Karen would need him in her bed when she got there. She needed to feel something other than constant rage, and he would enable that, for a couple of minutes at least!

"I expect the same degree of loyalty from you as well," she said looking directly at the three girls in front of her. Aerial still had her hand to her cheek, which made Karen smile.

"Yes, Miss Karen," they all replied in unison.

"Good, we understand each other. Now you should all get some sleep as you look like shit."

———

Harriet looked around the dreary little coffee shop which stunk of grease. At this time of the morning it was relatively quiet as the pre-work trade had now passed and it was still too early for the trendy types to have their brunch – which was just the latest excuse to eat whilst having a so-called business meeting. This enabled them to expense the ten quid they spent on avocado and toast whilst using words like *synergy* and *holistic*. Harriet had suggested to Sandra and Aerial that they stop off somewhere or neither of them would get any sleep; they both seemed wired. No doubt wound up from Aerial getting another backhander off Miss Karen. Some people didn't know when to keep their opinions to themselves; these two were always getting slapped. Even though Miss Karen could be heavy-handed, there were times when Harriet felt they'd deserved it; this was one of those times.

"You good Aerial?" asked Harriet.

"Yeah, it's fine. It's stopped stinging now. Why is it me that always gets slapped?"

"Cos you back chat her," replied Harriet smiling.

"I just can't help myself. I speak my mind and she is just jel that I can still turn a trick, and nobody would even look at her."

"Why you stay then?" asked Harriet.

"Cos she's the best innit. She's a bitch, but she is well better than any of them other places. She's the only one I know that don't take no cut from your tips."

"You could go alone. You make big money."

"Fuck that. It takes well too much effort to pimp yourself out. Easier for the money to come to you. Besides the real money is in the clubs."

Harriet looked at Sandra who seemed noticeably quiet and withdrawn. The girl was incredibly attractive with her dark skin and blue eyes. A rare thing to see. Harriet knew that her family back home in Africa would see this as a sign of the devil, yet Harriet thought it made Sandra look even more beautiful, special even. She needed to do something with her hair though, as it was just a frizzy mop. Sandra had a London accent, although she was not as commonly spoken as Aerial. They were both twenty-five yet there was no maturity to either of them. Aerial was an attractive girl, but everything was fake – the blonde hair, the tan, the nails, just everything – except those breasts. That was all she had going for her, yet Harriet couldn't help but like her. She seemed almost vulnerable and put it all out there as a front and besides, despite her vulgar tongue she made Harriet laugh and that was always a way into Harriet's heart. She loved to laugh.

"You quiet Sandra. You good?"

"Sorry, Harriet, I was miles away. What was that?

"I said you good?"

"Yeah, just tired."

"Tired of the work?"

"I love my work," she laughed, although clearly, she didn't mean it. Nobody ever did. It was a means to an end, although sadly some of them didn't have an end and it was this until nature took its course.

"Well hopefully I do not do this for much longer."

"Are you leaving?" asked Sandra with concern in her voice.

"Soon hopefully. I need to talk to Miss Karen, but I have made the money I wanted to make and now I am going to buy a property and do it up to make money and then buy another."

"You need a lot of money to buy a property in London, don't you Aerial?"

"Yeah, you need well loads. It's like half a million for a shoe box."

"I do not buy in London for this reason. I move to the north of England and start there, then I am not tempted to turn a few tricks when things get tight. When I walk away, it will be for good."

"When are you leaving?" asked Sandra.

"Don't you worry, it won't be for a while yet. I wouldn't leave Miss Karen in the shit. With Becky and Giselle both gone, it is not a good time and she has been good to me letting me live above the club as well so I can save more. I want to leave as friends, so I go when the time is right. Not for a while."

"Do you think Giselle will ever come back?" asked Aerial.

"No, she is not the type to admit when she is wrong and besides Miss Karen will probably kill her."

"Yeah, but she was the best, so she might change her mind. Becky keeps coming back."

"Becky is different. She did not fuck over Miss Karen. Giselle will be thrown out if she ever steps foot in the club again. I believe that."

"Not by Sid though, he's still sweet on her."

"That is another reason then. Sid belongs to Miss Karen."

"She likes to think that, but I think Sid would leave if he could," replied Sandra.

"It is not a prison. He can leave when he wants."

"Yes, but she will *fucking kill him* if he does," said Aerial giving a great Karen impression, causing them all to laugh.

Harriet had been with Sandra and Aerial in the coffee shop for over an hour. She should have left ages ago to get some sleep. She just didn't like to miss out on any of the gossip.

"I was getting a MOT at the clinic the other day and there was some guy actually wearing a face mask in the waiting room," said Aerial who was in full flow. "It was well funny, I mean come on mate you're in the clap clinic, you need a rubber not a mask," she added howling with laughter.

Harriet laughed along with her. Well you had to be polite, didn't you? Sandra had cheered up a bit thanks to Aerial's anecdotes.

"So, where you think Giselle is?" asked Harriet.

"With Tony probably," replied Aerial.

"Tony is a gay boy."

"I don't mean she is shagging him. He's just the only one who puts up with her bullshit."

"Does she still do her training with Tony?"

"Not sure. I'd like to train with that Ryan. He is well fit."

"Good luck with that my dear. He like them young and firm..." replied Harriet

"You saying I is fat? That is well out of order." barked Aerial.

"No, my dear, he like the boys. That is what I mean." She wanted to defuse the situation quickly. Aerial could be a feisty one.

"That is so not true. You think everyone is gay. Ryan is bisexual."

"That just stopover on the way to gay town my dear. You got no chance with Ryan, you do not have penis," added Harriet laughing.

"We'll see my dear, we'll see."

"Want to make a bet?"

"I'd hate to take your money."

"It will be taking your money."

"Are you hearing this Sandra?"

"Sorry, what?" Sandra asked, who had clearly not heard any of their conversation.

"Seriously Sandra go to bed it you're that tired," stated Aerial sternly.

"Yeah, you look like shit my dear. Get some sleep," added Harriet.

"Cheers Harriet, love you too."

"I say it out of the goodness of my heart. In fact, we should probably all get some sleep. I see you both tonight."

She drained her third cup of coffee, not worried, as sleep would easily come. She said her goodbyes and left Sandra and Aerial in the coffee shop, hoping they would take her advice and get some sleep soon. They didn't live at the club, although Sandra had once and Harriet had given her a bit of a hard time at first, yet it was in the girl's best interest. She did not adjust well to being in the business to start. Some tough love had snapped her out of it and since then she had been great. She was still quiet and introverted at times, although she could put on a front for the customers. Sandra was currently sharing an apartment with Aerial, who was a bit more of a wild child. Aerial had come from a big family, the youngest of seven, and had nothing of her own growing up. It was always stuff that had belonged to her older siblings. She had turned to prostitution to get her parents to notice her. Sadly, they did notice, and they hadn't spoken to her since. Karen was very anti-drugs, as was Harriet, and she suspected that was what Aerial and Sandra where now dabbling in and it was why they had moved away from living at the club. That was not Harriet's problem. She shouldn't care so much. Soon she would never see any of these girls again. Her timing had to be right to leave on good terms with Miss Karen. It was always safer that way. Rumour was that Miss Karen's former pimp in Poland had been a ruthless bastard and one night she had slit his throat, took all his money, and fled to London. Whether it was true or not Harriet didn't know, but she could tell intuitively that Karen hid a dark past.

———

Karen was thinking about how she could salvage the situation she was in following Giselle's disappearing act. There were clients to satisfy and she had Mr Yatumoshi due that evening. He would be expecting Giselle. He had been extremely disappointed when Becky was no longer available, and he was now settled with Giselle. He was one of her best clients and she didn't want to disappoint him again. Perhaps Karen could call in a favour. She knew it was wrong, but she had little choice.

Karen looked at Sid who was sitting opposite her looking his usual dreamy self. He might be thirty-two years old, yet with his dark Latin heritage, he looked in his mid-twenties. He had worked for Karen for years, for a while as one of her boys. However, the straight boys could only do gay for pay for a while before it started to affect them in the head. Karen had suggested Sid work the door for her and paid for his security accreditation. He'd lived in London all his life although he could put on a great South American accent and he'd used it to make the clients weak at the knees. The boy had talent, yet Karen didn't want him to be turned from the kind person he still was. The industry could harden the softest heart – she knew only too well herself.

"I will give Becky a call," she said.

"Becky hasn't worked here for over a month, Karen. You can't keep asking her back. She wanted out and you agreed."

"Bullshit, nobody leaves Karen. She will come. She knows what will happen if she doesn't."

"Even the punters don't ask for her anymore. You can't keep threatening her. I thought you liked Becky?"

"I love Becky like she is my own daughter, I only ask a favour. The customers like the exotic type, I give it to them."

"Can't you use Sandra?"

"That stupid bitch, she is not a professional. The skin may look the same, but inside Sandra does not have the power to turn men into the putty in the hands."

"Not like Giselle then, the human Slinky."

"Do not speak her name in front of me," spat Karen. "She

will regret crossing me. Nobody fucks with Miss Karen. You hear me."

"I hear you. It's just you know Giselle was the best you've ever had. That's why you're so pissed off. Girls and guys have left you before. They are all just passing through."

"No, the good ones stay. They are loyal to Miss Karen. Like you."

"I just work the door now Karen."

"I know, but they do not make them like you anymore Sid."

"Yeah well, we all got to retire someday."

"You will not leave me will you Sid?"

"No Miss Karen, I won't leave you. We've been through too much for that," he smiled, that lovely sweet smile. "I need to get back to setting up."

"Go, I need to make a call."

Karen watched him leave. He kept in reasonably good shape. He was wearing a vest which showed off his toned and tattooed arms. He was developing a bit of a belly, she liked that. She knew she had to be cautious with Sid as sometimes she unintentionally pushed him too much. She couldn't imagine life without him, besides Sid was one of the few people who knew her secret, and if that were to ever come out then her world would be shattered forever.

CHAPTER THREE

Detective Chief Inspector Eric Fenton looked down at the body. The woman's face unrecognisable, although he doubted it would be long before they had an identity. The whole scene stank of whore. A generalisation of course, yet he was usually right about these things. He used to state out loud that he was always right, however, from bitter experience he had learnt to keep such sweeping statements to himself.

"Can we ensure that Manning is the lead on this one?" he asked Detective Sergeant Gary Brennan who was stood to his left.

"I think she's already been assigned, Guv. I'll check, though I thought you weren't a fan?"

"That's irrelevant, she's good and if this is not some straight-forward bust up with the pimp then we need the best on our side. Besides, she's mellowed since she's been with Deidre."

"Bit gutting that isn't it, Guv – I mean she's something that Deidre. What a waste."

"What about your coffee shop girlfriend?" replied Fenton, humouring his Brennan with the delusion that he would ever stand a chance with Dr Deidre Peters, even if she wasn't a lesbian.

"Binned her off, she was getting on my tits."

"Yes, you are looking a bit busty at the moment."

Fenton saw Brennan blush, then realise his boss was taking the piss and laughed, whilst grabbing his chest and giving it a jiggle. To make inappropriate remarks at a murder scene was a typical reaction to something so horrific. It normalised the situation, well as much as you could when there was a dead whore in a back alley with her face smashed in.

"You've been with her a few years though," said Fenton.

"Well why do something today when you can procrastinate and put it off for months, or in this case years," he replied.

Brennan lumbered off with his usual ape-like walk. His short and stocky frame doing him no favours, yet he had charm and the gift of the gab. He was an asset to Fenton's team. Brennan had tried for promotion to detective inspector a few times although hadn't managed to succeed yet. It had been a while since his last attempt, so Fenton thought he'd probably given up, besides at thirty-two Brennan still had plenty of time.

Fenton looked round the scene. What a place to end up − a grotty alley. The place stank. There was rubbish strewn on the floor that had clearly been left for weeks. The alley had a slight bend to it so anyone walking past wouldn't have obviously seen her. She wasn't completely round the corner so surely it would have warranted a double take. The alley walls were daubed with the usual graffiti - *Bob woz ere*, *Social Justice* and *Jay is a pervert*.

There was no obvious weapon near the body. Several things could have been used to cause that amount of damage. It was a tragic end to someone who had no doubt led a miserable life. No matter what bad choices you made, nobody deserved to end up like this. He walked round the scene, keeping out the way of the forensic officers who were busy hunting for clues. He was still surprised it had taken until after ten o'clock in the morning for her to be found. He suspected that others had seen her and being typical Londoners had not wanted to get involved. He doubted it would have made much difference as whoever had done this would have made certain she was dead before leaving the scene. The intention was clearly to kill.

"We heading back now, Guv?"

"Yeah, there's little else we can do here."

"Did you get a new DI?"

"Yes, he should be waiting for us back at the station."

"Maybe this one will last beyond one case, Guv," Brennan smiled.

"Let's hope so Gary."

"None of them come up to Taylor's standard then?"

"Stop stirring it, you know that's not it. Besides Lisa Taylor has been a DCI for almost five years now. Is that fresh piss over there?" Fenton asked pointing in the corner.

"Yes Guv, the guy who found her said he was bursting so still went after he called us."

"Well if you've gotta go, then you gotta go."

"Bit warped though isn't it?"

"I think warped can be a term saved for our killer. This guy either knew her, or is a complete psycho, but I think it's the former... maybe a bit of both." He was thinking aloud, which was safe with Brennan.

"How come, Guv?"

"Her face, it's so personal. Some of it probably happened after she was already dead, although Manning will be able to confirm that. I wonder if she has developed her sense of urgency"

"I think after the *Diversity Slayer* she has learned to listen to us when it comes to prioritising."

"You're deluded!"

The Diversity Slayer case had been challenging. It had caused a moral panic in the press around hate crime. Three murders in a London hotel and all the victims were from minority groups. Fenton had felt that there was more to it than a hate crime as that didn't make any sense given, they all worked for the same company and knew each other.

Polly Pilkington, an antagonistic journalist, who was trying to make a name for herself, had run a press campaign that was very personal against Fenton and his ability as a detective. He was certain that there was a leak from within his team, as Pilkington knew everything that was going on before he did in some cases. He became convinced that Pilkington was having an affair with Manning and she was the leak, only to find out later that his boss and mentor Chief Superintendent Harry Beeden was the one having the affair and giving her all the latest on his case. He'd felt deeply betrayed by Harry and a friendship of over twenty years had been virtually destroyed. It had turned out that Pilkington and Manning were sisters, much to Fenton's humiliation when he had confronted them in a Pizza Express; he'd never been able to look at a dough ball again. He'd been very wrong about the situation and was lucky Manning had decided not to take things any further. They'd always clashed, yet respected each other professionally.

The case had not been helped by the politicians wading in to win political points and the whole fiasco had resulted in a change of government. However, the new Prime Minister had been overthrown by his own party after being exposed for his private sexual indiscretions, which nobody had really cared about until it was all over the press and screaming in their faces. It had been Pilkington who had brought him down.

Once she'd recovered from her fall from grace, she had realised that the Prime Minister in waiting had used her like a puppet and she had seen to it that her revenge was served chilled and dripping in satisfaction. Since then, Fenton hadn't heard from her. Apparently, she'd moved to Australia and he'd been meaning to ask Manning. They hadn't worked together in a while as Fenton had asked to be moved on to cold cases so he could have a break from the long hours and spend some time with his wife and daughters before the latter all left home. However, Beeden had heard *dead whore in alleyway* and Fenton was suddenly back in the thick of it.

Fenton's determination on the Diversity Slayer investigation had allowed them to come to the truth. The whole case had been over in a matter of weeks, yet it had felt like a lifetime. Something in that case had then triggered Fenton to take a new line of enquiry in an unsolved murder that had troubled him for a long time. This finally resulted in a conviction once he had re-opened the case. Beeden was only too willing to co-operate following Fenton's discovery of him and Pilkington. Fenton still shuddered when he remembered the suction noise as they unlocked from each other as he'd entered the Chief Superintendent's office. Fenton's record was now perfect regarding murder enquiries and he had always secured a conviction, even on his cold cases. He'd been recommended for promotion and politely declined. He was flattered and although he may be rapidly approaching fifty, he wasn't ready for the desk job just yet, in fact he didn't think he ever would be.

Later that morning, they were setting up the incident room for the murder investigation. Fenton was introduced to his new DI, Jack Jacobs. He shook Fenton's hand in a firm, yet friendly manner.

"Welcome to the team Jack. Have the others brought you up to speed with the case?"

"Yes sir, I also went down and had a look at the scene as well. Always better than looking at photos if you get the opportunity."

"True, so what did you think?"

"She was dressed like a whore, but that doesn't mean she was. Killer could be a pimp, ex-boyfriend, or it could be some random attack. If that's the case, we may get more."

"Was the body still there when you left? Fenton asked, mentally agreeing with his quick observations.

"They were just moving her. Ms Manning was on the scene and said she'd call you later. I wasn't sure who she meant at first, as she called you Eric."

"Yeah she does that," he smiled.

Fenton looked at the young man in front of him; well anyone under thirty was young. Here was another of the fast-track ambitious types who was DI at a young age. He reminded Fenton of Lisa Taylor, who was now a DCI and doing very well. Fenton was watching her career from the side lines and knew that soon she could be his boss. Jack was a very fit young man. Even in his suit, you could tell he was a guy who kept in good shape, yet he didn't seem to give off the vibe of being a brain-dead moron as many of the gym types did. Jacobs was over six-foot-tall, and Fenton thought his heritage was probably Caribbean, yet he had a strong East London accent. Him and Brennan would be an interesting combination, although he noticed Jack called him sir, rather than Guv.

It was obvious the guy was eager to please, although going off to the scene without letting anyone know wasn't a great start. Fenton decided let it go this time, as he didn't want to pull the lad up on his first day on the team, although suspected he'd need to keep an eye on him to ensure he showed himself to be a team player. Jacobs had worked with DCI Taylor before, so Fenton would be able to get some background information on the newest member of his team.

Fenton watched as Jacobs introduced himself to the rest of the team. Brennan looked like he was forcing politeness given he was a clear six inches shorter that Jacobs; every man had their insecurities. Even the confident and cocky Brennan had his Achilles heel and here it was in shape of tall, dark and brooding. Even from a distance, Fenton could tell that the handshake had attempted to be one of those let me try and break your hands types. Fenton saw Brennan wince, so it had clearly backfired.

Detective Constable Emma Shirkham stood up and gave one of her beaming smiles. Jacobs was clearly enamoured by the young lady. Fenton knew that Shirkham would not be interested in any fraternising. She was very dedicated to her job, in fact Fenton knew next to nothing about her private life as she kept them very separate.

———

Jack Jacobs was ambitious, and he wanted to get to the top. He was what people described as a university copper and he wasn't precious about that or how others viewed him because of it. He'd completed his two years on the beat as a uniformed PC and then swiftly moved into CID. He was sergeant at twenty-five and DI three years later. At twenty-eight he already had his eyes on his next career move, although he knew he had to put in a few years at this rank to truly earn his stripes. He'd been told that if he wanted to become a good DCI, Fenton was the guy to work with. Fenton's reputation was exceptional, and Jacobs had heard of how DCI Lisa Taylor was promoted at the age of thirty-two under Fenton's guidance. Her career was flying, and he'd just come off a case with her involving the death of a child. The case had been horrendous and taken its toll on all of them. Taylor had been honest with Jack and told him that although he was an asset to her team, he needed experience of working with other DCIs and should jump at the opportunity to work with Fenton if it arose. She'd pulled a few strings and here he was.

What Jacobs hadn't expected was to see such a stunning beauty in Shirkham. That natural long blond hair that seemed to float as if caught by a gust of wind and her deep green eyes meant she was not his usual type and yet here was the proof, the validation that nobody really has a type unless it's for recreational purposes only. Perhaps it was true that in love there are no deal breakers. When Shirkham spoke, her Irish lilt was still evident, although there was an aura about her that said she was streetwise, and certainly not some naïve girl who was new to the big city. This was a woman who could hold her own against any man. Jacobs felt his heart stammer in his chest and for the first time that he could remember, he found himself getting tongue-tied. He was staring intently at her and knew he should stop looking but couldn't help himself. She must have noticed, but she hadn't said anything, or given him one of those *back off* looks. Maybe there was a glimmer of hope!

"Let me update you on the case, sir," said Brennan snapping him out of his trance.

Brennan gave him a stern look which then turned into a sly smile. The bloke had clearly been intimidated at first, given he had tried to break Jacobs' hand, causing him to retaliate by squeezing back twice as hard. However, Brennan had obviously seen the reaction to Shirkham and knew Jacobs was just another typical red-bloodied male. The smile was the sort that only male coppers can give to each other, it could be best described as brotherly. They were going to get along fine.

"Call me Jack, don't worry about rank, unless the boss is around."

"Oh, he doesn't care about that either when we're indoors."

"Cool – but I don't think I'll call him Eric."

"Yeah, it doesn't apply to his rank."

Jacobs laughed; he could see why Taylor had spoken so highly of Fenton. He wasn't a formal stuffy DCI, yet still maintained a professional distance from the team, which commanded him the respect that was evident from the people around him.

"So where are we with identifying Jane Doe," he asked Brennan.

"We're getting prints taken from her so we can check against the database. If she was a whore, then she might have a record. Dental records may be a tricky one given how badly her face was smashed in, Manning will be able to confirm that."

"She's quite formidable that one. I've worked with her a few times."

"That would be an understatement, but she's good. It's always entertaining to see her and the Guv in full flow when they clash. We've been working on cold cases for a while, so we haven't used Manning. Taylor used to keep them in check, so it could get interesting with her no longer around!"

"Sounds like you enjoy it?"

"You'll see. I hear you've been working with DCI Taylor. How is she doing?"

"Excellent – best DCI I've ever had."

"Until now..."

"So, I'm led to believe."

———

Fenton called the team together to go through what they had to date; it would be a short meeting. This was always the case in the early part of an investigation when you had no ID on the victim and were waiting on the forensic report to come in.

"So how are we going with the ID?"

"They're going to lift her prints and see if she has got any previous, Guv," replied Brennan.

"What about missing persons?"

"We've got in touch sir, but aren't hopeful," said Jacobs.

"Why is that?"

"It looks like she was killed where she was found, so has probably only been missing since last night. She can't have been there longer than that given how public it is. Mispers won't have anything until at least forty-eight hours are up."

"Fair point, but if she was underage they might. Any idea how old she was?"

"Manning thought she was late teens, early twenties."

"Has Manning submitted a report yet?"

"No, I asked her at the scene, sir."

"And she gave you an answer just off the cuff? She must be ill."

Everyone laughed.

"Any answers on the race of the victim?" Fenton asked.

"She was black, Guv," stated Brennan.

"Yeah, I got that from looking at her this morning, I mean do we know anymore?"

"Not yet, Guv," replied Brennan smiling.

"Are you taking the piss?"

"Would I, Guv?"

"Well we need to do something. We can't just kick up our heels until Manning comes back to us, which could be tomorrow," said Fenton smiling. "I want Gary and Jack to start talking to the local club owners. She may have worked at one of them. Soho is a close-knit community, so if one of their own is missing then they'll know about it. Emma can you use your charm to get us those fingerprints today so we can hopefully save a lot of legwork. We're holding off on any press until we have an ID. They may get wind of it and they'll be interested. This was a brutal murder so there is someone out there who is dangerous. We need to find this guy. Right let's get to it."

They all disappeared to get on with their assigned duties, leaving Fenton to return to his office and update Beeden. There was nothing significant to update him on yet as they didn't even have a name for their victim, but it was best to keep him sweet and subsequently far away from his investigation.

"Her name was what?" asked Fenton.

"Giselle Gorge." Shirkham replied

"I assume that wasn't the name she had at birth?"

"It was sir. I've checked and double-checked. That was her real name."

"Poor cow never stood a chance, then did she? Seriously, what is wrong with parents today and the names they give their kids? Was she a whore then?

"Not sure, sir as her record was for petty theft. I've asked Vice to check if she was known to them. She has also spent her childhood in the care system, so there is no known next of kin to contact."

"Do we have an address?"

"No, she wasn't signing on at the dole, there's no income tax records for her with HMRC either and she's never been on any electoral roll. It's not going to be easy to find out who she knew."

"How old was she when she got her record?"

"Fourteen."

"So, she was what, nineteen when she died?"

"Looks that way."

"Well thanks Emma. Can you let Gary and Jack know the name and email the photo to them? It might be five years out of date, but it will give them something when they're doing the rounds at the clubs. I'm guessing though with a name like that, people will either know her or they won't."

"Any idea when we'll have a better idea of how she died sir?"

"I'm seeing Manning first thing in the morning, so if we can arrange to have the team assembled by nine then I'll have something to share hopefully."

"Leave it with me," she said, before leaving his office.

Fenton knew that this case would have the press crawling all over it, especially with a victim with a name like that. They would make assumptions about her, especially given where her body was found. The girl didn't appear to have any family, yet there had to be someone who cared. Everyone had someone, didn't they? It was a horrible feeling to think that someone could die like that and nobody would miss them.

CHAPTER FOUR

Jacobs was back in his old territory, with Brennan, making discreet enquiries around the Soho clubs. The clubs were always irritated when the police started sniffing around and weren't quiet about it either. They also had to consider their colleagues in Vice. They were extremely territorial about their whores and pimps. However, Jacobs had made a couple of calls and let them know what they were doing and why; murder tended to shut people up from raising any issues about territory.

"I've just got a text from Shirkham," remarked Brennan. "They've got a name – Giselle Gorge."

"Working name?" asked Jacobs.

He recognised the name straight away and chose to say nothing. That was the safest way to play it for now.

"Apparently not, that was the name given to her at birth. She's sent more on email to both of us."

They both looked at their phones scrolling through what Emma had managed to pull together from Giselle's shoplifting conviction when she was fourteen.

"No next of kin that they know of," said Brennan. "She was nineteen."

Jacobs could read it all for himself, although Brennan continued to call out snippets.

"At least we've got a name now for her and a photo, albeit a mug shot from five years ago."

"You're a bit posh for a Cockney ain't ya?" Brennan asked in his jovial way.

"Just a good education, Mum wanted to me to do well when Dad did a runner back to Antigua."

"Is that where your mum's from as well?"

"Nah – mum was London through and through."

He noticed Brennan's face change when he referred to his mother in the past tense. However, he didn't say anything, and Jacobs was glad about that. It had been a couple of years now, yet the pain was still there, every day.

"You got any brothers and sisters?" asked Brennan

"Two younger sisters, one's at medical school and the other's a barrister."

"Would be a bit awkward if she ever had to cross-examine you?"

"Yeah," he laughed, "she doesn't do criminal law though, says there's no money in it."

"Not in it for the love then?"

"Definitely not, she's an ambitious one."

"How old is your younger sister?"

"Same age as Giselle was."

"Ah, shit mate, you alright?"

"Yeah – I'll give her a call later though."

"Call her now, I'll go and get us a coffee."

"Surprised your heart's still beating the amount you've already had today."

"Blame my ex, she worked in a coffee shop."

Jacobs laughed. "I'll call my sister later as she'll be in classes. Coffee sounds good though and then we might want to pop back to the two clubs already visited, now we have name."

"Oh great. I can't wait. Which shall we do first? The one which stunk of BO, or the one with the fifty-year-old woman lap dancing at three o'clock in the afternoon?"

"Your choice."

"I'll let you pull rank on that one mate," laughed Brennan, as they went in search of a caffeine fix.

They found a chain nearby, one of those who might use the same coffee everywhere, yet it still tastes like shit if your Barista burns the milk. Jacobs noticed Brennan ordered a large latte for himself and a double espresso on the side, which he downed in seconds. Soon he'd probably stop blinking. Jacobs was going to say some glib remark, but he wanted to keep Brennan in a friendly mood whilst he asked him a few questions.

"So, tell me more about Emma," asked Jacobs.

"You mean Emma Shirkham?"

"Yeah."

"Ah, you like what you see huh?"

"Well don't you?"

"I've worked with Emma for too long, she's like a sister."

"But you can see the appeal?"

"Of course, but I don't fancy your chances."

"Why not?"

"Well she's never been one to mix work with pleasure. I mean we've worked together for about seven years and I hardly know anything about her private life. They are very much separate."

"Seven years and she's still a DC?"

"That's what she wants. Fenton has tried to promote her a dozen times and she's not interested. Says she's happy being at that level. I bet she'd be at your rank at least by now if she was interested."

"Well maybe I'll just ask her for a drink."

"Good luck with that," Brennan laughed. "Anyway, we better get to the next club, the Guv will be waiting for an update."

A couple of hours later they'd been round what had felt like a hundred different clubs, yet it was only six. There were still a lot to check off the list.

"Perhaps this will be lucky number seven," remarked Brennan hopefully. "These places stink."

"I know what you mean, can't think of what the smell is though."

"Sin!"

They both started laughing, then regained composure quickly when they owner of the club approached them. He was built like a brick shithouse and looked almost seven foot tall. He had a black eye with a cut under it. His face was streaked with oil, yet that didn't hide the grey stubble sprouting through his skin. Jacobs suspected he was the wrong side of forty, yet his dark brown eyes looked even older. Jacobs believed that the eyes told a lot about a person. Sometimes you could just look at someone like he was doing now and know that this was a man who had lived through some shit.

"How can I help you officer?" he asked, with a hint of caution in his voice.

Clearly, he didn't want police in his establishment, yet

knew it was in his interest to co-operate, especially if he wanted to stay in business.

"We're investigating a murder," remarked Brennan setting the tone of the conversation immediately. It also implied that co-operation was not a requirement, it was an expectation.

"Did you know a woman by the name of Giselle Gorge?" asked Jacobs.

"What? Something's happened to Giselle?"

"You know her?"

"If it's the same woman then yes I know her."

"Not really a common name is it sir. Can I show you a photo?"

"It's not of her on a slab or something is it," he said, with fear in his voice.

"No, it was taken five years ago. It's a mug shot. It's all we have on file."

He nodded and Brennan approached with the photo. The man immediately broke down in tears. At least poor Giselle had one person who would mourn her.

"So, Andy, how did you know Giselle?" asked Jacobs softly.

The man was still in a state of shock and kept breaking down. It had taken them half an hour to get him into a state where he could talk. It was an odd sight to see, given the intimidating presence the man had given at first.

"We used to be together," he responded.

"When was that until?"

"About six months' ago."

"When did you last see her?"

"Yesterday."

"What time was that and where?"

"You don't think I killed her, do you?" he responded defensively.

"I didn't say that. I asked you when and where you last saw her. We need to get an idea of her movements."

"Of course, sorry. It was at lunchtime in the gym."

"Which gym?"

"Ryan's Retreat in Covent Garden. Do you know it?"

"I know of it yes," replied Jacobs, hiding the shock in his voice and being grateful that Brennan was looking the other way when Ryan's place was mentioned.

"Well it was there. She was having a row with her personal trainer."

"What's his name?"

"Tony Leopold, although that is a working name."

"Is he still a working guy?" asked Jack, keeping his face impassive after hearing Tony's name also mentioned.

"I don't believe he is. He used to work at Karen's Klub. Have you heard of it?"

"Oh yes, run by Karen Kowalski. I remember it well from my days in Vice."

"I thought you looked familiar. You see a lot of different faces here. Can't remember them all."

"I guess not. So, Karen's Klub?"

"Yeah, well Tony used to work for her. She's one of the few that has men and women on offer in her place, so she does well with the bisexual businessmen. The working guys are too flighty for me, and prefer to work for themselves, so I'm not interested in having them here. Anyway, Tony gave up that line of work and became a personal trainer. Giselle used to work for Karen as well, but she binned it off recently as well."

"How did Karen feel about that?"

"What do you mean?"

"Well I hear Karen doesn't like people to leave her."

"I don't know, I haven't spoken to Giselle other than briefly at the gym. She wanted out as she'd been with Karen since she was fourteen. Nobody stays at the same place for five years, but she did. She was loyal, although she'd had enough."

"So, what was the row about with this Tony?" asked Jacobs.

"No idea, they weren't shouting or anything, you could sense that things were tense between them."

"In what way, tense?"

"You could just see from their body language that there was a problem."

"Did you speak to her and ask her what it was?"

"Yeah, she said it was nothing and I should mind my own business."

"How did that make you feel?"

"Nothing, she was always speaking like that. That's just Giselle, or was..." He swallowed and looked like he was about to break down again.

"So where were you last night from nine o'clock onwards?" asked Brennan.

Andy's eyes narrowed. "I was here. How many witnesses would you like?"

Twenty minutes later Jacobs and Brennan were heading back to the car.

"Why did you ask him where he was?" Jacobs asked

"Because he's clearly a suspect."

"Perhaps, but he was talking freely. Now we're getting nothing from him."

"How do you know this Karen Kawasaki?"

"Kowalski! Our paths crossed a few times when I was on Vice. Hard bitch. Looks after her girls and boys. Expects total loyalty from them in return though."

"Is that what you meant when you said Karen doesn't like people to leave them?"

"Something like that."

They got in the car. Brennan was driving. He was clearly one of those types who had the attention of a flea, so you couldn't speak to him when he's driving, or death would become an inevitable outcome. They drove in silence back to the station and this gave Jacobs time to consider what they had so far.

They now had an identity for the victim, and she'd worked for Karen Kowalski and apparently left her employment. Something people rarely did. It looked like he would have to pay Karen a visit soon, perhaps alone to ensure their agreement remained in place. However, he'd need to be careful as if she was involved it could get difficult, especially as Ryan's Retreat had also been mentioned. He would need to give Ryan a heads up as well as Karen. He owed them that after all this time. It would be good to see Ryan even though they had all agreed not to contact each other again. Perhaps a phone call would be safer. This murder was encroaching into his old territory and a past he thought he had put behind him when he transferred from Vice. He'd have to be careful about doing anything alone though. DCI Taylor had pulled him up on it several times and told him to stop acting like a one-man-band and always ensure he had back up, but he had no option but to speak to Karen and Ryan. He had to warn them what was coming.

———

Fenton strode into Manning's lab bright and early. The place was as immaculate and sterile as ever. No amount of disinfectant could rid the stench of death which hung in the air as a reminder of your own mortality. This place always reminded him of a horror film about dentists. He'd eaten breakfast as he knew after this meeting he'd have little appetite for some time and just in case, it was always good to have something that you could actually throw up – although it had been a very long time since that had happened in his days as a rookie.

"Robes," shouted Manning, which was her typical greeting whenever anyone walked into her lab.

She didn't even look up from what she was doing, so Fenton stood waiting for her to give him her undivided attention. Fenton had a low boredom threshold, so after thirty seconds he gave a not so subtle cough.

"Eric, good morning," she said looking up. "I must say you've got one sadistic son of a bitch who did this one."

It must be bad if she was saying that. Usually nothing phased the woman. It was part of what made her so annoyingly brilliant at her job.

"Any idea what was used?" he asked.

"A brick."

"Shit."

"Hmmm – shit indeed."

Her girlish voice was always something that Fenton found unnerving as it just didn't suit the person. At over six feet tall, she was broad and reminded you of a Russian shot-putter. Her black rimmed spectacles gave her a rather severe look and her short haircut was still very mannish. Clearly Deidre had done nothing to feminise the woman. It was that sweet sickly girlish voice though that still baffled Fenton, even after all these years of working together. At first, he thought she put it on in order to tone herself down. Then he'd seen and heard her in full throttle when she was angry - it was very real. If you were watching her on screen though you'd be certain that she'd been dubbed.

"You've got a name, I understand?" asked Manning

"Yes – Giselle Gorge."

"Prostitute?"

"Seems so. The lads found her ex-boyfriend, who was pretty cut up."

"Suspect?"

"Doubtful, given the reaction."

"Still?"

"Yes, we've not ruled him out and we're arranging swabs. So, what you got for me, other than she was beaten to death with a brick.

"There was no sexual attack, so that probably rules out that motive."

"Not even with protection?"

"Not a trace of any latex. She hadn't had intercourse since she last bathed, although she'd certainly been around."

"What makes you say that?"

"Her vaginal and anal muscles show a lot of use, given she was still in her teens, I'd say she started early. It's also clear to me that she has given birth at least once."

"Jesus Christ."

"I doubt the second coming would be spawned by this wretched soul."

"You're certainly on form this morning."

"When am I not?" she laughed.

Fenton couldn't help but laugh with her. Perhaps she had mellowed.

"Indeed, so anything under the nails?"

"Not a sausage and she hasn't been scrubbed. Judging by the lack of bruising I would say she didn't even put up a fight."

"Any sign she was drugged?"

"Nothing on the preliminary toxicology, but you know these things take time."

"You'd think that's something they'd have been able to speed up by now wouldn't you."

"Well this isn't a television show where you get full forensic results within a four-minute ad break."

"Yeah, yeah," he smiled

"She may have known her attacker," Manning added.

"What makes you say that?"

"Erm..."

"Pillow talk?"

"Don't be impertinent Eric, I won't stand for it," yet she was smiling.

"Hmmm – what's Deidre said anyway?"

"Ask her yourself."

Deidre appeared from Manning's office. Even after a few years Fenton was still struck by her presence. Her jet-black hair bounced like a *L'Oréal* advert as she walked. She had attractive brown eyes, light olive skin and was also around six feet tall. It was strange being in the presence of two women who were at the same height as him. Deidre was in a different league to Manning though who looked like a Rottweiler – still it took all types he mused.

"Deidre, how are you?" asked Fenton extending his hand.

"Her name is Dr Deidre Peters," remarked Manning.

"Oh, forget all that nonsense Mandy," retorted Deidre.

Fenton always wondered why Dr Shirley Manning insisted on being called Mandy by women and Ms Manning by men. It was a question he would never ask though. It was one of those for the *too hard basket*. They'd clashed many times over the years, yet they'd always maintained a mutual respect for each other's work ethic.

Manning blushed and went back to her work. Very unlike her!

"I'm very well Eric, thank you," replied Deidre. "How are Mrs Fenton and the girls?"

"All very well, only got one at home now and soon she'll fly the nest."

"They all do. You've got an interesting one here Eric if I do say so."

Dr Deidre Peters was one of the best criminal psychologists in the country, if not the world. How her and Manning ended up together beggared belief. Still it kept Manning mellow, which could only be a good thing.

"I would love your insight Deidre, although I don't want to blow the budget on the first day."

"Call it a favour."

"Really?"

"Well you'll be pandering to my morbid fascination."

"Well it's something if she knew her attacker I guess."

"What do you mean?"

"Well if she knew her attacker, it reduces the possibility of it being random. I was starting to worry that this could be the start of a spree."

"Still could be – many serial killers start with someone they know. And if you want my professional opinion, I do think this is part of something bigger."

"You think he's a slow burner, or we'll just see a slew of bodies turning up. I mean he could have taken them all already and will stagger them out."

"Unlikely given this one wasn't staged and the first is often quite significant. It can be more personal than any future victims. She could be your link. You need to find out all you can about her."

"Could it be linked to the baby she's had?"

"It's possible. That could be some time ago though and I think your killer will be closer to home. There's clear evidence of psychopathic tendencies here. The frantic attack and how they continued to smash in her face even after death shows a terrible temper that took something this extreme to satiate it."

"Do you think we'll get another body soon?"

"I'd say if you don't get one within forty-eight hours then you will be looking at a slow burner which will make then harder to catch, as each murder will be carefully planned. That's not to say this one wasn't. The kill itself may have been planned; the way it was executed was not. It's too messy and frenzied. However, they were rational enough to ensure they would not be traced from the scene afterwards. The fact that someone can become so calm after such a vicious attack tells me that you are dealing with an extremely dangerous person, possibly even a sociopath."

"Do you think we're looking for a man?"

"It's highly likely, but let's not rule anything out. The lack of any sexual attack shows that we could be looking at a woman. It would take someone with incredible strength to inflict these injuries. I'd keep an open mind for now, as you never know. History has taught us that women are also capable of anything," she laughed.

"Right let's see our girl, I'm due to brief the team at nine," remarked Fenton.

They moved over to where Giselle was lying. Manning had tried to tidy up her face, but she was still barely recognisable. Fenton really felt for whoever was going to have to identify her. His phone rang and he gave an apologetic look to Manning who glared. Deidre clearly hadn't mellowed her enough to relax the *no mobiles in the lab* rule.

"Fenton... What? Where? I'm on my way." He snapped the phone shut. "Shit, we've got another one."

"Go – I'll send you my report by lunchtime."

"Thanks," he shouted as he ran out of the lab.

———

Manning came out of her office with her coat on.

"Where are you going?" asked Deidre.

"To the crime scene of course," replied Manning. "They want me on this one as well. I hope this isn't another spree. Eric Fenton has a habit of collecting bodies."

"Damn, I'd love to see the crime scene."

"Well you're not officially on the case are you, so they won't allow you anywhere near it."

"Have a word with Eric and get me on it then."

"Don't be ridiculous they couldn't afford you."

"Well like I said, it'll be a favour."

"If you start giving out favours, you'll never do paid work again."

"Well we don't get serial cases in the UK very often."

"It's not a serial case yet is it? It's only a double murder and we don't have definitive proof yet that they are linked. It's just circumstantial at the moment. Now I need to get down there."

"Let me tag along and I'll disappear if I'm getting in the way."

"Alright," Manning, sighed. "But speak to Eric first, we've been on good terms for a while and I'd like to keep it that way."

"Why is that? I thought you said he was a dinosaur."

"Yes, but a good one," she laughed. "Besides, I still feel guilty over that business with Polly."

"Have you heard from her lately?"

"Not for ages. She's still in Sydney, living the high life. Lucky bitch."

"I thought you loved your work?"

"I do, but who on earth would keep on working if they didn't need to?"

"I would."

"Not if you had the sort of money Polly has."

"How much money did she make for bringing the Prime Minister down?"

"Enough to never have to work again. Served him right though, bloody pervert."

"Ah well, there is a dark side in all of us my dear. Just some aren't so good at hiding it as others."

"Not with my sister around."

They both laughed as they walked out the lab.

CHAPTER FIVE

Fenton walked up to Jacobs, Brennan and Shirkham. He looked down at the body and saw a practically identical scene to the one he'd been less than twenty-four hours ago. It was a different alleyway in a different part of the West End, but he didn't need forensics or a criminal psychologist to tell him that they'd met their end at the hands of the same killer. Still, they did come in handy when you needed them – reasonable doubt and all that.

"Any idea how long she's been here?" Fenton asked no one in particular.

"They think just a few hours, sir," replied Jacobs.

"I was just with Manning when I got the call so no doubt, she'll be on her way soon."

"I believe she is, sir. She was called not long after you."

"Speak of the devil," remarked Brennan. "And look she's got that Deidre sort with her. Jack, just look at how fit this woman is."

"Gary!" remarked Fenton sternly.

"Sorry, Guv. Sir, would you look at fit this woman is," he said to Jacobs with a cheeky grin.

Fenton chose to ignore Brenna's humour. He watched Manning approach with her bag of tricks, or tools of the trade as she referred to them.

"Ms Manning, we could have driven over together. I see you've brought company." Fenton remarked as Manning walked over. Deidre had remained in the car.

"Yes, well..."

Fenton still enjoyed watching her squirm. "Well if she's still pro bono then by all means she's very welcome."

"Thank you, Eric." She looked over at the car and jerked her head.

Deidre got out of the car, causing Brennan to make a dog-like sound, much to the annoyance of Manning who gave him a withering look.

"This is a crime scene Gary, stop behaving like a juvenile or you'll never get promoted. There's a time and a place to be the team clown," Fenton hissed in his ear.

"Sorry, Guv," Brennan replied, going bright red.

He gave a look which made Fenton think of a puppy which had just been kicked. Not that he would ever kick a puppy, although he might kick Brennan if he carried on acting like a tit.

"Right shall we get started. Ah, DC Shirkham. Good to see you again." Manning shook hands with Shirkham a little longer than necessary who didn't seem at all phased. "I saw DCI Taylor on a case a few weeks ago. She is doing very well. I understand she is going for Superintendent. Is that true Eric?" Manning asked.

"Yes, it is."

"That will be strange for you won't it?"

"How do you mean?"

"Well you former protégé becoming your boss. Must smart a bit," she added with a snort.

"Not at all. You know I have never been keen on the

higher ranks. We'd hardly ever see each other if that happened," he replied sharply.

He hated the fact then when they were in front of his team, she had to stamp her authority. The old Manning was still there, and it pissed him off. Still now was not the time to rise to it if he wanted to solicit the services of Deidre Peters for free, so he switched into polite mode as she approached. He also wanted to retain the moral high ground after pulling Brennan up for his behaviour.

"We meet again so soon, Deirdre."

"I said you might get another kill didn't I Eric. I must say I didn't expect it to be so quickly. Thank you for letting me view the scene."

"Not at all. You know the drill. Let's get the suits on."

After ten minutes Deidre had finished making her notes and was ready to talk to Fenton and the others.

"Eric, you're looking for someone here who has a purpose," remarked Deidre.

"But you said the first was personal."

"Yes, it was, and so might this one, but there is still an end goal."

"Do you think they'll stop when they reach it?"

"That's always a possibility and would show a high degree of self-control. This person has been planning these killings for a long time. I believe there will be more, and soon. I don't think you'll have the luxury of waiting on forensic evidence this time, as the body count is just going to mount up whilst you do. It'll have to be like the good old days before you had all this fancy lab work."

"I can hear you, you know," retorted Manning in the background.

"Do you think we'll have another tomorrow?" asked Fenton.

"It's possible. These first two may have been significant for the killer, and it's possible given the timeframe in which they were killed, they are interchangeable. In other words, it didn't matter which was first. It was probably whoever was in the right place first."

"Can you come to the station later when I brief the team?"

"What time is that?"

"I was hoping to do it by noon."

"I need to be somewhere else, but I could do four."

"That'll work, we'll see you then."

"I'll see you later Mandy. I need to get going."

Manning gave a thumbs up from where she was working, and Deidre walked off.

"Ms Manning is it the same murder weapon?" asked Fenton approaching her.

"Not literally, although it's likely the same type. I can see the brick dust residue around the wounds."

"Can we get all the bricks in the nearby area bagged and tagged please?"

"I do know how to do my job you know Eric."

"Of course, you do," he smiled. "I'll catch up with you later. I need to get back to the station. Gary you're with me. Jack you stay here with Emma until they're done. Briefing at four."

"Okay, sir," replied Jack.

"What are you smiling for?" asked Fenton.

"Nothing, sir."

Fenton noticed Brennan was smiling as well, although he had no idea what about. Probably some shared joke that he'd missed. At least they were getting on and the macho handshake from yesterday had not impacted their ability to already form a bond. It was important for a team to get along, even if they disagreed with each other at times.

―――――

Jacobs couldn't stop staring at her. He was acting like a frisky adolescent and she was clearly not interested. Her aloofness didn't give the cold presence she was clearly aiming for. To him she radiated heat and beauty. Well something like that. He'd read it in a magazine or something, in reality she was just fit!

"How long do you think we have to stay here for?" he asked.

"Like the boss said, until they're done," she replied.

"Do you think they'll be done before the briefing at four?"

"I have no idea," she replied bluntly.

This was going to be no easy catch, still he liked a challenge and he was welcoming the distraction from the anxiety he felt after contacting his old friends last night. He had used his untraceable mobile phone and told them of Giselle's murder. It had not gone down well, although Karen seemed to regard Giselle's murder as more of an inconvenience than a tragedy. The reality was that Giselle was linked to both places and there was no way of keeping them out of it. Especially now – he looked down again at the body and despite the severe beating she had obviously taken he was certain that it was Becky. It was yet another person that connected them all. He couldn't give her identity to his colleagues. They would need to discover that themselves. He hadn't recognised Giselle. This one was different. Who could be doing this? Could someone know what happened, or was it just be a fucked-up coincidence? This murder investigation had the potential to bring everything he had built up for himself, crashing down, and then where would that leave him?

Fenton stood at the front of the incident room and everyone fell quiet. A lot had happened in twenty-four hours. They were now working on a double murder and everyone knew that that results were expected and fast. One dead prostitute was of no interest to the press in all honesty. However, two victims was a different matter. They had to catch this killer before it happened again, and if they were carrying on with the same pattern then their next victim would be breathing her last in a matter of hours.

"So, our second victim has been identified as Becky Best. Again, that's her real name. She recently left employment at a place called Karen's Klub, which is where our first victim also worked. Becky was then working at a gym called Ryan's Retreat. The same gym that our first victim was a member of. Now both our victims worked in the sex industry, although we hear they had both put their pasts behind them. Has it come back to haunt them? I want to know more about the woman who runs this club, a Karen Kowalski."

"Jacobs, knows her, Guv," piped up Brennan.

"Jack, how are you two acquainted?"

"From when I was with Vice, sir – Karen runs a smooth operation, all legitimate. Although we know there is more to it, we were never able to get her on anything."

"Drugs?"

"No, she hates them, she was always drying girls out, the hard way. If they fell back into old habits, she would never give them a second chance, no matter how much they begged."

"So, what else was she into then?"

"The illegitimate side of the sex industry. She also had guys working for her as well. It wasn't just girls. Apparently, the guys don't do any private dances though. They aren't based in the main club."

"Dances?"

"That would be the legitimate side, sir."

Everyone laughed.

"Right let's settle down. Well we need to talk to this Karen, so we'll head over in the morning. Jack, you can come with me."

"Why not tonight? If there is going to be another victim tonight, then surely we need to move quicker?"

"The last thing I want us to do is piss off the Vice squad. We need to let them know what we're doing. Jack, you've got the contacts. I also hear this Ryan Killarney who runs this gym has a lot of whores as members?"

"That's probably just because of where it's located."

"Still we hold off on that one as well until we've spoken to Vice. Right Emma, what have you got for us?"

Shirkham stood up and walked to the front.

"So, the methods in which both girls were killed was identical. Both appear to have been continually beaten with the weapon, in this case a brick, after death as well. This one was different in that she was found with her handbag which is why we were able to identify her so quickly. It's possible that Giselle may not have had a bag with her when she met her killer, rather than it being taken."

"Good point, still we should find out what sort of bags she had and see if we can find them in her flat. If one is missing, then it still could be significant. Anything else?" asked Fenton.

"It appears that she would have been killed between three and seven in the morning, although probably closer to three. A homeless guy was sleeping in the alley until about three when he moved on somewhere else. He came back for some stuff when we were at the scene. She was found at seven o'clock this morning and the first forensic officer at the scene said she was already cold to the touch and it's been fairly mild lately, so she'd been there a while."

"Okay, well that helps until we can get an accurate time of death from Manning. Did we swab this homeless guys hands for brick dust, on the off chance?"

"Yes, that's being checked now sir."

"Excellent. Gary?" he said looking at his DS.

"We've not been able to trace any family for Giselle, they're either dead or have disappeared," he said, as he stood up thumbing through his notebook. "So, there's nobody even to claim her body."

"What about that guy Andy who was pretty cut up about it?" asked Fenton.

"We could start there, but I doubt Manning will have the body ready for release for a few days so one to come back to. Nothing on the baby she had. Can't find her registered as the mother of a child on a birth certificate and there's nothing on the adoption register. Manning says she delivered the baby so I'm checking death certificates as well, but that'll take a while given we don't have a first name or date."

Fenton saw Deidre enter the back of the incident room.

"Okay you'll see we have been joined by Dr Deidre Peters who is able to share her expertise on this case. I'm sure if any of you haven't met her, then you'll know her by reputation at least."

"Thank you, Eric," Deidre replied weaving her way to the front of the room. "Your killer is probably a man. Given the frenzied nature of the attack and the brutality caused after death, I'd say it was statistically likely that you'll be looking for a White male, aged between twenty-five and forty. He will be known to the victims as neither of them put up a fight. He could be a former punter, but I think it may go deeper than that. These are both former prostitutes who worked in well-established places. They earned top dollar and would not go with their clients in back alleyways. They will have known and trusted their killer. It is likely that they would have been incapacitated by the first blow, due to the lack of defensive marks, whether the first blow rendered them unconscious is something we'll never know. As I said to DCI Fenton earlier today, these kills were probably interchangeable. It's possible you may get another body soon, but if you don't then your killer will have either changed their approach or simply be trying to keep one step ahead of the police. They will have been aware that little could have been done to track them after the first victim, so to act again so quickly was clever and bold. This individual has no fear. They are not scared of being caught. However, do not expect them to walk openly into your arms."

"Both victims are connected in many ways. What would you suggest is the first one to start at?" asked Jacobs.

"This again is very deliberate. I strongly believe these victims have hurt your killer but have also been chosen to have you all chasing your tails. This is also why you received a second victim in quick succession. They are goading you because they know they can. I would follow up all leads. The club seems more obvious than the gym, although they could both be significant. Find out in what other ways these two places are linked and through which people. Believe me, this individual still has more to do, and we have no idea when they will strike again. The only thing we are certain of is that they will do it again... and soon."

After the briefing had ended Fenton thanked Deidre and saw her out before returning to his office. The team had a few last things to do before the end of the day and he wanted an early start in the morning. Manning had promised him some results. This case was in danger of getting out of hand. At present there had been no press release. Chief Superintendent Harry Beeden had made it quite clear that one was needed to warn the other girls off the streets. Not that it ever made the blindest bit of difference. These women had a living to make – children, or a habit to feed; usually both. They hadn't fled the streets when the Yorkshire Ripper or Suffolk Strangler were at large, and they certainly weren't about to change the habit of a lifetime now. Fenton pondered his next move and then picked up the phone. He needed to bend the ear of an old friend.

CHAPTER SIX

DCI Lisa Taylor walked into Fenton's office. Another tall woman. Those piercing blue eyes still caused you to be drawn to them and she had clearly not let a relationship get in the way of her keeping in shape. That was always most people's excuse; when you're with someone, you don't need to be fit and healthy in order to attract a mate, so what was the point in bothering. They seemed to forget that being fit and healthy isn't just about getting laid. Fenton still played squash regularly and he'd been married for almost thirty years, although it was once or twice a week now instead of the five times he did right into his mid-forties.

Here she was anyway. The best detective he had ever worked with. She became DCI at thirty-two, which is impressive and even more so for a woman. The short dark hair finished off her look and she had that razor-sharp mind to go with it. The only things that let her down were her penchant for bad boys, although her current squeeze at least had no criminal connections – Fenton had checked. She was originally from Bolton and despite living in London a long time, the accent was still strong, and it certainly made an impression.

"DCI Taylor, how are you?" beamed Fenton with pride.

"I'm good Eric, how about you?" she asked.

"Not too bad."

"Well clearly that didn't work?"

"What?"

"I were told that when someone asks you how you are, you say *good* and then they'll say the same. It stops them saying *not too bad* and then you don't feel you have to ask what's wrong and lose an hour of your time."

"Interesting theory."

"Yeah, load of old shit clearly. I see you put your stamp on this place?" she said looking round his office.

She was right. Ever since they had been solely based out of one police station, this had been Fenton's permanent office. He liked it in Kentish Town, and he had slowly added a few personal possessions to the office, such as a mini golfing hole, which he had used for about a week after he bought it. He had pictures of his wife and daughters on his desk, a few pictures on the wall to brighten the place up and his own coffee machine, so he didn't have to drink the instant crap from the canteen which hardened like treacle.

"So, what can I do you for?" she asked.

"Nothing really, I just heard your case had wrapped up, so thought we could catch up before you're assigned the next one."

"I got some down time to prepare for exams."

"Superintendent? I heard about that."

"Yeah whatever. Anyway Eric, I've known you a long time and you can't fob me off. What's wrong? I hear this case you've got is a tricky one."

"Still too early to make that judgement. We're hoping not

to have body number three waiting for us in the morning. We've got Deidre Peters to profile."

"How d'you swing that?"

"Freebie, I think she's probably got a new book in the works. Still Beeden's not complaining. While you're here though, I've been meaning to ask you something."

"Here we go," she smiled.

She'd always had a great smile. One of those few people who could smile, and it made everyone in the room feel cheerful.

"You've got me," he said holding his hands up in mock defeat. "Jack Jacobs?"

"He's good Eric. Got a sharp mind. I know how you feel about academic route detectives when they get fast-tracked, but he's proved himself time and time again on my cases."

"I don't doubt that, but there's something I can't quite put my finger on."

"He can be a bit maverick, wander off on his own. I've told him that it's got to stop if he wants DCI. He gets results, but I worry for his safety. I've told him that he'll never get up the ladder without sorting it out."

"I've already picked up on the maverick thing. No, it's something else."

"I know what you mean. I've worked with him a long time now and never been able to work it out. You're right though, there's more to that lad."

"Well I'll let you know when I work it out – I don't give up quite so easily!"

"Watch it, you cheeky sod!"

"Do you want to see the incident board? I would appreciate your thoughts on the case."

She nodded, so they got up and left his office. The rest of the team had gone home and there was a skeleton night staff who just ignored them as Fenton showed Taylor the incident board. He pointed out the two victims to date, Giselle Gorge and Becky Best, again clarifying that it was their real names. Taylor pointed out that it was a strange coincidence that they both had working girl names at birth and they both became them as adults. They also had first and last names starting with the same letter and jokingly suggested it was perhaps a lunatic who didn't like people with the same initials, and it was nothing to do with their work as tarts. Fenton said perhaps she had a point, as he didn't want to leave anything out. They then both laughed at the thought of how ridiculous that would be.

He talked through the investigation to date. It was helpful to do that with someone impartial at the same level. He was one of the few DCIs who didn't get all precious when those who once worked for him became peers, or even superiors. Fenton mentioned the links to Karen's Klub and Ryan's Retreat and Taylor mentioned the initials thing again. Perhaps it wasn't something to laugh about. Fenton hoped it was just the thing he hated the most - a coincidence, as nutcase killers with weird obsessions were not to be taken lightly. He'd have to talk to Beeden in the morning about how they handled the press release. It would only take one journalist to do some digging around and find the link with the club and gym, notice the similarities with the initials of those and the victims and start moral panic. Thankfully, Polly Pilkington was on the other side of the world – and there was another double initial!

Taylor asked if he had been to the club or gym yet and he told her that he was waiting until the morning when he had more forensic information. Given the gym had a lot of sex workers there as clients, and then the club itself, he knew they always closed ranks as soon as the police came sniffing round, so he wanted to have as much information as he could before he went in there for the first time.

He also told her that he'd arranged for more uniform to be out on patrol at night in some of the obvious areas where another victim may turn up. There was nothing more he could do, and Taylor agreed that warning the girls off the street was a fruitless task as they never listened anyway. Besides, neither of their victims had been street girls and supposedly they weren't even working girls at the time they'd died. This was another connection that Fenton and Taylor discussed. Could it be that these girls had been targeted because they had put it all behind them and was the old saying *once a whore, always a whore* being demonstrated here, although Fenton often wondered who came up with these old sayings and believed that most the time, people just made them up to suit their argument.

"If the connection is to do with them giving up the game, then that Karen should be your priority," remarked Taylor.

"She is, it'll be my first stop tomorrow. I'm planning to take Emma with me. We really need to get her promoted. I wish she'd change her mind about staying at one rank."

"Like you ya mean?"

"Touché."

"You could be Beeden's boss by now."

"You see, every cloud does have a silver lining."

They both laughed.

"How is Emma anyhow?" asked Taylor.

"Fine, why shouldn't she be?"

"Well she broke up with her husband."

"I didn't know that. I mean hardly anyone even knew she was married. You know how private she is."

"It were a while ago and she ain't told nobody. I only found out by accident, so I ain't spoken to her about it. Thought she might have said something to you though."

"Not a thing. Any idea when it was?"

Taylor shook her head. Fenton tried to think about a time

when Shirkham may not have been herself. There wasn't one. Always the consummate professional, never allowing her private life to interfere with her work. Still he would have hoped that she felt she could have confided in him. He'd have to talk to her, although choose his time sensibly. Perhaps taking her out with him would give him the opportunity for it to come up accidentally.

Just then his phone rang. It was Manning saying she had her preliminary report ready and was happy to discuss it tonight if he didn't want to wait until the morning. She would be at the lab for another hour. It was already past eight. Fenton asked Taylor if she wanted to come along. She agreed and said she'd drive herself, so she could head straight home afterwards.

Fenton and Taylor entered Manning's lab and went to grab their robes before they were prompted. However, Manning was nowhere to be seen, so Fenton assumed she'd be in her office. He walked over and heard raised voices. He beckoned Taylor over and it sounded like Manning and Deidre were having an almighty row. He couldn't work out what they were saying. They both agreed that it would be very inadvisable for both their careers if they were caught eavesdropping. Manning was still the best in the business, and the last thing they wanted was for her to refuse to work with them. They both sneaked out of the lab and waited in Fenton's car. After five minutes they saw Deidre come rushing out of the building, get in her own car and drive off. They left it for another couple of minutes and then went in.

"Robes," she hollered as they took them back off the pegs and put them on. Just one day he would get the robe on before she said anything.

"Ms Manning, thank you for staying on so late to see me."

"Not at all Eric and I see you've brought DCI Taylor with you. How are you?"

"Hello Mandy, and please call me Lisa. I'm really good and you?"

"Yes, all good," she replied, with her girlish giggle.

She was blushing, so still clearly had a thing for Taylor, who no doubt used it to her advantage on cases.

"Yes, it does work," Taylor whispered to Fenton, reading his mind.

You wouldn't have known looking at Manning that she'd been screaming and shouting a few minutes before.

"You two still whisper like naughty school children I see," she smiled. It always unnerved Fenton when she was being overly nice.

"So, what have you got for us?" he asked.

"Well your victims were both killed with a brick which I can definitively confirm. We also can't find the murder weapon at either scene, so it was taken away by the killer, yet they used a different brick for each victim. Read into that what you will."

"Perhaps Deidre will be able to give us some insight into that," he said provocatively. Sometimes he just couldn't help himself.

"No doubt she will," came the brittle response. "You will see that both victims are virtually unrecognisable given the damage that has been inflicted to their faces." She was pointing at photographs on the wall, which Fenton was grateful for. There was only so many times you could look at the real thing without it entering your nightmares.

"There is no evidence of any sexual assault on the second victim, which is the same as the first," Manning continued. "However, again this one has been very sexually active. There is no indication that this one has given birth, or even had a termination. Although if this happened in the early stages it would be nigh on impossible to tell."

"They both died from the blows to the face?" asked Fenton.

"Yes, they did. It is possible, and let's hope probable, that both victims quickly lost consciousness before the fatal blow was dealt, but of course we'll never know. One thing is certain though, is that after death your killer continued to inflict further damage to both victims. I suspect they may have just been wanting to make sure their victim was dead, and the attack was so frenzied that once they started, they couldn't stop."

"Any DNA on any of the victims?" asked Fenton.

"No and nothing to indicate a struggle, any form of restraint and or any drugs used to debilitate the victims. They may have been rendered unconscious with the first blow. That may perhaps be a small mercy."

"That still doesn't explain why there were in a dark alley," remarked Fenton.

"My job is to present the facts, Eric. As the detective it's your job to interpret them."

"I'm aware of my job thank you."

"So, any closer indication on time of death?" asked Taylor.

Fenton noticed she had been quiet so far and then quickly jumped in as she sensed things were getting tense. The last thing Fenton needed was the old Manning back. He hoped her altercation with Deidre was just a tiff.

"Yes, of course Lisa," Manning purred. "Giselle died between one and two o'clock in the morning. Becky between three and four."

"What time does the sun come up at this time of year?" Fenton asked.

"About five," replied Manning. "So, it was dark when they were both killed. Shall I continue?"

Fenton nodded.

Fenton had said goodbye to Taylor and reflected on the case so far. What sort of killer was he looking for? He didn't like coincidences and there was just too many here. He couldn't push resource into chasing down every coincidence that come up on a case, so which were the strongest ones?

Giselle and Becky had both worked for Karen Kowalski and had since left her employment. It was believed that she wasn't keen on people leaving her until their *debt* was repaid. Had Giselle and Becky repaid their debts? Did they even have one in the first place? They were also linked through this gym, Ryan's Retreat, although that link wasn't as strong. Becky worked there as a fitness trainer and Giselle had been a client. Not unusual really given they both knew the area well. The club was a stronger link and that would be where he would start first thing in the morning. He hadn't really got anything he could use from Manning when he spoke to Karen Kowalski, although he had been right to hold off and not rush in there like Jack Jacobs had wanted to do. He'd put him and Brennan on the gym and Fenton himself would personally meet Karen and take Shirkham with him.

He considered what the motives could be. Could it be personal? Both women probably knew each other and may have had potential enemies who knew them both. Fenton was not convinced it was random and this first and last initial thing seemed too ridiculous to contemplate, although until they had a tangible motive nothing could be ruled out. The fact that both victims were black couldn't be overlooked either. This didn't have the feel of a hate crime, although it would mean serious repercussions later on if that proved to be the case and he hadn't duly considered it as a possibility, so nothing could be dropped as a line of enquiry just yet.

This press release was of concern. He needed to talk to Harry about rethinking what could be released. The problem with press intrusion was that it forced you to follow lines of enquiry which his gut instinct told him were nothing. That's what detective work was about – following that gut instinct and uncovering the evidence to back it up. The waiting around for forensic reports didn't happen years ago and crimes were still solved. He needed to give the team a bit of a shake up tomorrow. They had made a few enquiries, although they had basically just taken it easy whilst waiting for the reports to come in. He was guilty of that himself, as were most police these days. What he would do after the interviews with Ryan and Karen is follow that gut instinct. It appeared that this case wasn't going to give him the luxury of time to solve it.

CHAPTER SEVEN

Karen was looking after the bar until ten o'clock, when her barman was due to start. The club was quiet, which was typical at this part of the evening. The early evening crowd straight after work had gone back to their wives having had their little treat – some of them with other men. Men were all the same, whether they be gay, straight, bi or miscellaneous. They were all the same: cunts! This was why she chose to remain single. The last man who had crossed her had come to regret it, in fact it he had never come again. She laughed out loud at her own joke. God, she was hilarious!

The police sniffing around after two of her girls had been murdered would be a problem for business. DI Jack Jacobs had already given her a discreet call and told her she couldn't buy her way out of this, as they were talking about murder. Those stupid bitches – if they had stayed with her, she would have protected them. Still it could be useful. She had warned them not to leave her and people might assume she was responsible. Well she had someone who could verify her whereabouts for last night at least so she was not unduly worried. There was an advantage to any rumours, as they would dissuade any other girls from thinking of leaving her. Becky, she hadn't minded so much as she had repaid her debt and sought a better life for herself. She had even helped Karen out the night she died, which was another problem. Becky had been here last night. Still the client would want complete discretion and the only other person who knew was Sid. She doubted Becky would have said anything to anyone else.

Giselle was a different story. She had still owed Karen and then fucked her over. Well the stupid little bitch would fuck with her no more. Karen was now seriously out of pocket – an occupational hazard when you drag people off the streets and groom them. For some inexplicable reason they could develop a sense of self-worth and believe there was something better for them elsewhere. It was pitiful and intensely irritating when you'd broken someone in so much that the customers literally queued around the block, which they did for Giselle. When it came to her work, Giselle had a raw and desirable sexuality, she was someone who could take people beyond their sexual limits and have them begging for more. As a person she was an arsehole, consumed by greed.

There was nothing Karen could do about Giselle now anyway. She wouldn't recoup her losses from the others as that's what she was known for – she was fair. She'd been there herself and if the girls or guys had pulled out all the tricks to get a good tip then that was for them, unlike restaurants who tended to use tips and service charges to top up the minimum wage for their staff. She would need to keep her people sweet for now, or she'd soon find herself back where she started – with nothing. She was less worried about the guys as they hadn't been targeted, and they didn't scare as easily. People were surprised at how tough a male whore could be, except with Karen, then they were all the same – pussies!

"Sid, why aren't you on the door?" she said, looking up as he approached.

"Detective Inspector Jacobs wants a private word. I've sent him into the back."

"Matt is not here yet to cover the bar and I need you on the door."

"Matt's out the back, just relaxing before his shift. I'll ask him to start early. I don't want Jacobs in the club."

"Fine... and Sid, be careful how you fucking talk to me. I know you are looking out for me, but you treat me with respect. You hear?"

He shook his head and walked off. She would have to have a word with him later, or people would think she was losing her edge.

Jack stood and kissed both her cheeks and gripped her hand firmly. They had known each other a long time. Karen trusted him, although she knew he would not think twice about turning her in if he thought she was responsible for these murders.

"What can I do for you Jack?"

"We've got a problem Karen. Two girls murdered in as many days, and both working at this club. It puts a spotlight on us that we could do without."

"The girls where no longer working for me. There is no connection."

"Karen, listen. They were both beaten to death in back alleys. Both murder scenes scream whore and they both worked here. The connection has been made, whether it's a valid one or not. My boss will be coming to see you first thing tomorrow morning."

"He can go fuck himself. I say nothing without my lawyer."

"You need to play nice with him Karen. He's good and he won't be frightened, fobbed or bought off. He knows that we know each other."

"What have you said to him you stupid boy?"

"Relax, he just thinks I know you from Vice. He knows nothing else, but I had to say something. I haven't mentioned knowing Ryan, as I think that's easier to cover."

"Why are they asking about Ryan."

"Becky was working for him. Giselle was a member of his gym. It's not a big leap to connect them all."

"But every whore in Soho uses that gym."

"It's still a connection that has to be checked out. I'm seeing Ryan after I'm finished here. I didn't want to meet him at the gym in case someone saw."

"He's not coming here is he?"

"Relax. I'm not that stupid."

"So, what will this...?"

"DCI Eric Fenton."

"I see, so what will this Fenton want with me?"

"To ask you when you last saw the girls, how long they worked here, when they left. The circumstances they left under. Any clients they had any problems with..."

"I will not name my clients."

"Be careful there. I agree, don't give them up too easily or it will look obvious. Perhaps let him persuade you it's in your best interest. You don't want him to get a warrant. It might have been a long time ago, but you'd be surprised what Forensics could still find."

"Don't threaten me Jack, you have just as much to lose and it will be worse for you in prison."

"Nobody's going to prison. You need to calm down. This will all blow over. It's just a coincidence. As soon as they find who did it then they'll leave you alone."

"And I will have no fucking business left and you will have

your career and Ryan will have his gym. It will only be Miss Karen who is fucked."

"Have you got any idea who could have done this?"

"No. For Becky I am sad, but that bitch Giselle is just lucky I didn't get to her first and I will tell that to this Fenton guy as well."

"That's good, as it will only take a few questions with some of the girls for him to find out how you felt about her."

"He is not speaking to my girls."

"He's investigating a double murder. He can talk to whoever he wants."

"I will tell him to go fuck himself. He leaves my girls alone. They are scared enough," her anger now palpable and she was pacing up and down, her bosom heaving as she breathed deeply trying to control her temper.

"Karen, listen to me," he said grabbing her arms, so she stopped and looked directly at him. "This is a murder investigation. You must co-operate, or the police will be all over this place like a rash. They will suspect you're hiding something, and nobody will be able to step foot inside without being questioned. Just play nice. Tell them you and Giselle didn't get along just don't get too carried away. Who is you alibi anyway?"

"I was with Sid."

"Why am I not surprised," he said smiling.

"The boy knows loyalty."

"I don't doubt it, still watch yourself Karen. The spotlight will be on you for a while and if anyone finds out about what happened then, well you know what will happen."

"Nobody will hear anything from me. You know that Jack, we all have too much to lose now."

"I'll see myself out."

He got up and held her for a second. He must have sensed

from her breathing that she was trying to hold it together, as he waited for her to break the hug.

"I'll be in touch. If you need anything leave me a message on my other phone, just in case."

"I will, Jack and give Ryan my love. Tell him I miss him."

He nodded and left.

Karen was sitting in her office. It was after two o'clock. It had been a surprisingly busy night, although things had been quiet for the last half hour. A few of the girls and guys had gone out for all-nighters so she had told Sid to close early. She wanted to be fresh for her meeting with Fenton the next day.

"Any problems with the customers for closing so early?" Karen asked Sid as he entered her office.

"No, there wasn't many. It's been quiet tonight. I've locked up and the tills are done as well. Matt has stocked up for tomorrow and left. I'm going to get off to bed."

"You are not going to look after me tonight Sid?" She resented that her voice sounded pleading. The last thing she wanted was to tip the balance of power.

"Let's just call last night a one-off, shall we?"

"How can it be a one off when you have been in my bed more times than I can remember?"

"You know what I mean? Let's be adults about this shall we?"

She slapped him hard across the face.

"You listen to me. It was lucky for you and me that you were in my bed last night when Becky was killed. I will also tell the police that you were with me the night that filthy whore was killed as well."

"You went out the night Giselle was killed."

"Well think yourself lucky that I can provide you an alibi as well. Remember they will be looking for a man, so it is for the best if you do as I fucking say and don't answer back. Now you come to bed with Miss Karen and see if you can last longer than five minutes this time. You may have retired, but that does not mean you act like a fucking amateur. Now get upstairs before I find another alibi for the night Giselle died."

"You won't do that Karen. You've got just as much to lose. Now I'm going out and I'll be back tomorrow."

"Please don't leave me alone Sid. I did not mean to hit you. I am just upset that the police will be here to question me tomorrow."

"I need my space Karen. I'll be back tomorrow for when the police get here," and he quietly left.

She knew not to go after him when he was in one of his moods. He would just walk the streets alone all night. He still did that from time to time to clear his head. She would now have to face the night alone. It was at night that she remembered what had happened in this very room. She sat back in her chair and quietly sobbed, making sure nobody could hear her.

———

Jack and Ryan were sitting at the back of the all-night Soho cafe. It was late and Jack knew there was an early briefing tomorrow. Despite that, he had to speak to Ryan before his boss did. He couldn't take the risk that Fenton wouldn't want to do the interview himself, or that he'd send someone else. Ryan had been late owing to a business matter he had to deal with, and they had agreed it wasn't worth the risk of Jack being seen at the gym.

They had known each other for almost twenty years and barely seen or spoken to each other for the last two. Jack was almost overcome with emotion when he saw his oldest friend who knew him better than anyone. That had to be put aside, as he had to be sure they were all protected.

"What's this all about Jack?" Ryan whispered as he sat down

There was a loud group of drag queens a few tables along, howling and shrieking, so nobody was interested in them anyway. Jack was casually dressed as he thought he might be recognised from his days in Vice if he remained suited up.

"You know about Giselle and Becky?"

"Well of course, you called me remember. I still can't believe it about Becky," he started crying.

Jack looked around worried they would attract attention. There was nothing to worry about. The drag queens were completely engrossed in their number one topic of conversation – themselves.

"Where you and Becky together?" Jack asked gently.

"No, but I wish I'd told her how I felt."

"I thought you were with Tony?"

"You'd be surprised what can happen in two years, besides Tony only loves himself. It was only ever a casual thing. Regrettable now when I think about it."

"What do you mean?" asked Jack suddenly interested.

"Not good for my cred. Tony's a good friend but he's not my usual type. He's got a great body of course, but that face left a lot to be desired though."

"You never struck me as being that superficial," Jack remarked.

"Like I said, a lot can happen in two years Jack. With Tony it was the personality that attracted me to him. I mean with that nose of his it was like being sucked off by an aardvark."

Jack roared with laughter and then quickly went quiet, so he didn't attract attention. He'd missed this guy and the hilarious things he'd come out with.

"Anyway, I needed to see you. I'm on the murder case and my colleagues are aware of the connection between Giselle, Becky and your place?"

"What do you mean?" asked Ryan.

He sounded worried, which was good, as it demonstrated that he was taking this seriously.

"Well Becky worked for you and Giselle was a member. My boss will no doubt be round to see you tomorrow."

"Is that DCI Taylor?"

"How do you know about her?"

"I still speak to your sisters from time to time. I missed you. I wanted to know how you were doing."

Jack smiled. He missed his old friend as well. Perhaps two years had been long enough and when this case was over it could go back to how it used to be.

"I'm not with Taylor on this case. It's being led by a guy called Fenton."

"I've heard about him. He's been in the press a few times."

"Yeah, they tend to give him the high-profile cases."

"So, what does he want with me?"

"Well you were Becky's boss. It's not unusual that someone from the team will need to talk to you and with Giselle being a gym member, it's another link. I've already had to warn Karen."

"What? She'll do her nut if they go to the club."

"They already are doing, so listen to me. Nobody knows that we know each other, and I want it to stay that way."

"Jack, we went to school together. What if they find out? It will look bad that we're lying."

"I've thought about that and we just won't volunteer the information but be honest if they ask you outright."

"What about Karen?"

"They think our dealings were professional from when I

was in Vice. She's too well known to the squad, so I had to say something."

"I don't like this risk. I mean even your Mum knew me."

"This is my career we're talking about."

"Yes, and it's my business. We've all got something to lose Jack."

"Yes, but it's me who will be dead if we end up in prison."

"Do you think it's all connected then? Becky and Giselle knew nothing about it."

"No, it's probably just some screwed up coincidence. We just don't want the police sniffing around and then finding something else, do we?"

"How did you get on the investigation?"

"I asked my DCI if I could work with Fenton at some point to get more experience. The timing just worked. I didn't even know it was Giselle. I recognised Becky though. I'm so sorry mate."

"I can't believe someone would do this to someone who was so lovely and sweet. She wouldn't hurt anyone," Ryan said getting upset again.

Jack glanced at the drag queens to make sure they weren't eavesdropping. Although they probably didn't even realise anyone else was in the café.

"Do you have a suspect?" Ryan asked.

"Well my colleagues haven't exactly ruled you out yet."

"What do you mean? This has got nothing to do with me. Why on earth would I want to hurt Becky?"

"Well I know that, but they don't know you. You got an alibi for the last two nights?" asked Jack.

"I was home, alone."

"Shit."

"Well I can get someone to say they were with me."

"Don't do that as it'll only cause you problems when they find out you lied. They need to prove you had a motive and you don't, so don't worry about it. We don't want them sniffing around too much. Just do whatever you can to divert them on to someone else. Anyone have a problem with them both? I hear Tony had a run in with Giselle?"

"That was nothing, just a bit of banter. I haven't seen Tony in a couple of days though. He's gone AWOL," replied Ryan,

"What? When did you last see him?"

"Monday evening."

"The same night Giselle was killed."

"You seriously think Tony?"

"Well, where is he? Make sure you mention this to my colleagues."

"I'm not dropping Tony in it. Besides, it will just keep the heat on my gym."

"Don't be stupid. You need to give them a distraction. How often does Tony go AWOL?"

"He's not done it in a while, but he's disappeared for two weeks before."

"Well it's your call. It seems straightforward to me. Just make sure that nobody links us together. Does anyone at the gym know about us other than Tony?"

"Ironically, it was only Becky and Giselle. Sid of course, but he barely comes the gym anymore. Oh, and Paul."

"Right, I'll need a chat with Paul then, what does he know?"

Just that we went to school together of course. He's away on holiday anyway."

"Where?"

"Gran Canaria, where else? The guy is a walking STI."

"Have you spoken to him?"

"No, I haven't been able to get hold of him."

"Is that not a worry?"

"No, he probably lost his phone in a dark room or sauna. You know what he's like. He's away until next week."

"Right well let's see how things play out tomorrow. We might need another meet. Let me contact you, although if something comes up, call me. Not on my main number. The emergency phone will be off, but I'll check it as often as I can."

"I miss you Jack."

"I miss you too. This was the right thing to do though. I need to go. I've got a briefing in less than five hours."

Jack stood up and gave his friend a hug. He put his baseball cap back on and pulled it down over his face and walked out of the cafe onto Old Compton Street. He needed to get some sleep. He couldn't risk getting a cab here, so he'd have to walk for a while.

The fact that both Tony and Paul were missing was a worry. Paul may just be on holiday and had lost his phone when his trousers were round his ankles. Still it wasn't helpful that neither of them were contactable. If Paul genuinely had lost his phone, then he was in for a shock when he got back. Everyone knew how much he thought of Becky as he had been the one to get her straightened out. Giselle, he wouldn't give a shit about, as nobody did. There was only Ryan who saw some good in her. His gut instinct told him that there was more to this case than the obvious and he didn't think it would be long before they found another body. The question was whose would it be? He just hoped that this one be not be even closer to home.

———

Tony looked around at his surroundings, the blood had matted in his eyes and his vision was blurred. He was still naked, and his ankles and wrists were bound together. This could be a typical Saturday night, if it wasn't for the blood, and the lunatic upstairs.

He wasn't sure how long he had been here; it must have been a couple of days at least. He couldn't be subjected to anymore pain. Why were they doing this to him? If he was going to die, he just wished they would get it over with. He couldn't bear anymore of this. Unfortunately, his pain threshold was high; that's what you got for being the masochist.

He heard footsteps getting closer and then the door unlocked. He couldn't cry out as he was gagged and he had to be careful, the last thing he wanted to do was choke. He knew he was going to die in this room, however, he wanted it to be as quickly as possible.

The door opened.

"Unfortunately, Tony, that stupid bitch has fucked up my plans and I have had to escalate my timetable. Such a shame as I had such plans for us to play together some more. Now I'm going to have to remove your gag. Please, no more pleading. It is getting tiresome. I know you are used to being the bitch, but for fuck sake, be a man for once in your life."

The gag was removed.

"Why are you doing this to me? I haven't ever done anything to you."

"Silence," he felt a hard slap across the face.

"Now I'd apologise for this, but I'd be lying. This is really, really going to hurt."

CHAPTER EIGHT

Fenton was in his office preparing for the briefing, which had been pushed back. There had been a late-night discussion with Chief Superintendent Harry Beeden regarding an early press release, which had to be dealt with first. Fenton was told that quick results were expected in this case – stating the bleeding obvious again. Beeden had raised his concerns that as soon as the information was released, they were going to be inundated, so he had assigned some additional officers to handle the phones. Fenton had decided to set up a visit with Karen Kowalski for the morning, although when he had called last night, he'd been informed that she was currently with another policeman. It hadn't taken too many questions to the girl who answered the phone to discover the policeman was Jack Jacobs. Fenton was furious and was ready to have it out with Jacobs as soon as he arrived. He was tempted to question him in front of the whole team. However, given Jacob's previous work in Vice; there could be something to it, so he'd speak to him one-on-one at first to find out what he was up to.

. . .

The press conference was tough going as they were so many questions they didn't yet have any answers for. They had identified their victims, knew that they had both worked in the sex industry and had since *retired*. That was all they released. They didn't mention the connection with Karen's Klub or Ryan's Retreat. They hadn't yet investigated it fully and the last thing they needed was a press storm waiting for them when they arrived to conduct interviews with the proprietors and staff. This was the problem with the press; they didn't do anything in moderation. If they find out about a dead body, they would be there like vultures before the next of kin had even been informed.

They put a warning out to the all the working girls, and any female alone at night given both victims had apparently turned their backs on prostitution. The message therefore was that everyone should be extra vigilant. The press conference had been conducted by Fenton, Beeden, Jacobs and Shirkham, much to Brennan's annoyance. Beeden had made his feelings quite clear that a press conference about dead female prostitutes being held by four male police officers would just be begging for a by-line.

Fenton had asked Jacobs to meet him in his office straight after the press conference, which would soon be hitting the breakfast news channels and evening papers.

"Do you have something you want to tell me Jack?" Fenton asked, getting straight to the point.

"No, sir, but I'm guessing by the look on your face that you do," he smiled.

"This is not a fucking joke. Where were you last night?"

"Ah."

"Ah, yes indeed. What do you think you're playing at?"

"Did you have me followed?"

"What? Don't be ridiculous. Why? Should I be having you followed? Do you want to tell me what was so important that it couldn't wait until today, as I specifically instructed?"

"I was just wondering how you found out, that was all"

"Does that matter? Would you have said anything if I hadn't? Did you get anything of any value from her then?"

"Who?"

"Who do you think? Karen Kowalski."

"Not really no, she seems to have an alibi. I haven't had a chance to properly check it out yet."

"No and you won't. I'll be interviewing Miss Kowalski later myself with Brennan."

"Okay, sir."

"Is that all you've got to say for yourself?"

"Well I thought given I knew her from my days in Vice, if I spoke to her one-on-one, I might get more out of her."

"And what if she or someone at that club is responsible for these murders? Did you for one second think about the danger you were putting yourself in? Added to that, not one person knew where you were going. As far as anyone was concerned, you'd gone home for the evening."

"It won't happen again, sir."

"If you ever want to progress up the ranks then this running off on your own won't get you there. I understand from DCI Taylor that this is not the first time you've done something like this. How can you be expected to lead a team, if you can't even act like you are part of one?"

"Is that all, sir?"

"Don't get pissy with me. You'll apologise to the team, for your behaviour, at the briefing and you can look through the CCTV whilst Brennan and I are out interviewing Miss Kowalski and this Ryan Killarney. I'll also be interviewing staff at both venues so don't expect us back until this evening. There'll be another briefing later as well."

"Why do we..."

Jacobs had started to speak and clearly thought better of it. As soon as he had mentioned apologising to the team Fenton had seen his face change slightly. He hadn't seemed particularly bothered by being given the hours and hours of CCTV footage to look through. It was clear that for the most part, he could control his emotional responses very well.

"Tell the team to get ready, I'll be out in two," said Fenton, making it clear that their conversation was over.

Following the briefing which had only recapped on the information they had, or didn't have at this stage, the team started to go about their assigned duties. Fenton and Brennan's first call of the day was Karen's Klub.

"Morning Ms Kowalski," remarked Fenton as he and Brennan were introduced to her.

Fenton looked around at the vibrant decor. It wasn't like your typical gentlemen's club with dark colours and velvets everywhere. It was decorated in a mix of bright pastel colours and she clearly had a thing for chandeliers as they were everywhere. Albeit tasteful, they were scattered around like you would with mirror balls and it reminded Fenton that you can have too much of a good thing.

The layout of the place was also different to what he expected. Instead of there being a discrete bar in the corner, it dominated the centre of the venue. Clearly the place could get very crowded. The bar was also chrome, glass and black leather. The place was bizarre. As well as the dozens of old-fashioned chandeliers, and an eighties retro looking bar, the booths had vibrant cushions scattered all over them. Fenton could see a popular colour was hot pink – he'd learnt the name of this colour from his daughter. She'd been through a phase, which had lasted over twenty years!

Karen Kowalski was around five foot eight with bright purple hair. Despite it being the morning, she was wearing what could only be described as a cocktail dress and she was done up to the nines. Was this normal or had she dressed up for their visit?

"I assume you are here about the girls who were murdered?" asked Karen. She had an East European accent, although she spoke perfect English, with not a stutter to her speech.

"What makes you ask that?" replied Fenton. He noticed she looked very tense.

"Well, I have seen the newspapers and the girls worked for me at one time. It is not difficult to guess why you are here Inspector."

"You guessed correctly. Is there somewhere else we could talk?"

"We can go into my office."

Fenton and Brennan followed her. They walked down a very plush looking corridor with fabric walls past the toilets and through a padded door marked *Staff Only*. They then walked down another corridor which looked like something you'd find in the basement of a hospital. The place was a lot bigger than it appeared. They climbed a flight of stairs and arrived at Karen's office. When Fenton saw the office, he was convinced Ms Kowalski had multiple personality disorder; it looked like a Parisian boudoir from the sixties.

"You like my decor inspector?"

"It's very... interesting."

"I bet you have been to a few shitholes in your time, but you will never forget Karen's Klub. It panders to my madness."

Fenton gave her a questioning look.

"Read into that what you will Inspector," she laughed.

A great big bellied laugh, which was so unexpected. It

caused her whole face to change from the hard-looking woman he'd met just a few minutes ago.

"Boy do you speak?" she asked Brennan.

"Yes, ma'am."

"Ma'am? I am not the fucking Queen you know."

This time Fenton laughed with her. He was beginning to like her. Brennan seemed to be in a daze. Maybe he should have brought Shirkham.

"I understand you spoke to one of my officers last night?" asked Fenton.

"No, I have not seen any police."

"DI Jack Jacobs? I know he came to see you last night." Fenton noticed she looked flustered. "He told me himself," he added.

"Well yes, but it wasn't a long visit. He just asked me where I was at the time of the murders, and I told him I was with Sid."

"Sid?"

"Yes, he looks after the door. On the nights you are talking about, he was looking after me," she laughed.

She tried to look all coy. It failed; she just came across as an old slapper who was past her prime. Fenton still found her fascinating though.

"Is Sid here now?"

"Yes, he will be in the cellar getting stuff ready for tonight."

"Any other staff here?"

"Only a few of the girls doing the day shift. Aerial, Sandra and Harriet. They'll be here in about thirty minutes."

"Gary go and speak to Sid and then get started on interviewing the girls when they arrive. You leave me with Miss Kowalski."

"Sure, Guv," he remarked as he loped off, closing the door behind him.

"Now Miss Kowalski, why don't you tell me exactly how well you know Jack Jacobs."

———

Jacobs was finding the CCTV viewing tedious. This was Fenton punishing him for going rogue. He couldn't believe it was known that he was in the club. He'd have to find out who had answered the phone as none of the girls had known about him other than the two and that were dead. Perhaps they had said something, but still how had he been identified? He couldn't go back to the club now as Fenton would be watching him closely. The last thing he needed was another fuck up. Still, at least he had managed to play it dumb until he knew who Fenton was talking about. He didn't want his relationship with Ryan being discovered, so in a way he had to be relieved, as he still technically hadn't lied.

"How's it going," asked Shirkham, poking her head around the corner, causing Jack's stomach to somersault, partly at being startled, and for other reasons.

"Slow, but then this stuff always is," he replied trying to remain cool – both types of cool.

"You recovered from your public apology," she asked with concern on her face.

"My own fault for running off on my own, the boss was only right," he replied, knowing she had a lot of respect for Fenton.

"I know you're pissed off. It's written all over your face. The boss cares about his team. He's only worried about what might happen to you."

Jack could see that she was being very genuine and perhaps Fenton wasn't a bad guy after all, yet he was still not convinced that the public humiliation ritual was the best way to endear you to someone.

"Do you want a coffee?" she asked. "Take a break from that for a while."

Perhaps being stuck in the station isn't so bad after all!

———

Brennan was starting his interviews by first speaking to Sid the doorman. He noted that he was a very good-looking man, and built like a brick shithouse, although there was a bit of a paunch showing so he clearly wasn't in the shape he once was. His hands were like shovels and he had this annoying habit of constantly cracking his knuckles.

"So where were you on Monday and Tuesday night between one and six in the morning," Brennan asked.

"I was with Karen."

"All night?"

"Yes."

"Do you have CCTV here?"

"Yes, but we don't video ourselves screwing."

"That's not what I was implying. Do you have it in the club?"

"Yes, but it's on a continuous loop so we only have the last seven days."

"We'll need to take them with us."

"You got a warrant?"

"No, but I can get one if you prefer and I can come back for this chat tonight when the place is busy and then do it down the station."

"I'll get them for you," Sid huffed, standing up.

"In a minute," Brennan remarked putting his hand up. "I've got a few more questions first. When did you last see Giselle?"

"A few days ago," Sid replied sitting back down.

"And where did you see her?"

"At the gym."

"Which gym?"

"Ryan's Retreat, it's in Covent Garden."

"Okay, so did you speak to her?"

"Only to say hello. She worked here and she stormed out after a row with Karen. We weren't friends or anything."

Brennan had a feeling the guy was lying.

"And what about Becky?"

"What about her?"

"Well when did you last see her?"

"Tuesday."

"The day she died?"

"I saw her at the gym as well. She was working there. She was a lovely girl. Had got herself proper sorted out as well. She was well happy with her job."

"How long had she been there?"

"Month or so."

"What terms did she leave here on?"

"Good. She worked to pay some debts off and when they were gone, she was out of here. It was all very amicable. She gave Karen plenty of time to replace her and was always honest that this was never a career and she just wanted to clear her debts."

"Any idea what the debts were for?"

"Not really."

"What does *not really* mean?"

"Well she never said, and I didn't like to ask?"

"Did you suspect anything?"

"Well I don't think it was student debt, or anything innocent like that."

"So why did Giselle leave?"

"No idea. She just upped and left. She dropped Karen in it as there were clients booked, which had to be cancelled. Not good for business. She wasn't happy."

"Did Karen track her down?"

"No idea. Karen told her never to step foot inside the club again when she left."

"And did she?"

"Not that I'm aware of?"

"It's a yes or no really isn't it?"

"Well I never saw her in here again."

"Did Karen?"

"I dunno."

"Clearly you two are very close then."

"What do you mean by that?"

"That's all for now, Sid. We'll be in touch if we need anything else. Just check that the girls are here will you and I'll see whichever is free first."

Sid got up looking confused that the interview was concluded so abruptly. Brennan wanted to unnerve him, as he was clearly nervous and showing classic signs of lying, particularly regarding anything to do with Giselle. He'd have another go at him but wanted to speak to the Guv first.

———

Fenton was still talking to Karen, a woman he was becoming more fascinated with every second he spent with her.

"Giselle and I were not on friendly terms. I will be honest about that. She dropped me in the shit when she left, but I would never wish what happened to her on anyone. No matter what they did."

"In what way did she drop you in it?"

Fenton sipped the tea Karen had made for him. He wasn't sure what it was; it tasted revolting and smelt like feet, still he smiled politely and nodded. Keep her sweet – something the tea was not.

"She just left without a word and left me with bookings

which I could not fulfil. They wanted her specifically. She was good and she knew it, but she was also a selfish bitch who only put herself first. I don't like to speak ill of the dead," she added, clearly as an afterthought as she evidently had no such qualms in attacking the young girl's character.

"So, when did you last see her?"

"Not since she walked out of here. I would not have given her the time of day after what she did, and she knew to keep away."

"And Becky?"

"Now that was a crying shame. She was a special young lady. She did not drop me in the shit when she left. She was always straight with me that she was not a lifer, she was only passing through. Such a shame though as she had real talent. She could make a man cum in his pants, just by running her tongue over her teeth."

"Sounds like quite a skill," Fenton smiled. He was shocked to see Karen in tears.

"She was such a special girl. Why anyone would want to hurt her, I don't know. If this was just Giselle, then I would say that you had your work cut out for you. She pissed off a lot of people, but Becky was special, and everyone adored her. Nobody here would have done this, you are looking for an outsider."

"Perhaps," but he wasn't convinced. Too many coincidences. "Do you know a Ryan Killarney," he watched her closely.

"No, I don't think so, wait... does he own the gym Ryan's Retreat?"

"Yes, he does."

"Then I know of him, but I would not know him to speak to."

Fenton kept watching her closely. If she was lying, then she was good.

———

Brennan's next interview was Sandra. She looked like she was in her mid-twenties, although he could never tell with Black women. Once he'd take a girl home thinking she was younger than him, only to find out she was forty-two. Sandra was quite small in stature, can't have been much over five foot. She had a mass of hair that was all frizzy yet didn't seem to move. The thing that struck Brennan the most was her piercing blue eyes.

"What would you like to know officer?" she asked.

"Did you know Giselle Gorge and Becky Best?"

"They both worked here, and I used to see Becky all the time, but Giselle I only saw now and then, usually at the gym Ryan's Retreat."

"So, when did you last see Becky?" he asked, wondering if every whore in London used that gym.

"Tuesday morning, she came here to see Karen about something. I'd been out with the girls for a coffee after finishing work and I'd forgotten my bag, so I came back to get it and saw her. We said a quick hello and she said she was here to see Karen."

"That was the day she died. So, any idea what she was here about?"

"No idea, like I said, I didn't stay long."

"And did you know anyone who had a grudge against her, a former client or something?"

"No, she was extremely popular, but she never took it all for herself. She was very fair with the other girls."

"And what about Giselle, did anyone have a grudge against her?"

"Take your pick. I mean, I never knew her that well as we never socialised, but she thought she was better than the other girls. She was similar to Becky in that she was good, but she made sure everyone knew she how good she was. The day she walked out, her and Karen had a screaming match at each other, which wasn't uncommon, but this one involved Giselle belting Karen across the face. I mean we were all shocked as its Karen who is known for her back handers. This was mega intense though. She walked out and told Karen to go fuck herself. She never came back and when I saw her in the gym, she would hardly speak to anyone. She was a strange one."

"Any idea what the row was about?"

"No, probably money though. That was all she cared about."

Brennan was now interviewing Harriet. Aerials was not available for interview, as she was feeling unwell and wouldn't be coming into work. Brennan noted that Harriet had a strong African accent and wore what appeared to be hundreds of bangles on her arms. She kept kissing her teeth, which gave Brennan the impression that she didn't think much of him.

"So, Harriet, what can you tell me about Giselle and Becky?"

"I see her on Tuesday evening."

"Who?"

"Becky."

"Where?"

"She here."

"Doing what?"

"Why else she be here?" she kissed her teeth and gave him a look of contempt. "She is working here."

———

Jacobs felt he was going square eyed from staring constantly at the screen and still nothing. He had seen Giselle on the night she died on the CCTV. It was brief and he hadn't been able to pick her up on any of the other cameras in the area. She'd been at Seven Dials near Covent Garden just after one o'clock in the morning, which was not long before she'd met her killer in the alley. She was walking away from Soho, which would make sense if she was heading home. Something, or someone must have made her turn round. One thing they knew for certain from Manning was that she had died where she was found, so if her killer had lured her away then a camera must have caught her somewhere. Added to that, it was someone she knew well enough to want to take such a detour.

"You must be getting fed up with that by now?" asked Shirkham, making him jump slightly and get all flustered again – what was wrong with him?

"Well it'll be worth it if we find something."

"Do you want a coffee again? A real one this time I mean. I'm just popping out."

"I'll come with you," he smiled, getting up and grabbing his coat. This was an opportunity he wasn't going to miss.

Jacobs and Shirkham were sitting in the coffee shop. An awkward silence between them, which Jacobs was desperate to fill, yet was dumbfounded at how tongue-tied he was over this woman.

"So..." he started.

She looked up from her coffee and gave that incredible smile. He felt like he was going to throw up, his stomach was so knotted, and he could feel the blood rushing to his face.

"So, do you think the boss will get anything from the club and the gym?" *Yes, talk about work stuff. Nice and safe.*

"Not sure, we'll certainly get some background on both our victims, which we desperately need. The boss always says coincidences are just evidence that hasn't been proven yet."

"Yeah, DCI Taylor used to say that a lot, must be where she got it from."

"She was here last night."

"Really? Seeing the boss?"

"Yeah, must have just been having a catch up. I understand she's taking time off between cases to move in with her boyfriend and prepare for her exams."

"Is that the biker bloke?"

"Yeah, she's been with him a long time now. Surprised she hadn't already moved in with him."

"Well she's always been career driven. I think she is going for Superintendent. They reckon she could take Beeden's job when he retires."

"If only!"

"What makes you say that," he asked.

He noticed two pink spots had appeared on her cheeks where she was embarrassed and had clearly said more than she meant to. This was good, Jack thought as she was clearly comfortable with him.

"Come on, don't stop now," he smiled encouragingly.

"Well when we were on the *Diversity Slayer* case, we had a press leak and guess who it was?"

"Beeden? Did Fenton tell you that?"

"No, the boss is more discreet than that, but you hear things," she giggled. It was such a warm endearing sound that Jack felt his stomach lurch again.

"You wanna have dinner with me tonight?" he blurted out without thinking.

She looked at him for what felt like an eternity, as if she was slowly registering what he has asked her and appraising him carefully whilst thinking of a polite way to reject him.

"I'd love to," she smiled.

CHAPTER NINE

The gym was busy with the lunchtime rush and there was nobody on the reception desk which irritated Fenton, given he had a scheduled appointment. Fenton and Brennan sat down on two luminous green plastic chairs. The kind which were oddly shaped and looked incredibly uncomfortable, yet when you were sitting on them, all was well with the world. A terrifying looking woman with piercings and tattoos glared at them as she made several attempts for her finger to be scanned; the method used to operate the entrance turnstile.

"At least you can't lose your finger like you can a membership card," remarked Fenton.

"A bit too *Big Brother* for me," replied Brennan.

"What do you mean?"

"Well you don't know what they are doing with your fingerprint do you?"

"Got something to hide, Gary?"

"You know what I mean, Guv. It's getting to a point where nothing is private anymore. Soon you'll have to masturbate into a cup to get a ticket for the bus."

"Since when have you ever got a bus?" Fenton laughed. "I

know what you mean though. I don't think this retains a fingerprint in the same way we do. Still worth asking in case a print comes up on one of the bodies."

"But Manning found nothing on Becky or Giselle."

"True, although I have a feeling our killer isn't quite finished yet."

———

DCI Lisa Taylor had seen some horrific things in her career. This one had to take the prize. She'd been called out early when the body had been found. It had been dumped on Hampstead Heath – so much for time off between cases!

"I have to admit Lisa that even this one makes me feel a bit sick," Manning remarked.

"It must be bad then. It looks like he either bled to death or he were choked."

"You're probably right. I will know in a few hours. You and Eric are keeping me busy at the moment, aren't you?"

"I wonder if it was a homophobic attack," Taylor thought aloud.

"Well that's your job to find out. There is one thing I am certain about though."

"What's that?"

"He didn't die here."

———

Jacobs felt his eyes drooping as he continued to watch the CCTV. He'd been checking all the other cameras around the same time to find Giselle. After what felt like hours, he finally spotted her.

"Emma, get over here."

"Have you got something," she asked.

"Did we get Giselle's telephone records?"

"Yes, there was nothing on it after ten on the night she died."

"How do we explain this then?" he said, pointing at the screen.

It showed Giselle on the phone at ten past one, according to the time stamp. She seemed to be talking very animatedly with expansive hand gestures. Without the sound it looked almost comical. She then put her phone in her bag, changed direction, and headed back towards Soho.

"There was no bag or phone found on her. We have her number and have checked it," added Emma.

"Is that inbound as well?"

"Do me a favour," she replied smiling. "I know what I'm doing, Jack."

"Sorry, of course you do."

He hadn't meant to insult her; it was just this was potentially a big break and could get him back in Fenton's good books.

"Are you going to call the boss?"

"Not yet,"

"Jack?"

"We'll put it on the incident board, and I'll text him. He's already left Karen's Klub so let's go there and speak to the girls. They may know about another phone."

He could tell Shirkham didn't like it, so he gave her a pleading look. She eventually nodded her head in agreement.

"I want to see you send that text though."

"I think you need to work on your trust issues," he replied laughing.

She laughed with him, yet her eyes implied he'd hit a raw nerve.

———

"Jack has found evidence that Giselle may have had another phone so he's taking Emma to speak to some of the girls at Karen's Klub," Fenton told Brennan as he read the text message,

"At least he's not going off on his own this time, Guv."

"It's a shame he didn't find that on the CCTV before we were there. Karen will be pissed off about getting another visit."

"She's got history with Jacobs, hasn't she?"

"Well only on a professional basis from when he was in Vice," Fenton replied.

Based on his conversation earlier, Fenton knew there was more to it, and he would have to speak to Jacobs later. He'd wanted to get some further background from DCI Taylor, only she had been pulled on to a horrific murder in North London. She had one sick killer to find, based on the sketchy details he'd already heard.

"DCI Fenton?"

Fenton turned to be met by a muscular young man. He was one of those fit and healthy types who made you subconsciously pull your navel in, attempting to give the illusion that you didn't eat carbohydrates.

"Mr Killarney?"

"Yes, please call me Ryan. Sorry you've been kept waiting. We're a little short staffed. One has gone AWOL, another on holiday and obviously Becky."

"Who's gone AWOL?"

"One of the personal trainers, Tony. He's done it before, so nothing we're worried about. Just bad timing really. Shall we go into my office? It will be better than sitting out here?"

Fenton and Brennan followed Ryan through the gym, which was still busy. They passed the weights section and heard the clanking of barbells on the floor, accompanied by heavy grunting. The guys seemed to be in competition with each other – he who grunts loudest, is the strongest. It sounded like American porn, the type where the cast simply can't keep their mouths shut or below eighty decibels – not that Fenton would know such things.

"Ryan, my colleague DS Brennan would also like to interview your staff. Is there another room he could use so we can speak to everyone as quickly as possible?" Fenton asked, as they sat down in the meticulously neat office.

"I understood you only wanted to speak to me?"

"One of the victims worked here and the other was a client, we will want interview anyone who knew either or both of the victims."

"Does that mean you need to speak to my clients as well?"

"That's highly likely yes, but we'll start with the staff."

"It won't be good for business if you start interrogating my clients."

"We are trying to catch a killer, and soon, before anyone else crosses his path."

"You think he'll kill again?"

"We are working on that assumption, given he has already killed twice in as many days."

"You can use the staff room. You'll find it near the changing rooms. Here's a pass to get through," he added passing Brennan one of those swipe cards – at least it wasn't a cup!

"Thank you," said Brennan getting up.

"There will be a guy called Steve in there. He's my assistant manager and he'll be able to arrange for people to talk to you between clients or classes."

Brennan thanked him and left, leaving a nervous looking Ryan Killarney with Fenton.

———

Jacobs had entered Karen's Klub with Shirkham, only to be greeted by an irate Karen Kowalski.

"What the fuck is this, Jack? That Fenton guy has only just left."

"You'll address me as Detective Inspector Jacobs, I'm not on Vice now Miss Kowalski."

"Are you taking the fucking piss? Get out of my club, or I will have Sid throw you out," she screamed.

Jack wondered what Fenton had said to her as he had not seen her get this angry before; not with him anyway.

"I'll only have to come back with uniformed officers," he replied.

"You do that, and you will regret it."

"You heard the lady," said Sid as he appeared behind them. "You'll need to come back with a warrant."

"We'll do just that," replied Jack.

He was fuming that he had been humiliated in front of Shirkham. Karen would not get away with this. He was going to have the place torn apart.

Back at the station, the news from Shirkham did nothing to improve his mood.

"The boss won't allow a warrant until he's come back and briefed the rest of the team. He's still with Ryan Killarney," said Shirkham, clearly trying to soften the blow.

He knew she could see how embarrassed he had been when Karen had kicked off on him.

"I'm going to go and see if they've found anything on the search for another mobile."

He didn't want her to think he was sulking, so he smiled before leaving.

It was already after three; the boss would be back soon and then hopefully they'd be out by six so he could dash home and get changed. He had a date tonight so needed to give himself a metaphorical slap across the face to snap out of it. Fenton was probably right; the last thing Jack should do was piss off Karen Kowalski. She knew too much, and he had too much to lose, although so did she.

———

Fenton was in Ryan's office. Nothing in the room gave any indication of the man behind the muscles – god, what a cliché. He sounded like Polly Pilkington. Thankfully, she was no longer around; she would have loved to have put her own personal spin on a case like this.

"So, Ryan, how long did Becky work here?" asked Fenton.

"About a month."

"Did you know her before then?"

"Yeah, she's been a member for a couple of years."

"How did she get on with people?"

"Becky got on with anyone and everyone. She didn't have a bad a bone in her body."

Fenton noticed he was welling up. He didn't want to appear crass, but he had to get back to the station to catch up on all the developments and didn't have time to do the fluffy stuff that came with policing and just about every human interaction these days.

"So, you can't think of anyone with a grudge against her?" he asked, to move things along.

"Not from here, no. I mean you know what she used to do for a living don't you?"

"Yes."

"Well she never spoke about her clients, so I don't know if someone from her past could have had a grudge against her."

"What would you say if I told you she was still working in prostitution and was so the night she died?"

"I'd say you were lying. She had some debts to repay and when she'd done that she stopped. She hated the job."

"But I have a witness who saw her at Karen's Klub the night she died."

"It doesn't mean she was working. Becky and Karen were still friends. She was probably just visiting."

"What was your relationship with Becky,"

"We were just friends. I had feelings for her, I won't lie about it. I just never had the balls to let her know and now I never can."

He broke down, much to Fenton's dismay. Fenton resisted the urge to look at his watch given he'd been told in the past that it could be considered rude, although he believed that people were too sensitive these days.

"Do you know Karen Kowalski?" Fenton asked deciding to change approach.

"Erm... not really."

Hesitation noted.

"I mean I know of her and she has been here a few times. Quite a few people who work there come here. I've probably had about three conversations with her. So, no I don't really know her."

Too much unnecessary detail.

"What about Giselle Gorge, how well did you know her?"

"She was a client. She didn't make friends easily as she was so unapproachable, of course she had her own demons."

"And what were they?"

"No idea, you can just tell when people are a little lost and clearly have some inner turmoil."

"I see and did you speak to her ever about these *demons* that you believe were there?"

"Well no, I just said she was very unapproachable. We only ever spoke about things related to her workouts, or classes."

"And how did she get on with Becky?"

"They were very close."

"How do you mean?" asked Fenton, leaning forward, his interest spiked.

"Well they had worked together for Karen and then Becky left. I understand Giselle wanted out as well. Apparently, Karen wouldn't let her go until her debt was repaid."

"What debt was that?"

"I don't know, I didn't ask at the time and I told you I don't know Karen," he snapped.

Fenton found Ryan's change in tone suspicious.

"Tell me the people who Giselle and Becky had the regular contact with here at the gym, especially if it was with someone who knew both of them?" Fenton asked.

"How on earth can I do that? Do you know how many people come through those doors every day?"

"Well surely you have a member list, although let's start with the staff, including any people who may use your premises on a freelance basis, such as personal trainers."

"I employ all my personal trainers directly."

"Then you should have no problem in providing me a list," Fenton replied, with one of his smiles, which he now knew unnerved people.

Ryan sighed and pulled his laptop towards him.

———

Fenton was leaving Ryan's Retreat with Brennan. It was coming up to seven o'clock and he still had to go back to the station and give a briefing. He was shocked to see DCI Lisa Taylor walking towards him.

"Lisa what are you doing here?" Fenton asked.

"I were going to ask you same thing."

"My victims both used this gym, well one of them worked here. What's your interest?"

"It looks like I may have one of yours then as my victim also worked here."

"You mean the Hampstead Heath one?"

"Yeah, victim by the name of Tony Leopold."

"The owner mentioned a Tony who had gone AWOL. Are you here to break the news?"

"Yes, we can't find a next of kin, so we're hoping his boss will be able to shed some light or at least give a positive ID."

"Different MO to mine though so you can keep it!" Fenton laughed.

"Ah, but you always said there are no coincidences, Eric."

"Bollocks, well you better pop over and see me when you're done then," he replied.

"Might be a while if we get an ID. I can pop over in morning if that would be better. If it is coming your way, I'll need to brief the team and handover anyway."

"I'll speak to Beeden when I get back. Give me a call when you're done. I may still be around."

"Will do."

Fenton had heard just how terrible that murder had been and the last thing he needed was a third victim, especially if their killer had changed the MO. If they were now going after men, then the link was the gym and not the club. He'd have to ease off on Karen Kowalski for now as he didn't want to antagonise Vice, especially if it turned out that the link to her club was just indeed another coincidence.

Fenton decided he'd delay the briefing until the morning, so told Brennan he could head off home and he'd make his own way back to the station. Apparently upon his announcement there had been a speedy exodus from the team. He was going to have to cancel weekend leave if they did have a third victim as they would need to go back through everything they had already done and see if there were now further links. What he didn't understand was how someone could go from violently beating two women to death to doing what had happened to Tony Leopold. At least this new victim didn't have a sexually suggestive name, or the same initials. Could a case ever be straight forward?

———

Ryan wiped his mouth as he looked in the sink; it had been a while. The visit from Fenton had unnerved him. Then he had heard about Tony. He had been asked to formally identify him as there was nobody else and that was true. Tony had no family, well none that would even care that he was dead. There was a sister Ryan believed, although Tony hadn't spoken of her in years. The policewoman had been so kind and gentle, unlike that Fenton who just had one of those tones in his voice which automatically made you feel guilty and this was when you hadn't even done anything. Imagine if he had? The guy was intimidating, although he suspected it wouldn't be easy to mislead DCI Taylor either. He knew Jack had worked with her and that she had once worked for Fenton, so Ryan had to be careful. Effective policing – who needed that?

He stuck his fingers down his throat and vomited again.

"I thought you had stopped doing that shit," came a familiar voice from behind him.

"What the hell are you doing here Karen? If someone sees you, we're fucked," he said spinning round in a panic.

Ryan rinsed his fingers under the tap and then dried them on his top, before wiping his mouth.

"Relax, I'm not stupid. Nobody saw me come in here."

They immediately smiled at each other and embraced in a hug. It had been too long for such good friends.

"So why are you here?" he asked.

"I've heard a rumour. About Tony?"

"It's true," he replied.

Karen couldn't speak. Ryan could see her mouth was moving, yet no words came. Suddenly she was in a heap on the floor as her legs gave way. Ryan rushed over and helped her to a seat. He held her. No words were spoken. There didn't need to be. They had known each for so long and been through so much that words were not necessary. In those few second Karen's bravado had dropped. Ryan knew she was a very caring woman, who fiercely looked after her own, yet it was very few people who saw this side of her and knew the Karen behind the madam. Ryan was one of the select few. Tony had been another. Neither of them could cry. The numbness and reality of what had happened slowly dawning on the pair of them. Then the dam broke and Ryan sobbed. Karen rocked him like a baby. Her turn to comfort him. She kissed the top of his head, rocking him back and forth gently.

Ryan had no idea how much time had passed, although it felt like hours. He could see Karen had also shed tears for their mutual friend. A man who knew them as well as they knew each other, shared the same secret and who they could only mourn for together in private, given the promise they had all made to each other two years ago.

"Do you think this is linked to Giselle and Becky?"

"I hear the police are not looking at it that way. They have another detective heading up Tony's murder,"

"Yeah, it was her who came and told me. They want me to identify him."

"Let his bitch sister do that. She did nothing for him all his life, so let it be her burden."

"I don't know where to find her. I wish you could come with me."

"I do too, but that is not possible. The police have already made thee link between my club and your gym. We will need to be extra careful. Just wait and see if the police find her first before agreeing. Doing this will not be good for you."

"But why would anyone want to kill those three people?"

"I don't know. We are dealing with a very fucked up person. I have heard that Tony was mutilated."

"What?"

"I don't know all the details and please don't ask me how I know what I know, but there is something going on here. Someone is trying to destroy us. Someone knows what happened."

"Then why have they gone for Giselle and Becky. They had nothing to do with it?"

"Yes, but they must know how much I hated that bitch Giselle. Perhaps they are trying to frame me."

"But why Becky?"

"You were in love with her, perhaps this is to get at you in a different way."

"How did you know about that?"

"Ryan, please. You have known me a long time. I know everything. I don't know who is responsible for these murders though. I am just trying to work it out before anyone else gets killed."

"Have you warned Sid?"

"Of course, but what about Jack?"

"I've seen him, and he is on his guard. Is that how you found out about Tony?"

"No, I have other sources."

"Who?"

"Like I said, best you don't know. Can't get you into any trouble then. I need to go, will you be okay?"

"I don't know but go before someone comes back here."

"I will go out the back again."

She left.

Ryan couldn't believe what had happened to Tony. They had shared a dark secret and their friendship had evolved to one of family. They were like brothers. He was one of those friends that you can be as close as you can be to someone else without being a blood relative. They'd had their misguided on and off fling, as had done with many of his friends. He couldn't make the link between the three people who had been killed. With Giselle and Becky that was obvious. Where did Tony come into it? Was he even linked, or was it just a horrible coincidence? Had Karen raised a good point? Could the past now be catching up with them?

———

Fenton was sitting in his office reflecting on the day and all the people he had spoken to with Brennan when the phone rang. He looked at the screen and with some trepidation he answered it.

"Hi Lisa, what can I do for you?" Fenton asked, knowing what was coming.

"Eric, I've just spoken to Beeden and he wants me to hand this murder inquiry over to you."

"The guy on Hampstead Heath?"

"Yeah, it appears that not only did he work at Ryan's Retreat but he's another retired whore. He worked for Karen Kowalski until about two years ago."

"Shit, has she been told?"

"Not yet. We've told Ryan Killarney and we've located a sister who lives in Yorkshire, so the locals are taking care of that."

"It's a completely different MO though isn't it?"

"Yeah, but if we've made a link then the press is gonna do same, so Harry wants one team working on it. You're getting a few more detectives that were working with me. He wants me free for something else, but you've got me tomorrow, so I can brief the team on what we have so far if that'll help, or do you want to do that yourself?"

"Happy for you to do it. Let's catch up beforehand. Shall we say eight o'clock in my office?"

"Make it seven and I'll buy you breakfast. You won't want to eat after you know all the details so you may as well get a good feed in early," she remarked, in her matter of fact tone.

"Usual place?"

"Yep – see you then."

Shit!

He'd heard only some of the details and they had sickened him. He couldn't work out why Beeden had automatically moved the case over when the links may well be circumstantial. It was usual practice to wait until at least forensic evidence had come in to make a clear link. He'd better go and see Manning straight after the briefing tomorrow and wondered if he may be able to get another freebie consultation from Deidre. They were clearly dealing with a psychopath and that should be enough of an enticement for her to agree.

CHAPTER TEN

Emma looked around the restaurant. Despite being tucked away down a side street the place was busy and she was pleased that Jack had pre-booked their table. She loved Thai food, although she had no recollection of telling Jack, so he'd either done his homework or had a lucky guess. Or perhaps he just liked Thai food. This would a refreshing change from her ex-husband, who couldn't eat anything remotely spicy without putting a toilet roll in the fridge, in preparation for the following day.

Jack had made a lot of effort with his attire for the evening. He was wearing one of his suits, but not one he usually wore for work, which tended to be navy blue or black. He was wearing a grey suit, but without a tie. It was clearly tailored as it fit him very well. He had the top two buttons open on a simple white shirt. Emma wished she'd made a bit more effort. She was wearing jeans and a new top she'd bought but compared to Jack she felt a little underdressed. This was despite Jack saying she looked great when they'd first met that evening. She could tell if someone was being disingenuous, and she knew he'd meant it.

It was interesting to see someone like Jack who came across as very self-confident, appear nervous and fidgety. He was engrossed in his menu, so she studied him subtly. She'd already made up her mind on what she wanted. She had a rule with new Thai restaurants. She always had the Tom Yum soup with prawns followed by the Pad Thai with chicken. These were the basics and very unadventurous for her, but her logic was that if they couldn't get these staple dishes right, she wouldn't return. If they did, then she would be back, working her way through the entire menu over time. She must have had Thai food at least three times a week since she'd become single again. Was she single or divorced? She preferred single; it sounded younger.

Emma continued to glance at Jack as he concentrated on the menu. His expression looked forced, so it was clear that he could sense her looking at him; that didn't stop her. He was such a handsome man, rather than what young people call *fit* – there was something almost gentlemanly about his look. He looked up from his menu and smiled, she could feel her cheeks reddening, yet held his gaze. As is the norm in any restaurant, the waitress then arrived ruining the moment. On the plus side Emma could feel the heat leaving her face. They ordered their drinks and food at the same time as they both knew what they wanted, although Jack was going to change from the Thai fishcakes to the Tom Yum when he heard Emma order it. She suggested they get the fishcakes as well and share them. Another staple dish they would need to get right for her to become a returning customer.

The waitress returned shortly afterwards with their drinks. They were both on the Singha beer. They could now finally talk without interruptions – well until the starters arrived. At least it wasn't a Japanese place, where the efficiency, albeit impressive, could soon verge on irritating, particularly on a date. As soon as you order, the meal is in front of you, and once you have taken the last bite and laid down the fork, she didn't do chopsticks as it took her too long to eat with them, the plate would be whipped away in a second and the bill presented. You always got the feeling that they wanted you to leave – or perhaps that was just her analysing it too much.

"Where in Ireland are you from?"

"A place called Castleisland in County Kerry."

"Nice and quiet I bet, compared to London?"

"Nice and quiet compared to anywhere," she smiled.

It was her main reason for leaving, although the chaos of London had been quite a culture shock.

"So how long have you been in London?"

"Just over ten years, since I joined the police."

"What made you want to join the police here and not at home?"

"It's a small town, so not much action!"

"I hear you're only still a DC because you're not interested in being promoted?"

"That's true. As the DC on a case you're the hub of everything and everyone relies on you to make sure all the new information is shared amongst the team quickly. Added to that you can sometimes spot things that the more senior detectives don't. I like that."

"I never thought of it like that. I just wanted to get out there and move upwards as quickly as possible."

"You don't want to race to the top too quickly."

"Don't I?"

Their starters arrived and they started to eat. The smell of the Tom Yum hit her nostrils and the colouring of the soup told her straight away this would be good and after the first spoonful she wasn't disappointed. Jack was already dipping his fishcakes in the sweet chill sauce provided, although Emma preferred them with soy sauce, which the waitress kindly brought over within seconds of her requesting it.

"So why don't I want to get to the top too quickly?" he asked getting the conversation back on track.

The waitress had gone to get them another beer each. Emma didn't usually drink so fast, something people found ironic about her, before claiming they didn't stereotype.

"Well if you get there too quick, you'll no longer have ambition fuelling you and those at the top who have slogged it out for years on the streets get the most respect. Not like Beeden who has never run a murder investigation in his life."

"Seriously?"

"He worked in internal investigations and then moved across when he got to the top. The boss and he go way back, although their friendship hasn't been the same ever since what happened on the *Diversity Slayer* case."

"Who was that woman who was writing all the stories in the press?"

"Polly Pilkington."

"That's the name. I heard she's from London but talks like a Swedish prostitute."

Emma nearly choked on her second beer, which had appeared beside her. She was drinking faster than usual given her nerves, and the soup had a fantastic kick to it.

"Well Pilkington was getting all her information from Beeden. Apparently, they had a scene going and Fenton walked in on them."

"Not when I'm eating please," Jack replied, causing them both to laugh.

After a wonderful meal they decided to go somewhere else for coffee. Neither of them fancied another drink after guzzling four beers with the meal. Jack was so easy to talk to and she'd had chance to ask him about his family background. He spoke with such devotion about his mother who had died a couple of years ago, after spending a few years in a care home, despite only being in her fifties. She had been ill for some time and it had clearly taken a lot out of Jack. With no father around, him being the oldest and the big brother, he had taken on the burden to look after her and made sure his sisters were not distracted from establishing themselves in their chosen careers. He evidently had a great relationship with his sisters, another endearing quality. Emma had become pessimistic in her old age and since her marriage breakdown. She felt that if this guy was too good to be true then he probably was. There had to be something, but she wasn't going to dwell on that tonight, she just wanted to enjoy herself.

"So, are we allowed to talk shop?" Jack asked.

"I don't mind at all," she replied.

She wondered why he was moving away from talking about his own private life. However, so far, she had mentioned nothing of her divorce, but then neither of them had spoken about previous relationships.

"What's your gut feeling about this case then?"

"I don't believe it's as straight-forward as some guy with a pathological hatred towards women or prostitutes, or both even. There are too many coincidences and the way in which the victims were killed shows an uncontrollable frenzy and yet so far there is no forensic evidence."

"They might find something yet. It's still early," he added.

"True and if anyone will find it then it will be Manning. She is brilliant, although a little feisty at times."

"I've heard her, and the boss are infamous for their run ins?"

"True. They respect each other which makes a big difference. They'll never be friends, yet they know the other will do all they can to progress the case. It's not as bad as people make out."

"Brennan seems to think they're overdue one of their clashes."

"Gary's a bit of a drama queen. Don't get me wrong, he's great and I won't hear a bad word said against him. He just likes a bit of drama to break the tension. He's worse than women with gossip."

"Yeah, I've picked up on that already. He's gone for DI a few times, hasn't he?"

"Yeah, but he's no good at exams and that's where he always flunks, although I'm sure he doesn't revise as much as he should."

"How long have you two worked together?"

"About seven years. Ever since I was brought onto Fenton's team."

"Is it usual to stay on one team for so long?"

"It is when it works so well and the boss is a great DCI to work for, although I suspect DCI Taylor would be very similar."

"Like two peas in a pod," he said laughing.

They carried on talking; it was so effortless. She didn't want the evening to end as she was enjoying his company so much. It had been a long time since she had felt this spark with anyone. The last time wasn't even with her ex-husband. They'd been introduced by mutual friends and had slowly built up to their relationship until they became comfortable with each other and then it was just the accepted thing to progress onto marriage. Look how that had ended! This was different; there was an instant connection and it felt good.

They'd finished their coffees and she knew she should be making a move. She had an early start and it was going to be another long day on the investigation. The coffee shop was quiet, with just a few customers remaining. It didn't close for another half an hour, but the staff were already starting to clean up and close off sections. No doubt, so they could be out the door the moment the shop closed. Emma remembered working in a bar when she was young and the fact that she didn't get paid for setting up the bar or tidying up. She wondered if that was still the case here, or perhaps they just wanted all the customers to bugger off, as they had been on their feet all day.

The conversation had stalled slightly, and there were a couple of moments of awkward silence. She could see that Jack was trying to pluck up the courage to kiss her. She contemplated letting him sweat it out and then thought she'd put him out of his misery. She gently stroked his arm and turned her head to one side, which was a big enough signal. He leaned forward and kissed her. It wasn't a slobbery passionate kiss, but it wasn't gentle either; it could only be described as intense and exhilarating. Despite her best intentions Emma knew that tonight she was going to break her golden rule about first dates – if the opportunity presented itself of course!

CHAPTER ELEVEN

Fenton walked into the cafe and saw Taylor sitting in their usual spot. They'd been coming to the same cafe near Waterloo station for the last five years since she had become a DCI. There was no need to order, he just gave the owner a nod and Betty went into the kitchen bellowing, "Usual for the coppers," with a strong Liverpudlian accent. It was early and the building trade were still having their lumberjack breakfasts, even the ones who were still in shape. He had no idea where they put it all and longed to be young again with hollow legs.

"So, you officially get the case today, you lucky, lucky man. I'm off to see Manning in a bit. She's expecting you as well of course," Taylor said with a sarcastic smile.

"Suppose I better eat a good breakfast then," he replied smiling. "Three sausage and three bacon please Betty," he said to the owner as she brought their tea and toast.

"No probs Eric. You want anything else Lisa?"

"I'm good thanks."

"Won't be too long, we're a bit busy today." She bustled off into the kitchen.

"You'll need a strong stomach for this one I'm telling you," Taylor remarked.

"Don't let Betty hear you say that about her breakfast," he laughed.

"All jokes aside, if this is the same person then we're dealing with someone who's sick. I mean this stuff is warped."

"But could it be the same person? It seems strange to just suddenly switch."

"Well it could be a woman who has a hatred of men and that's why she's gone to extremes with this one."

"I'm not convinced we're looking for a woman, more than happy to be proved wrong though."

"Are you taking the piss?" Taylor asked with a stunned look on her face.

"Of course," he replied with a deadpan look which caused her to smile. He missed working with her.

Their breakfast was put in front of them. Fenton glanced at his watch; it had been less than three minutes since Betty had informed them there would be a delay. If only everywhere else regarded three minutes as a delay, people would be a lot less irritated.

"I hear you and Mike are moving in together," Fenton asked whilst taking a bite out of his sausage. This was the best breakfast place in the world.

"Yeah, it's not too soon is it?" she asked genuinely worried.

"What, after five years? Mrs Fenton and I were married with two kids and a mortgage after five years."

"How are the kids?"

"Great, just Emily at home now. When she goes to university the house will be noticeably quiet."

"Are you looking forward to retirement?"

"Are you taking the piss again? I've got years left in me. I'm not even fifty yet."

"Any plans for big day?"

"Not if I'm still on this case. It already feels like a month, and we're not even a week in."

"You think there'll be more?"

"I'm certain of it. The first one had all the signs of a serial case. It's why Beeden pulled me off cold cases."

"How are things between you two now, it's been a long time since that Pilkington business."

"Professional and courteous. We'll never go back to what we had."

"That's a shame. He clearly still thinks a lot of you giving you a case like this."

"Do I detect a tinge of jealousy?" he mocked.

"Not in the slightest and you'll see why when we get to Manning's lab."

Fenton shrugged and then continued to eat his breakfast. He thought about the case and what they had so far. Extraordinarily little if he was honest. Yes – the victims could all be connected through Ryan's Retreat and Karen's Klub, although that was just circumstantial. They literally had nothing. He'd have to tell Jack to pull his finger out with the CCTV. This was London, there were cameras everywhere, so there had to be something.

"I'm not sure Jack's as great as you make him out to be you know," Fenton remarked to Taylor.

"In what way? I told you he were a bit maverick."

"A bit? He went and interviewed a potential suspect, on his own, at night and without telling anyone, and after I had said to leave it until the morning."

"That's extreme even for Jack. He is known to go off on his own, but he's never put himself in danger before. I mean that were a stupid thing to do. He keeps things close until he knows he's got something to share. You won't hear any supposition from him."

"You know I like people to tell me what they're thinking, even if it does turn out to be nothing."

"Did Jack really do that? Who did he interview?"

"This brothel madam, Karen Kowalski."

"Brothel madam?"

"Well in all but name, she's the owner of a gentlemen's club on her tax returns."

"And this is that Karen's Klub?"

"That's the one, not very inventive a name is it?"

"No. Anyway, I'm worried about Jack. This really isn't like him, Eric. Did he say why he spoke to her?"

"He said he knew her from when he was in Vice and thought an informal approach may prove more fruitful."

"And did it?"

"Not really, although this Karen knows Jack a lot more than he makes out."

"What do you mean?"

"They've definitely got history between them, although she wasn't giving anything away."

"You mean sexual history? I don't see Jack with some old boiler who runs a knocking shop."

"Nothing like that. He's trying his luck with Emma you know. I heard they went out for dinner last night."

"Really? Good for her, she's had a shit couple of years. I'll have to give her a call. Look, Eric I've known Jack a long time and he's a good detective. He spots things others don't, and I include myself in that, but I think something must be going on with him. Would you mind if I had a chat with him and see if I can find anything out?"

"Be my guest," he said, as he looked at his watch. "We'd

better finish up or we'll be late for Manning. We can walk from here. I could do with the cardio after this breakfast."

"You're late Eric. You might be trying to collect every dead body in London, but I do have other cases to get to," Manning barked as Fenton and Taylor walked in.

He glanced at his watch; he was only three minutes late. She was clearly in one of *those* moods and hadn't received the memo from Betty! Fenton chose not to bite back. They pulled their robes on, after being prompted.

"Nice to see you again Lisa, although I don't suppose you're too upset about off-loading this one to Eric," she tittered. "Well I've been doing this a long time, and this has to be the first that has put me off breakfast. Shall we have a look at him?"

Fenton nodded and they went over to the table where the body had a white sheet over it. She pulled it back to his chest and he looked peaceful, not a mark on his face. The guy was clearly in shape as he had prominent muscle definition, then he did work in a gym, so perhaps that was to be expected. However, the receptionist at Fenton's gym was always talking to her colleague about trying this or that diet whilst scoffing a Snickers – although that was a Local Authority gym. It was important to add that part whenever he told someone about his gym and how much the membership was per month; in a way this justified why it was so shit, like many cheap things in life.

"Do we have a confirmed cause of death yet?" Fenton asked.

"Yes – choking."

"You mean from the..."

"Yes, your killer cut off the victim's genitals and then choked him with them. I wasn't sure what would have killed him first – that or him bleeding to death. He lost a lot of blood before he died. The blocked larynx got to him first though. I can't tell if he lost consciousness before he died, let's just hope the poor guy did. Be good if you catch this one Eric."

"When have I not caught a killer?"

"A fair challenge, I'll let you have that one," she smiled at him, which was unnerving. Her mood seemed to be all over the place.

"I wonder why someone would switch from a brick over the head to this," Lisa pondered out loud.

"Who knows Lisa, I just tell you how they died. The rest is for you to work out. I hear you are moving in with your man finally?"

"Yes – how did you hear?"

"Ah, you know me. I hear all!"

"Of course you do," Taylor laughed. "And how about you? How is Deidre?"

"Ask her yourself," Manning gestured towards the door, as Fenton and Taylor turned to see her walk into the lab from Manning's office.

"Your case is becoming more fascinating by the day," remarked Deidre, as she strode in.

"What do you make of our killer switching?"

"It's unusual and perhaps not the same killer. I say perhaps as you never know with serial killers. There is always a new mutation, doing things differently. If it is the same person, then I would say you could be looking for a woman."

"Why?"

"I just can't see another man doing this to another man. Your killer clearly hates men."

"Could be a gay guy then."

"That's a fair point Eric, it could well be. It's a good point actually. He'd have the strength to cave the women's heads in, although I'm not saying a woman couldn't do it."

"Well we better get back to brief the team, now we have the report," Fenton remarked, picking up the file off the table.

"This press coverage certainly will keep your incident room busy won't it? I mean it's ridiculous what they come up with nowadays,"

"We are trying to keep press coverage to a minimum at the moment," replied Fenton.

"So, you haven't seen today's papers?" she asked.

He gave her a questioning look. He hadn't seen the papers, although felt a familiar dark feeling in the pit of his stomach. Was it apprehension about what was to come, or the dead male prostitute with his genitals stuffed down his throat that was making him feel queasy?

"The Alphabet Killer?"

"The what?"

Deidre handed over the national paper which had *Police Hunt Alphabet Killer* as its headline, Fenton read the article quickly, getting angrier by the second. He had an over-whelming sense of déjà vu and looked at the by-line for who had written the article. The journalist was named as *Daisy Dixon.* That wasn't fooling Fenton.

"Your sister up to her old tricks I see," Fenton snapped at Manning.

"The journalist is Daisy Dixon," Deidre remarked.

"This has got Polly Pilkington written all over it. I see she's had a pop at me again. What is it with her? Did she not learn her lesson last time?"

"Eric, I have not spoken with Polly in about two years. As far as I know, she is still living in Australia. This is just someone copying her style. She's not the type to change her name. She has no shame."

"Bullshit, I want to see her – now!"

"Just watch who you're talking to Eric, remember this is my lab," Manning barked.

"Call her and tell her I want to see her in my office this morning," he bellowed, as he stormed out with Taylor following closely behind.

He could hear Taylor trying to keep up with him as he marched off towards his car. He checked his phone and there were seven missed calls, all from Beeden. This was going to be a bad day.

"Can you find out who this Daisy Dixon is? If it is Pilkington, you'd better be there to stop me doing anything stupid!"

He hadn't been her boss for five years, but he knew she'd do as he asked. It wasn't an authority thing; he just knew she'd have his back. He then braced himself as he prepared to call Beeden.

———

POLICE HUNT ALPHABET KILLER
Daisy Dixon

Police officers hunting a serial killer in London continue to draw a blank. The killer has now struck three times in as many days and the investigation has barely started. It appears all victims had previously worked in the sex industry, although it is understood that the police aren't pursuing this as a line of enquiry in their investigation. The victims to date are Giselle Gorge, Becky Best and Tony Leopold. However, Leopold's birth name is Frances Fullerton. He changed his name by deed pole when he worked as a male prostitute. His surname was in honour of Leopold von Sacher-Masoch, a 19th century Austrian journalist and writer. His name was where the term 'masochism' was derived from. It is well known that Leopold sold himself for masochistic purposes from a young age.

This means all victims have the same initial for their first and last names which is a concerning development the police are not pursuing. The victims also once worked at notorious gentlemen's club Karen's Klub which is known to cater for its high-profile clients and their varied sexual perversions. All victims were also members of the gym, Ryan's Retreat. A gym known to be frequented by prostitutes and the gay community who fraternise openly in the gym's sauna and steam room. The names of these venues are again another indication that the killer has a warped vendetta against letters of the alphabet. Does that mean we can expect another twenty-three victims until the entire alphabet has been exhausted? It means that the existing victims links to the sex industry could merely be a coincidence, and those of us with matching initials should be staying out of dark alleys and gay cruising areas, the latter being were the latest victim was found by a man 'walking his dog'.

The exact circumstances of how the victims have been murdered has not been released, yet sources close to the police indicate that Leopold was killed in a different manner to Gorge and Best and suffered some form of mutilation prior to death. Fenton was investigating the case of Gorge and Best, with the Leopold case being originally assigned to DCI Lisa Taylor. It is believed that Fenton demanded he take over both cases insisting they were all linked, yet his immediate team have their doubts. An officer assigned to the investigation commented that Fenton was 'out of control' with his obsession in having an exemplary record for solving murder cases and taking on those with a high profile. It is understood that his bullish approach is the reason why every murder enquiry lead by Fenton has been resolved. Whether or not the right person was convicted is questionable, yet his record is known to be something of an obsession. His approach to an investigation is believed to alienate those around him, yet the powers that be only care about the results and the metaphorical bodies which lie in his wake are disregarded.

Fenton was responsible for leading the investigation which brought the Diversity Slayer to justice five years ago. The case was so high profile that it was instrumental in bringing about a change in government allowing the worst Prime Minister in a generation to seize power. Fortunately for the British public this was a short-lived time in office, and he was ousted by his own party within a year when revelations came to light about his sexual deviances.

CHAPTER TWELVE

Polly Pilkington, or Daisy Dixon, as she was now known, walked into Fenton's office as confident as ever. Fenton loathed the woman. Twice she had tried to ruin his career and here she was again, albeit under a new guise. She wasn't an unattractive woman, although she had become a brunette since they last met. Annoyingly it suited her. Her hair was still short, yet without the blonde, the orange tan appeared less severe. She still had her hourglass figure and it was still impossible not to be drawn to her enormous cleavage as it was just there, mesmerising like a pendulum.

Polly still had that conceited smile plastered over her face. He'd seen other people smile in the same way – sociopaths! He'd always believed the woman to be unhinged and obsessive about her career. He could feel his face reddening as he remembered one of their last meetings many years before when he had confronted her with Manning, believing them to be having a scene together. The humiliation was still raw. It wasn't because he had made a complete tit out of himself in a packed restaurant; it was that he had been wrong. Polly was Cockney through and through, yet when she spoke her fake accent made her sound like a Scandinavian whore, quite apt given the reason she had unfortunately appeared back in his life.

"Eric, darlink, it has been far too long."

"I thought you had moved to Australia. Did they deport you?"

"I see you have not changed. Still an uptight prick. No doubt to compensate for your small genitals."

"What?" he spluttered. "You do realise who you're taking to don't you?"

"Sit the fuck down Eric, I didn't come here to waste time going over old ground."

He was so stunned at the way she had spoken to him that he just sat without question. She was always a hard-nosed bitch who embroidered the truth for her own gain, yet she had never been so crass and downright rude, especially to a senior police officer. She wasn't that stupid, or did she still have Beeden in her pocket? Technically he could arrest her for speaking to him in that way, although he wouldn't. The paperwork would be too much of a headache.

"I have come here on serious business, darlink. As you can see, I have rebranded. That jumped up little pervert ruined my good name, so I have had to start from scratch again."

He assumed the jumped up little pervert she was referring to was the former Prime Minister who had used her for his own climb up the political ladder and then turned on her when Fenton had solved the Diversity Slayer case and brought her vindictive personal campaign against him to an end. It had been a wondrous moment. Still she'd had the last laugh.

"He didn't last very long in power though once you had finished with him," Fenton retorted.

"Perhaps not, but the damage was done. I hold no grudges against you Eric. You see, you did not fuck me over out of spite. You did it to solve a crime. You were just doing your job."

"One of the last times we saw each other, you were doing a job as well."

He was referring to walking in on her and Chief Superintendent Harry Beeden in a compromising position. At least it had answered the question of where she was getting all her insider information.

"Don't be so crass Eric, it doesn't suit you."

"It's been five years Polly, or do I call you Daisy now? Anyway, like I said it's been five years. Perhaps I have changed as well."

"Your type never changes Eric. You are a dying breed though. You have never been one to love the PR side of policing. I see your little protégé isn't quite so camera shy."

"So, DCI Taylor is your new target now that you know you can't bring my career to a crashing halt?"

He was getting irritated with himself, as he was finding it difficult to keep his temper in check and he still hadn't got to the real reason as to why she was here and why she had so willingly agreed to see him. Even after all this time, this woman could still push all his trigger buttons in a nanosecond.

"My, my Eric, we are on edge today. I have no interest in Lisa Taylor. She is a very capable officer who will no doubt make her way to the top. I believe she is up for promotion to Superintendent. Won't that be interesting for you? Having your former subordinate as your boss?

"Nothing would make me prouder," he said, firmly with conviction.

"How sweet. Anyway, I did not come here to discuss the fascinating career of some northern DCI who has made a name for herself in the Met. We have far more important things to discuss."

"It was I who requested your presence here, and I who will determine what is to be discussed," he said, holding her gaze.

There was a brief second of hesitation, only fleeting and if he hadn't been watching her so intently it would have been missed. It boosted his ego, not that he had one.

"Well perhaps we want the same thing?" she replied, regaining her confidence.

"I doubt that, considering I want you to stop with this ridiculous *Alphabet Killer* nonsense as all it is going to do is terrify people. You have no evidence that suggests it is a motive and you are merely grasping at straws in some futile attempt to try to resurrect your defunct career. Well nobody is interested in your provocative and vile sensationalistic bull-shit that you try to palm off as journalism. The days of being able to whip up a moral panic in the media are on their way out. People aren't as gullible as they once where and won't be swayed by some two-bit writer who things she can change the word with an over and incorrect use of exclamation marks!"

He was impressed at her resolve. She hadn't reacted in the slightest at his rant, which is what it was – still, it felt good though.

"May I have my turn now?" she said, smiling sweetly. It was the sort of smile *Hannibal Lecter* probably gave before he decided who would be that evening's dinner.

"I wanted to see you Eric as I believe you have a dangerous killer on the loose. The *Alphabet Killer* angle sells papers. This could become profoundly serious."

"I have three dead bodies. It doesn't get more serious."

"You will soon have more I believe."

"Again, you are giving me nothing that I haven't already considered as part of this investigation."

"I think your killer is on a mission."

"Really? You shock me."

"Eric, listen to me and don't interrupt," she shouted.

There was something in her tone that made him stop and listen.

"I think your killer is on a mission to eliminate people who have either wronged them or have a hold on your killer. What concerns me the most is that I don't think this is your typical serial killer"

"What makes you think that?"

"I've been studying criminal psychology whilst I was away and for it to be a typical serial killer it doesn't make sense that all the victims would be so inter-linked. They may start close to home and then widen the net. This person continues to be attacking people from that club. It is like they have a specific mission to complete."

"There is also the gym as well, which is what you mentioned in your article."

"I think that is just a coincidence. A lot of whores use that gym."

"I don't believe in coincidences."

"Yet you disregard the *Alphabet Killer* motive?"

"Because that's ridiculous."

"Perhaps, but if you don't believe in coincidences, then explain it."

"I can't... yet! I'm surprised you haven't gone for a race angle after last time."

"The male victim was white."

"True, but he was killed in a vastly different way. It was up close and personal. Whoever killed Tony, or Frances, or whatever his name is, they held him and carried out a sickening murder."

"What did they do?" she asked leaning forward.

"You know better than that Polly, we need to hold some things back. Not just to help us catch this sick fucker, it's so people can still sleep at night."

"You can't blame a girl for trying, darlink."

"You going to drop this alphabet shit then?"

"If you have another victim and they don't match up then I'll try another angle, until then a girl's gotta eat."

"And to hell with the repercussions?"

"As you said, nobody is so easily swayed by the media anymore so why do you care?"

"We're done," he replied standing up.

"I guess we are for now," she said standing up and walking towards the door. "Be interesting to hear what Deidre thinks of my theory, but no doubt I'll have to use my own contacts to find that one out. See you soon no doubt, Eric."

Then she was gone.

Fenton leaned back in his chair trying to work out what, if anything he had gained from that meeting and how she knew about Deidre's involvement in the case. The obvious place to look would be Manning, although he knew better than that. She was professional to the end and besides, he didn't think she held her sister with much regard anymore given he believed her when she said they hadn't spoken in a long while. He could look at Beeden, although he doubted Harry would be so stupid to risk his marriage again. His wife had made him pay dearly when she found out and he was still up to his eyeballs in debt for all the *gifts* he had bought for her. How she had found out, Beeden didn't know. Fenton had a fairly good idea though!

"What did she want?" asked Taylor.

"The usual, to tell me how to run my case."

"What's kicked her off on this alphabet thing?"

"Nothing, she admits it's a coincidence. She thinks our killer is on a mission."

"How incredibly insightful of her."

"Oh, and get this, she's been studying criminal psychology, hence the sudden wealth of insight, or so she thinks. She knows about Deidre Peter's involvement as well."

"Manning?"

"No, I don't believe that. I hope Deidre is still willing to do a freebie. My budget won't stretch to her normal fees."

"A serial killer and they won't pay for a profiler?"

"You sound shocked Lisa, I thought I'd taught you better than that."

She laughed. "Sometimes the old idealism creeps back in. Better stamp that out of myself if I want to become Superintendent."

"Only for the interview please, especially if you're going to be my boss!"

"I'll go and give Dr Peters a call for you and then be on my way."

"Thanks for sticking around whilst Pilkington was here again. I saw you hovering outside the door. Like the good old days."

"Not quite. I hardly heard you raise your voice. You must be going soft."

He chuckled as she left. He then called his wife to let her know that it was doubtful he would be home for tea. It wasn't even lunchtime, yet instinctively he knew that it was going to be an exceptionally long day. He sat back in his chair and mulled over the case. One thing he hadn't shared with the rest of the team was his belief that they might be dealing with two killers. The way the women and then the man had been killed was so different, albeit both violent. The murder of the women was frenzied, whereas the man had been killed in a planned and controlled manner. Pilkington had given him nothing new and they still had no suspect in the frame. He got his notebook out and listed the people he thought could be involved – Karen Kowalski, Ryan Killarney and this Paul

Johnson who was apparently abroad, yet nobody could get hold of him, He also suspected something was going on between Karen and her doorman so he added Sid Verpa to the list as well. That was four people who warranted further questioning. He knew the team were flat out, yet they had nothing, so they needed to up their game. Some obvious things had been missed in the commotion of having three bodies in quick succession. The investigation needed a break-through. Fenton hoped that wasn't going to come in the shape of another victim.

———

Jacobs was in the canteen grabbing a late lunch. Fenton had torn strips off him about the CCTV and the lack of progress and then put more men on it given the latest Giselle sighting. He'd asked Jacobs to co-ordinate it. They needed Giselle's other phone found as the caller could have been her killer, something Jacobs had surmised himself. Still he allowed to let Fenton rip into him without responding as it was easier. Jacob's head was all over the place and he needed to get it together. The situation with Ryan and Karen was of great concern. Between them, they had the power to end his career and no doubt put him behind bars. However, he knew it was unlikely as they would also end up doing a long stretch as well. If one of them was responsible for these murders though, they now had nothing to lose. He was sure they didn't, as he knew them both and had seen their fear when these murders started. Neither of them knew who was doing this, Jack was sure of that. Fenton wasn't so convinced that they weren't involved though. There was nothing he could do to dissuade him, without suspicion being raised and nothing got past Fenton. Jacobs was also falling for Emma Shirkham in a big way. He was scared of the way he felt, yet he believed she felt the same way, especially after they had spent the night together. That was not typical behaviour for her and what an incredible night it had been. He hadn't felt such a strong emotional connection like that with someone in a long time, if ever. If she knew what he had done, then she would want nothing more to do with him and he wondered if she would turn him in herself and then dismissed the thought. She would not get the chance, as he would never put her in that position. He had to make sure that all the loose ends were tied up and nothing could ruin the future he dreamed of; the senior rank, the perfect woman and one day, his own family.

———

Fenton had given the team a brief update and mentioned the CCTV footage, which they now had several officers searching through in order to find where Giselle had gone and perhaps who she had met on the night of her death. He handed over to Deidre Peters who had agreed to discuss a potential profile. Rather than take information away and report back in a few days like most profilers, she had suggested they work *organically*. Fenton wasn't sure what she meant, and half expected her to bring out a bag of overpriced carrots that hadn't been washed. She'd clarified that the technique worked well, as it meant the team were given the opportunity to be honest about what they were thinking, even if it was still supposition.

"Let's start by building a picture of our killer," Deidre said. "Do we think it's a man or woman?"

There were mutterings around the room, whilst they talked amongst themselves. Clearly nobody was willing to stick their neck out first and Fenton was deliberately holding back, as he'd agreed with Deidre. He caught Shirkham's eye and gave her a subtle nod.

"I think a woman could be involved," Shirkham said loudly, causing everyone to stop muttering and focus on her.

"Involved, as in not the killer?" asked Deidre.

"When it was just Giselle and Becky, I was convinced it was a man as the attack would have taken incredible strength. I'm not saying a woman isn't capable of that, but I believe for a woman to do that to another woman, would be because of such a deep personal hatred that it would be someone close and that would mean we wouldn't be in the position we are now."

"You mean you'd have a motive or a suspect?"

"Yes, or even both. If it was just Giselle, then the story would be quite different. You then add in Tony's murder and that's where I think the woman comes in. I think we're looking for two killers working together."

Fenton was impressed. He hadn't vocalised his theory of two killers to anyone and Shirkham was thinking the same. Why he couldn't get her to go for promotion he would never fathom out. Still, he would try again once the case was over. The rest of the team, he could tell from their faces, were waiting to interject. It only took one person to get the momentum going.

"Does anyone else think we are looking for more than one killer?"

Fenton was pleasantly surprised to see half a dozen hands go up. He noticed Jack's hand didn't and his body language made him look distant. He didn't look bored, but it was clear his mind was elsewhere, Fenton put it down to the bollocking he had given him that morning, although hoped he wouldn't remain in petulant child mode for too long.

"Does anyone want to suggest a different theory?" Deidre asked.

Brennan put his hand up, like he was still at school, causing Deidre to smile encouragingly.

"I get the two-killer thing. I just find when there are two killers it's harder to not leave a clue. Could the cases not be linked like we think they are, and I know what the Guv will say about this, it could just be a coincidence?"

Sharp intake of breath around the room and then laughter, to which Fenton joined in.

"Another possibility is that it could just be one killer and it's a gay guy," Brennan added.

"Say more about that," Deidre prompted.

"Well we know that this Tony was that way inclined and our killer could have a pathological hatred towards whores, perhaps his mum was one, or his neighbours' cousin."

Everyone laughed again, even Deidre which caused Fenton to like her even more. It showed she understood that the team needed the humour to break the reality of the horrific things they often had to deal with each day. Fenton had come across many in Deidre's profession throughout his career and most of them, albeit good in their own field, had zero personal skills and felt their intellectual superiority elevated them above everybody else. They didn't last long. This woman was different though. She had everyone's attention.

"Right, building on what DS Brennan has just said, what could be the motive?" she asked.

"I think it's personal," replied Shirkham.

"What makes you say that?"

"The damage to the faces of the two women, most of which was done after death. Then we know Tony was held long enough for his stomach to empty and bound in some way. He then had his genitals removed whilst he was still alive. That's very up close and personal. Unless…"

"Go on?"

"You're dealing with a complete psychopath, the link between these people is another coincidence and then we've been looking in completely the wrong place."

Everyone gave an *oooh* and again laughter. Pilkington would be in her element observing this, as it would be another thing to report out of context.

"It's an interesting alternative," Deidre remarked. "However, I believe your first theory is correct. This is a personal agenda. I could believe in one coincidence between victims, especially with sex workers. It's a strong possibility that they may have all been working from the same club at one time, as they tend to move around. I don't think you should disregard the theory of a gay man acting alone, even if there are strong indications that you are dealing with two killers.

"The killer of the women is interesting as they are disorganised and get into a frenzy when they kill. However, they can calm themselves quickly as they leave no evidence at the scene. They may even be familiar with police procedure. I still wouldn't rule out that this killer is a woman, although I agree DC Shirkham makes some very valid points, it's best to consider all angles whilst you don't have a suspect to give you a strong line of investigation. I would suggest looking through any recently released male sex offenders, or it could even be someone who was acquitted or had the charges dropped. Violence will feature. I would also suggest looking for any women who have reported a sexual assault and had the case dropped or their assailant was also acquitted. I don't think you need to cast the net too wide as your killer knows the area well and clearly knows how to avoid detection from CCTV."

"Do you think we will find them on CCTV then?" asked Fenton.

"I think it's unlikely, or you would have found it now. They could have missed something in their planning and they also can't have predicted the route Giselle may have taken to meet her killer, so keep looking just in case. The unregistered mobile phone is critically important. Nobody she worked with or at this gym knew the number?"

"No, she had another mobile which seems to be her regular number which everyone knew and that has been checked," replied Fenton.

"What about the man who identified her, has he got that number? He works in one of those clubs, doesn't he?"

It was a good shout out. Fenton admitted they hadn't checked and asked Jacobs to investigate it as soon as their meeting was over.

"Your killer or killers could be motivated by a need to eliminate those who have wronged them, which means it may not be a case of them not stopping until they are caught, they may just stop once they have completed their mission so to speak."

Fenton found the use of the word *mission* interesting as it was identical to what Polly Pilkington had suggested earlier and now Fenton had a suspicion about where she had got her information from. Fenton would have to let Dr Peters know that now she was officially helping on the case, albeit for no fee, she needed to show some discretion.

Once the meeting broke up, the team went about their assigned tasks and Fenton asked to see Deidre in his office. She was less than impressed with his accusation, stating quite clearly that she had only met Polly Pilkington on two occasions, and that the last time was before she moved to Australia. She was not even aware of her return to London as Manning had received no contact from her sister, and even if she had, she would never discuss the case with anyone else. She was a consummate professional and if he were to make

such unfounded accusations in the future, she would with-
draw her support on the case. She didn't storm out but left
quietly leaving Fenton feeling even worse. She had said the
one thing only women can say that leaves you feeling totally
wretched –she was *disappointed* in him.

CHAPTER THIRTEEN

Sid was stacking up the crates in the cellar to keep busy. Ever since the murders, the club had been rapidly losing customers. He hoped it was just a blip, as Karen had worked hard to get where she was. Her mood hadn't improved, and she seemed to be being more secretive than ever. Some of the girls had left her already and she didn't appear to be the slightest bit bothered. Sid was worried that she wouldn't recover from this mentally, let alone financially. The deaths of Becky and Tony had hit them all hard. Only Sid really mourned for Giselle. He knew her in a way that others didn't, as he'd seen her vulnerable side in the limited times they had been alone together. She'd had a shitty life in and out of care with nobody wanting her from the moment her mother dumped her, until she ran away from the care home at the age of fourteen. Somehow, she had ended up with Karen and she had looked after her and taken her in. Karen was adamant that Giselle wouldn't entertain any clients until she was sixteen and only if she wanted to. It was this, that made Giselle feel like she had a debt to Karen. If Giselle had walked out at sixteen then Karen would probably have wished her well. However, by this point she had seen too much. She happily let Karen sell her virginity on her birthday, although Sid and Giselle had already been close for a few months by this time, so her virginity was merely symbolic. It didn't matter as Karen sold Giselle's *virginity* at least a dozen times.

Slowly over the next two years, Giselle became a woman. Sid was alarmed at the how much she changed in that time. He had seen it before with other girls, but this was different. The business broke her, with every emotion she ever had, being literally screwed out of her. She was good at her job and word spread. Everyone wanted a piece of her, and she was more than happy to sell it for the right price. It broke Sid's heart to see her deteriorate. The other girls turned on her through jealousy and Karen began to resent her as she strived for independence and to break the hold the club and its madam had over her. Giselle knew that she held the power and she didn't have to rely on anyone to get what she wanted. In the end, it was Karen who needed Giselle, not the other way around: Karen hated that, and it was the source of their many arguments. Sid had seen this industry destroy people before, although nothing like what it did to Giselle.

Giselle was someone else who shared his secret. Nobody knew about their relationship, and he couldn't keep anything from her. He adored her too much and she knew him better than anyone. When the nightmares came, she had held him and reassured him that he was safe. It was in one of these moments that he told her about that fateful night. There was no judgement, even when they saw less of each other and the industry changed her, she kept his secret.

Their relationship was never the same after she found him in Karen's bed. It was not something he was proud of, it was just a necessary evil he had to do from time to time, to ensure he had somewhere to stay. It was also supposed to mean that he wouldn't have to entertain male clients again, although

Karen still coerced him out of retirement when she was stuck, but these instances were becoming less frequent as the years ticked by. He had never had an issue with sleeping with men for money. He just saw it as just a job, but he knew deep down it was affecting him mentally and he needed to get out. However, this was the only industry he had ever known and when Karen offered him the option to work on the door instead, in return for a steady wage and the occasional *personal service* for free bed and board, he took it without hesitation.

Despite Giselle's animosity with Karen, she never revealed that she knew the secret Sid held with Tony, Karen, Ryan and Jack. Now two of the people that knew about it were dead. Did Becky know anything? Had Giselle broken her promise? Sid doubted it. Given the ferocious rows Giselle and Karen had, she had never said anything. He also knew Karen was a lot of things, but a cold-blooded murderer was not one of them.

Sid wanted to run, but he couldn't. If he ran, he wouldn't know what was going on and when they might be coming for him, or even who *they* were. The situation was becoming such a mess. Work was not giving him the distraction it usually did. Perhaps this was a big hint for him to finally get the fuck out of the place. He had his security certification and plenty of experience. There would be no problem getting another job, but would it pay as well, and would he have free accommodation; he doubted it. Karen had given him a good deal for a reason and that was because she had wanted to keep him around. It was the same reason Tony had gotten such a good deal at Ryan's gym; qualifications paid for, great wage and flexible schedule. The lifestyle fitted around Tony's social side. That guy got around, but he had such a charm about him that he never came across as sleazy. Sid missed their friendship greatly and after what had happened, they had been told to keep their distance from each other. They couldn't risk being seen together. It hadn't stopped them still meeting up occasionally, away from everyone. They didn't speak about what had happened; it was just good to be with someone who wouldn't question Sid on why he had suddenly gone quiet. At times they would simply meet up to sit in silence as they both reflected on what had happened and pondered on what their future could hold if anyone ever found out. It was impossible to get away from it.

Sid remembered their last meet up away from everyone. It had only been a month before the murders started. They had spent the day at a Spa in Essex. This was very out of Sid's comfort zone, but Tony had suggested it as a way for them to relax and not risk bumping into anyone like could sometimes happen in a bar, or even a coffee shop. They'd had a relaxing afternoon and Sid had been surprised about how much he had enjoyed the spa treatments. They'd agreed to make this their new ritual and to try and do it at least once a quarter. It was now something they'd never do again. Sid felt the tears sting his eyes and used his t-shirt to wipe them away. He didn't want to get emotional and knew the only way he could do that was to focus on his work.

He started to unpack the recent delivery. This would keep him busy for a while and the physical exertion was always good for quelling any emotional spillage. The last thing he needed was Karen offering to *comfort* him. He'd have to say something if she started to take the piss with her demands, but then he knew he was just kidding himself. He didn't have anywhere else to go. He wasn't great with money, so he had never saved anything; he couldn't run even if he wanted to.

He heard a bang behind him, which made him jump. He went to the cellar door and opened it. He looked around and couldn't see anyone. It didn't look like anything had fallen, so he dismissed it. He picked up another crate and heard

another sound, but this time it sounded like a shuffle of footsteps. He swung round and there was still nothing there – he
was getting paranoid.

He bent down to pick up another crate and someone
grabbed him from behind. He went to cry out, but they stuck
a cloth over his mouth. He went to shake them off, but he felt
a needle go into his neck. Within seconds the room became
blurry and he dropped to his knees. He stumbled on the floor
and managed to turn around; the last thing he saw before
blacking out was a pair of high heel shoes.

Sid rattled the chains which bound his hands and heard
the same clink of metal as he moved his legs. He wasn't going
anywhere. Where he was though, he had no idea. One minute
he had been stacking crates and the next he had woken up
here. He had not heard another person and wondered if he
had just been left to rot. He was thirsty and had already
pissed himself. He was naked on a stone slab, so it wasn't like
he was comfortable to begin with. His legs were now starting
to chap in the cold.

He looked around, the light was limiting and there wasn't
much he could see. A door was about twelve foot away from
him so the room was a decent size for what could only be
described as a dungeon – certainly bigger than your average
cell in a police station.

He remembered the first time he had been in a police cell
when he was fourteen years old. This was the one time he had
been arrested when he hadn't done anything wrong. Two of
his friend's girlfriends were having a catfight in the town
centre and everyone was drunk on cheap cider. The police
had arrived and pulled the girls roughly apart, to which Sid
had merely said, "Eh mate, they're only girls you don't need to
be so rough." The police had viewed this as a sign of aggres-
sion, as they had sprayed him with Mace. The pain had
brought him to his knees, and he had little recollection then

of what happened after until the pain started to subside, and he found himself in a cell with a few digs to the ribs. When he asked if he could wash his face he was told to, "wash it in the bog you little shit." He hadn't stooped to that. His mother had arrived after what felt like hours and was her usual brilliant self. Sid remembered her tone to the desk sergeant was clear, authoritative and to the point when she took one look at Sid's face...

"I assume there will be no charges against my son, and we shall respond with the same degree of hospitability, now where do I sign to release him?"

She hadn't chastised him for what had happened, merely given him the advice that once he started working he would come across people who didn't like to be told how to do their jobs and he should probably get into a habit of not doing that. This would ensure a quieter life when he was working in an office. Sadly, his mum had died when he was eighteen. At least she had never seen him become a male whore and then a doorman; a far cry from the office his mother had craved for him.

He didn't know why he was suddenly thinking about his mother, perhaps it was because he felt totally helpless, and the only person you could ever do that with and receive no judgement for being scared, was your mother.

Sid heard a noise. He couldn't cry out as he was gagged. He listened with trepidation as he heard footsteps getting closer. They stopped outside the door. There was a rattle of keys before the door opened. Sid's eyes needed to adjust to the light, so it took a few seconds for him to register who was stood in the doorway. When he did, he realised who it was. He knew that this was the last person Tony had seen before he died. He also knew that after years of looking over his shoulder, it was finally over.

CHAPTER FOURTEEN

Karen was worried. Business was falling and she suspected this wasn't the usual end of the month lull. They didn't exist in this industry. If you could afford her girls and guys, then you weren't living in the red. No, these murders were keeping people away. It wasn't out of fear for their personal safety. It was fear that with the police snooping around, their perfect little suburban lives could be shattered by the revelation of their perversions. Added to that Sid had taken it upon himself to do one of his disappearing acts at one of the worst possible times. She was down on staff as well. She only had six girls, which was half what she usually had and there were no guys left, Details of how Tony had been killed had been reported in the press and the guys had freaked. Maybe they weren't as tough as she had thought. The women were used to beatings, sexual assaults and even the odd murder. The guys were never targeted, so this was something new and terrifying for them. Karen had never known the men's toilets at Piccadilly Circus to be only used for what they were built for. This wasn't just affecting her; she had spoken to many of her counterparts and they were suffering the same drop in trade. The blame was laid squarely at Karen's door as all the victims had worked for her at some point. She was hoping she could have tempted Sid out of retirement for the night, as she needed a man with certain qualities for a demanding client. He wanted two of the girls and she had lined up Sandra and Aerial for that. He was also quite specific about the sort of man he wanted. It would need to be someone with a penchant for the weird and wonderful. She would need to call in a favour, although they were fast running out.

———

Harriet was sitting at the bar talking to Darren. He was the new barman and extremely cute. She knew Karen all too well and that he'd soon be turning tricks. The *gay for pay* ones all started on the bar.

"How are you finding it Darren?"

"It's not as busy as I thought it would be," he replied.

He was well spoken and seemed out of place with what were basically the dregs of humanity. She liked the way his hair flopped forward as he was stacking the fridges ready for what was supposed to be an evening rush, although she doubted it would come. Still, if she did two customers tonight it would be enough. She always had some extra funds tucked away in case of slumps like this, so she didn't have to dip into her main stash. She had a few clients on the side as well. She had met them at the club and then exchanged details. Strictly against the rules, however she had been sensible with the oncs that she did this with; she had chosen those who had enough money to still attend the club regularly and see her outside as well, so no suspicion was aroused.

Harriet loved the doleful brown eyes on Darren. They

gave him an air of innocence – it wouldn't last long. The city sucked that out of the innocent very quickly. Come to Karen's Klub and it's gone in about ten minutes.

"You alright Harriet?" asked Aerial, as she sat on the next stool.

"Yes, I just wonder if it will pick up later. I thought you had Mr Yatumoshi upstairs?"

"Just waiting on Sandra. Karen's trying to get us a bloke who measures up if you know what I mean," she snorted.

The woman was common and repellent. She was surprised Karen hadn't tried to persuade Sid to do a comeback. He'd come back more times than Barbara Streisand. He always said this would be his last one and then Karen would be in a fix and poor Sid would dutifully oblige, yet again. She asked Aerial about Sid.

"Done one of his disappearing acts so Karen is in a foul mood, and I mean worse than usual."

Harriet was half listening as she heard Aerial muttering on with pointless drivel. There seemed to be no end to the amount of absolute crap that came out of the woman's mouth. Harriet knew that Aerial didn't like her. In fact, she knew most of the girls didn't like her. It was because, for Harriet this wasn't a way of life; it was a means to an end. She already had enough put aside to set herself up as a property developer. She saw herself as the next Sarah Beeny, although without the half dozen kids. That wasn't for her and besides, she couldn't have kids, not after what had happened to her when she was young, although she had made her peace with that a long time ago.

She'd been worried that with business the way it currently was, Karen would be reluctant to let her go. She had been straight with Karen from the start that this was just to set up a business, Karen had appreciated Harriet's honesty and they'd spoken earlier with Karen remarking that no matter what happened, a deal was a deal.

———

"You will just have to make do with what you are given," shouted Karen at Aerial. She noticed Sandra standing by the door out of arms reach.

"The gay guys don't work on this kind of gig Karen. Where the fuck is Sid?"

"Don't speak to me that way or you will pay."

"Seriously, are your fucking joking? You need us more than we need you. Haven't you noticed, nobody wants to come to this club anymore and we get a big spender who wants two ladies and a guy, and you get us some poof. They scream when they see a bit of minge. Are you for fucking real?"

Karen was furious and slapped Aerial hard across the face, although she didn't seem to be in the slightest bit perturbed.

"Is that all you can do, shout and hit. People won't stay you know. Look, a straight guy works better on this type of job and you know that. The straight guys can do gay for pay if they are the top. The gay guys think a minge is a nuclear weapon and will run screaming from it. This guy wants everyone involved. It's not going to work."

"Then you will make it work, if you want any more jobs at this club."

"Don't threaten me Karen, as I am this close to walking out," Aerial retorted, holding her finger and thumb about a millimetre apart.

She stormed out slamming the door with Sandra following her. Karen slumped back down in her chair and wept. She had managed to hold it together whilst they were in the room, but she was struggling as everything was falling apart. The only hope she had left was that the secret she had buried long ago would remain where it was. Tony's murder had scared her. Could someone really know what happened?

Aerial was a mouthy little bitch, even if she was right. This wasn't a job for a gay guy, they had their purposes and could do some pretty fucked up shit, although put them near a naked woman and they're likely to pass out. Still she had it on good authority that this guy had double dipped for pay before, so Karen kept her fingers crossed. This was a particularly important client that she could not afford to lose.

———

Aerial gave the guy the once over. Well he certainly looked the part. She walked straight up to him, no introductions and stuck his hand in her knickers. He smiled, clear on what she was asking him to do. He started to move his hand and within a couple of minutes Aerial's body shuddered. This guy knew what he was doing; perhaps Karen hadn't lost her touch. Sandra had stood in the doorway the whole time, looking awkward.

It was a short while later when Aerial realised that the guy was deaf. *Deaf?* Was this a joke? She took back everything she had just thought about Karen. The woman was an actual fuckwit.

"Can you believe this?" she asked Sandra. "How are we supposed to instruct a deaf gay guy on where to put it and when?"

"As long as I can see your lips it'll be fine," he replied in a clear and strong Lancashire accent, causing them both jump and laugh.

"Come on, let's do this," Aerial said moving her lips slowly. She couldn't help it. He gave her one of those *don't take the piss* looks and then smiled.

. . .

Aerial had met Mr Yatumoshi before. He had unusual and demanding tastes, nothing perverse, although Aerial knew her definition of perversion was for beyond the realms of anyone's imagination. Mr Yatumoshi himself was quite different. He was very precise in what he wanted. He always had three *toys* as he called them. Aerial had been called worse in her years. It was always two women and one man. The man was always white and had to be hung like a donkey. The women's ethnicity was often inter-changeable, although at least one of them had to be black. He had a thing about white on black skin. The male whore did most of the work, as he would have to have sex with both women and then with Mr Yatumoshi. In fact, Mr Yatumoshi only touched the women during his inspection stage, when he would wash them very gently to ensure they were clean. However, during the whole scenario, which would last a couple of hours, Mr Yatumoshi would be blindfolded. His hearing was very astute, so he would know if his instructions were not being carried out and this would reduce the tip. The tip would start at a hundred per cent of the already astronomical fee. He'd pay a thousand pounds, which would be two hundred for each individual and the remainder going to the house. The tip was shared equally. Karen never encroached on the tips. If the tip was bigger than the fee, she would simply say *well done* and that would be the end of it.

Mr Yatumoshi said little. It was only to give out instructions. He was a young man, compared to most of the clients at this club and Aerial believed he was in his early thirties from what she had been told, although she found Asian men always looked like teenagers, until they looked about ninety. There was no middle ground. He was almost six feet tall, so Aerial suspected there was some European heritage. If they played this right, then all three of them could be five hundred quid up in a couple of hours. A lot rested on the deaf guy being able to deliver the goods!

"Did you hear that Sid has gone missing?" Sandra whispered to Aerial as they were being washed.

Mr Yatumoshi had given them permission to talk amongst themselves. Red Rum had been washed and was lying on the bed naked, reading Heat magazine – *seriously?*

"He's always going walkabout, so nothing new there. Probably knew Karen would have had him playing the part Red Rum is playing," Aerial replied quietly.

"Red Rum?"

"Well I thought it suited him... a horse from Lancashire!" she added, when Sandra clearly wasn't going to be able to work it out for herself.

Sandra looked at the naked guy on the bed and then laughed.

"You are in good spirits I see. Shall we begin our evening?" Mr Yatumoshi remarked smiling. "You are now as I say, Yatumoshi clean."

Aerial and Sandra moved over to the bed and awaited their instructions. They were now going to be shagged by a deaf gay guy from Lancashire whilst a blindfolded Japanese man gave instructions of what they were to do. One thing was for certain, you could never get bored in this job.

———

Harriet was sitting at the bar still ogling Darren, who was keeping himself busy at the other end. Perhaps she had come across as too predatory – oh well, no freebies tonight. She looked up as she heard someone rush into the bar and was surprised to see Paul, her personal trainer from the gym. She thought he was on holiday. He looked terrible.

"Harriet where's Sid?" asked Paul.

"Paul, you're back. Have you heard what's happened? It's terrible," replied Harriet getting emotional.

"Yes, I've heard, but I'm in a rush. Now where is Sid?" he said bluntly.

She had never known Paul be so rude. He had an intimidating presence as he was six foot four and ripped yet had always come across as the clichéd gentle giant.

"I have no idea. He has gone on one of his walkabouts, and you don't be so rude to me."

"Shit, right well if you see him tell him it's urgent."

"Why don't you tell me what you need to see Sid for," came a familiar voice behind them.

Harriet could tell by the look on Paul's face that Karen was the last person he wanted to see.

"I don't have time Karen, I'm in a rush."

"Get in the fucking back or I will have you arrested you little cocksucker"

"This better not take long," he sighed, before storming into the back.

Damn, Harriet thought. She didn't like to miss out on the gossip.

———

Karen could see he was on edge, as he was pacing up and down in her office. He was always a fidgety queen, although she was starting to feel dizzy. She couldn't believe how bad he looked, what had he been up to?

"Will you sit still. You are getting on my nerves with all this pacing."

"I have places to be Karen. Yes, I've heard about Giselle, Becky and Tony. No, I have no idea who did it. I just need to see Sid."

"Where have you been? Ryan has been trying to get hold of you."

"On holiday."

"You lie, you did not go to Gran Canaria."

"What?"

"Well you don't look like the contented slut you usually do when you come back from that place."

"Cheeky bitch, what I do on holiday is my business. The *Madame Rasputin* thing doesn't work on me you know. Remember I was never one of your boys."

"No, you were too busy giving it away. I am surprised you do not need a trailer to pull your arsehole behind you."

"Go fuck yourself."

She went to deliver one of her trademark slaps, yet he was too quick for her and grabbed her arm, before letting go. He hadn't hurt her, but she knew not to attempt it again.

"I know you too well Karen, you can't bully me like the people here. Now if you don't know where Sid is then I am going. I need to see Ryan, then I'm off."

"Off where?"

"I've got plans and they don't concern you. Why don't you concentrate on keeping your business afloat, if anyone will ever work for you again?"

He stormed out and slammed the door.

She burst into tears again. What was wrong with her lately? She was getting emotional about everything. Sid had done a disappearing act. The girls were speaking back to her and now Paul, who she had known for years, had spoken to her like she was nothing. She had never known Paul to be so angry, almost fearful. Paul was the nicest guy she had ever known. He was so gentle and would never raise his voice. She had met him through Ryan and him, Tony and Paul had been inseparable, and they had made Ryan's gym what it was today. That was what had upset her, someone she loved was in trouble and instead of coming to her for help he'd taken it out on her. Right, she couldn't wallow in this self-indulgent bull-shit, enough people did that these days. Emotions were for the bedroom, not for the workplace.

She picked up the phone – Ryan would need to be warned about Paul, so he knew what was coming.

CHAPTER FIFTEEN

Ryan hung up the phone. What was Paul up to? He'd screamed at Karen and slammed doors. That was not Paul. He couldn't think about it now as he had a client due. One of those slightly overweight types who visited the gym three or four times a week, yet their diet was so bad, they never lost any weight. They would spend a lot of time, money and effort to just maintain a podgy middle. Still business was business. This woman had a thing for him though, as did many. She wasn't his type. He liked his women lean and his men podgy. It always confused the shit out of the beefcakes as he rarely touched them. Any way business and pleasure shouldn't be mixed – well not all the time anyway. He'd had some fun in the women's sauna earlier. His bulimia had been bad since the murders and he always gravitated towards women when that happened. They were more caring and considerate, even if it was for instant gratification. The men tended to say crass lines like, "Those are the sort of shoulders I could rest my ankles on." Women didn't say things like that, well not the women he was interested in anyway. He needed their kindness when his emotions were up and down like this. He was prone to bursting into tears. The women didn't mind that. They knew how to handle it. Men just seem to think that if they kept slapping you around the face with their knob then you'd stop crying. Gay or straight, men were all the same when it came to sex – all about them. On the gym floor though, there were no tears: Ryan's alpha male side roared.

"That's six... and seven... and eight... come on lift, come on Tamara lift... don't give up... come on, just two more to go... and nine... and ten. Well done, now jog round the gym come back and give me ten more."

She looked like she was about to collapse, and he could see her legs were shaking as she jogged off all wobbly. They'd only been going for five minutes and she already looked like she was going to faint. He knew what it was. She had done her usual thing of thinking that because she had a personal training session that night, she could have a lunch full of saturated fat, that she could then work it off. It didn't work like that. It just made her sluggish and not able to reach her full potential. He'd been working with her for three months and there had been no progress. She did two spin classes a week and saw him once a week. He also saw her come in at other times and workout on her own. She should look different from when she started, yet her weight had hardly moved; neither had her body measurements. Her endurance should also be up, although that wasn't as strong as it should be. She was clearly ruining everything with her diet, and it angered him. This was just a waste of his time when he could be helping people who wanted to change rather than just pant over his body. He would have to push her to her limits tonight to see just how dedicated she was. He was going to enjoy this.

. . .

"Why are you crying Tamara? Lift. Come on, lift. Look every time you complain and cry it just makes me want to ruin you even more... and not in the way you're thinking." Ryan quickly added, noticing the glint in her eye.

She laughed and then finished the set and collapsed in a heap. He passed her the water bottle and she drank like a man lost in the desert – all dignity gone. Mascara had run on to her top. Why did women wear makeup in the gym?

"What is your ultimate goal Tamara?"

"I wanna be able to walk out of here, into that dirty chicken shop over the road and feel no guilt."

He'd heard worse goals.

"Fine, well if you want to do that then don't go there tonight."

She blushed, although it was hard to tell, as her face was purple. He just knew that was her plan. He'd seen it too many times.

"Have you heard of the weekend off diet?"

"No, I ain't."

"Well you're good Monday to Friday with your diet and eat what you want at the weekend, but don't go completely stupid. We'll do your weigh-in on a Saturday morning and I'll give you a calorie goal for the week, rather than daily and if you blow it all on the weekend then you'll have to burn even more in the week and be tougher on yourself with your diet in the week."

"But I go out with me mates on a Friday."

"Then be good Sunday to Thursday," he added exasperated. "And weigh-in on a Friday morning. Can you come in here on Friday morning?"

"Yeah, before work, at about half seven."

"Right come here on Friday and don't eat anything before you come in. We'll weigh you and take some measurements then we'll move your sessions to Friday morning. I'll then give you your calorie goal for the week and it's up to you how you use that. If you don't stick to this one Tamara, I'll have to consider whether you're dedicated or not. I've got a long waiting list."

She looked upset, but said she'd do it, with a determined look on her face. He doubted her motivations, and this was proven a few minutes later when he watched out of the window as she left the gym and went straight into the chicken shop. If she didn't lose any weight in the first week of their new routine, then she was off his list.

He walked into his office and there was Paul. They hugged. Something wasn't right. Paul looked different. He was always so polished. His ash-blonde hair perfectly styled, with his face slightly tanned. With his height he always had a striking presence about him and although he had a London accent, it was subtle and cultured in tone, which just added to his attractive aura. Ryan saw a shell of that man in front of him. Hunched over, eyes red and puffy as though he hadn't slept in days, his hair greasy and he was unshaven. Sadly, Paul had never been able to grow a beard, despite being in his mid-thirties, it still grew like bum fluff and in patches on his face. It really wasn't a good look. He also looked wired.

"Are you on something?" Ryan asked.

"No, I'm just wound up because Karen was giving me a hard time. You know where Sid is?"

"Not a clue. Where have you been?"

"Holiday."

"No Paul. I tried your phone and it was a UK ring tone."

"Shit."

"What is going on? Please tell me you've got nothing to do with these murders?"

"You'd better sit down so I can explain."

Ryan was still sitting in his office. He was in shock. He'd known Paul a long time and couldn't believe he would do this. It felt like the ultimate betrayal. If he'd been honest with him from the start, then perhaps he wouldn't feel this way. Ryan could feel the anger inside of him. He opened his desk drawer and pulled out the three large bars of chocolate and started to gorge. The chocolate melting in his hands. He was about to start on the second bar when the door opened, and Karen walked in. She snatched the chocolate off him, disappeared out of the office and came back seconds later with a wet flannel telling him to wash himself up. There was no sign of the chocolate.

"I need to go to the bathroom," he said getting up.

"You have a body like a Greek God. A bit of chocolate won't do you any harm, Sit down. I have heard from the killer."

"What?" he said, sitting back down.

"Yes, she called me at the club. She has Sid." Karen broke down.

"Is he dead?"

"I don't know, probably. Oh, my Sid. We have been through so much together. Why would anyone hurt my Sid?"

"You said she?" Ryan was dumbstruck.

"The voice was disguised with a machine, but I knew it was a woman."

"Could it be one of your girls?"

"I can't believe one of my girls would do this. Perhaps I am wrong. I don't know what to do. Do you think the police are looking for a woman? They could assume it is a man and be looking in the wrong place."

"I don't know, but we can't involve the police."

"Especially not Jack!"

"I agree we need to be careful where Jack is concerned. He has too much to lose and probably won't think twice about handing us over if he can keep himself clean from it all."

"He is in it up to his neck," she retorted with bitterness.

"Perhaps but we do need to speak to him somehow. Karen the only people who knew besides me, you and Jack were Tony and Sid. Do you think it is related?"

"Becky and Giselle knew nothing about it."

"Not that we know of. You know what Sid was like for getting into the girls, perhaps he had a thing with one of them and said something. They could just be eliminating everyone who had anything to do with it, or knew about it?"

"I don't think it is about that."

"I don't think we can take the chance and we both need to be careful. We need to warn Jack."

"I do not want to speak to Jack. He threatened to search my club."

"We don't have a choice. He needs to know. He might be able to do something. He's got inside information. He's just doing his job. Better him be on the search than not."

"That is up to you then."

"I'll talk to him."

Karen got up to leave.

"And Karen, when they come to tell you about Sid, you need to act surprised. You don't want them suspecting you."

"I don't think that will be too difficult," she snapped, her eyes watering as she spoke.

Ryan sat back after she had left and tried to think who it could be that was doing this. There was nobody else who knew what they had done so perhaps it wasn't related and there was another reason why Tony, Sid, Giselle and Becky had been targeted. Surely it was too much of a coincidence that Tony and now possibly Sid had been murdered. Was he next? Was it really a woman? Could it be Karen who was doing this? She was reluctant to involve Jack and that didn't make any sense given how Jack had helped her in the past. Perhaps Karen knew more than she was letting on.

———

Sid had taken a long time to die, in fact so long it had become rather tiresome. However, there was no way things could be rushed this time. She wanted to enjoy this. The body would have to wait until tomorrow night. All she wanted now was sleep. There was still one thing that had to be done. She picked up the phone and dialled.

"What is happening with that bitch?"

"Soon, it'll be soon. She's on her guard, so it's not as easy to get her away from the club. She keeps getting taxis everywhere," came the reply.

"That's why I told you to do it straight away, before people started taking precautions."

"Sid is missing. Nothing to do with you is it?"

"I ask the questions. Now I want her gone by the weekend. I want this over."

The phone went down.

CHAPTER SIXTEEN

POLICE FLOUNDER IN ALPHABET KILLER CASE
Daisy Dixon

Police are no closer to capturing the killer who continues to stalk the streets of London, targeting victims with the same initial for each of their names. The police continue to focus their attentions on the sex industry, ignoring the chilling possibility that the killer may cast their net wider to complete their 'mission.' A source close to the police indicates that they believe the killer may claim twenty-six victims in order to complete the alphabet in its entirety. However, it's impossible to predict where the killer will strike next as there is no logical pattern to the order of their victims so far.

The investigation is led by DCI Eric Fenton, 49, who was given the investigation due to his experience at tackling high profile cases and being able to handle cases with such intense media attention. There is now serious doubt about whether he is the right man for the job and a replacement is being held off taking up other cases so they are ready to step in when Fenton is moved aside, which is said to be imminent, if an arrest isn't made soon.

The body of the first victim Giselle Gorge remains unclaimed and it seems it is destined for a pauper's grave. A tragic end for a young woman institutionalised by a failing social services system throughout her childhood. She found herself in the depravity of prostitution and yet although she was able to leave that behind her and consider the possibility of a new life, this was cut short, as she was brutally beaten to death in a back alley by a crazed psychopath. A devastating end to a devastated life!

———

Fenton looked over the incident board as the team gathered behind him, ready for the morning briefing. He would not allow the latest Pilkington article to rile him. He wanted to remain focussed. She was right in one way; he needed an arrest, or they would soon start scrutinising his investigation. He suspected that was why Taylor was being given time off to move and prep for her exams. Beeden wanted her clean in case she needed to be brought into this one. She was the obvious choice to replace him as she had briefly worked on Tony Leopold's murder and most of the team knew her. He couldn't blame her, although it would sting and he knew she would feel terrible about replacing him, if it came to that. She was up for Superintendent and he would tell her not to do anything to rock that. This would not be a time for the moral high ground, over friendships. She needed to play the game, so they could have people at the top who weren't wankers, like Beeden.

Fenton heard it go quiet behind him, so turned to start the briefing.

"Right, let's see what we have so far and then crack on with the day. Before we do that, let me allay your fears about the scaremongering in the latest article by Pilkington or

Dixon, or whatever she is calling herself this week. I am going nowhere. The article was right about two things. The first is that we need an arrest and we need one soon. The second is that the powers that be are circling as they do. Thankfully, the politicians are keeping out of this one as much as they can, probably because they know Pilkington is leading the press storm and we all know how that ended for the last Prime Minister.

"She is also right about Giselle's body not being claimed. My only concern is we'll now have every pervert and lowlife calling to claim her body. Gary will you go and speak to the guy who identified her, perhaps he wants to claim her body, then I'll need you to come with me as I want another session with Karen Kowalski and Ryan Killarney. Kowalski and Killarney – sounds like a crooked firm of solicitors. Anyway Gary, can you do that?"

"Sure, Guv."

"Do you want to give us an update from your side?"

"We've managed to find something out about that Paul, the personal trainer who was supposed to be abroad," said Brennan getting up.

"Supposed to be?"

"Yes, I know they don't have a Passport Control in the Canary Islands, but we have been able to confirm that he did not take his scheduled flight out of the country. We then sent a ping to his mobile and he was in London last night and he isn't supposed to be back until next week."

"Any idea where in London?"

"He was in the Covent Garden area so he may have been to see Killarney."

"Right, we'll speak to him straight away. Jack can you handle the Giselle thing as you were with Gary when she was identified. Take Emma with you. Excellent work, Gary."

———

Jacobs and Shirkham went to visit Andy, to see if he would be willing to claim Giselle's body. He was terribly upset that nobody had come forward for her. It was why he had resisted doing it himself as he thought there would be someone else. He knew her family were non-existent, as she had spent her childhood in care homes. His anger was aimed at Karen Kowalski. According to Andy, Giselle had been with Karen since she was fourteen and earned a lot of money for her. Giselle just wanted out, but Karen wasn't prepared to let her go. Giselle had talked to Andy about blackmailing Karen about the disappearance of one of her former doormen, a Gregory something. Andy couldn't remember his surname, although knew it involved the Irish guy, Ryan who ran the gym which all the whores use in Covent Garden. Apparently one night the guy had disappeared after a row with this Ryan guy and Karen was involved. Giselle thought it might be enough for Karen to back off and let her go.

Jacobs was now getting increasingly nervous. He was thankful that Gregory's last name hadn't been revealed. The problem was that Shirkham now knew about it and it would arouse suspicion if he didn't act on it. She was questioning Andy on what else he knew about the disappearance of Gregory, and exactly what Giselle knew about him.

"I don't think she knew a lot, but she could have been holding back the details from me. Our Giselle didn't miss a trick. She was always listening."

"Did she say how Karen reacted when she quit? Did she follow through on the blackmail?" asked Shirkham.

"She went ballistic, I heard, but I don't know if you she went through with the blackmail threat. If she had, I doubt Karen would have badmouthed her all over Soho in the way that she did."

They got as much as they could from Andy, which included an alarmingly good description of Gregory. It took every effort for Jacobs to remain impassive. He knew he would have to go and see Ryan and Karen as soon as possible.

Shirkham asked if he wanted to grab a coffee. He wanted to get back to the station and find an excuse to sneak away. She looked hurt when he said no, so he kissed her to allay any fears she might have. He was still interested in developing things further and knew their night together had been a big deal for her, as it had for him. She had confided in him about the breakup of her marriage which only endeared her more to him. They made plans for the following evening.

Back at the station, Jacobs wanted to check something before he disappeared for the rest of the day. He had something important he needed to take care of that afternoon. He needed to check something on the CCTV again. The guys who were working on it had gone for lunch – not really a surprise. The office-based coppers knew nothing outside of flexitime. That would make things easier, as he didn't want to explain anything until he was sure. Jacobs was able to find the DVD with relative ease and find the place he was looking for. How could he have missed it? The Tony thing still didn't make sense, but he believed he now knew who had killed Giselle and probably Becky. He quickly ejected the DVD so nobody would be able to track what he was doing, just as Shirkham appeared from around the corner.

"Do you want to go for lunch?" she asked.

She'd seen him messing with the CCTV but had hopefully missed which DVD he was working on. He didn't want her to feel compromised. He'd also made another decision which she would never understand, although he hoped she would once the case concluded.

"I need to dash off, personal matter."

"Nothing wrong I hope?"

She sounded concerned and he instantly felt guilty. He quickly looked around, stood up and then kissed her again. He was falling for her in a big way and hated lying to her.

"Just one of my sisters. Can you cover for me? Might not be back until tomorrow. Can you update the rest of the team on what Andy told us?"

"Of course, I've already started some subtle inquiries to try and find this Gregory chap, without asking directly."

"That's a good idea," he said, not meaning it.

She asked him to text her later, and with that he took off.

———

Fenton hurried into Manning's lab. They had another body and Manning had agreed to see Fenton straight away. The body had already been moved from where it was dumped. It had not initially been linked to Fenton's investigation, due to its location.

Manning, as usual, made it clear that her findings would not be confirmed until she had completed her whole report and therefore, he couldn't *hold her to anything*. It was now nine o'clock in evening. It had been a long day, even though it felt like only five minutes ago when he was briefing the team. Jack had taken off early on a personal matter, so he had left it to Gary to run the briefing. He would have a word with Jack in the morning. He knew personal matters came up, but he should have at least called or text to say he was going, rather than leave a message with a junior colleague. A junior colleague that Fenton suspected there was more than just a professional relationship going on. Something else for the Jack list tomorrow. Fenton hoped he hadn't gone off all maverick again. His phone was switched off, which wasn't a concern if he was dealing with a personal matter, yet Fenton's intuition said he was up to something else.

"Eric, you do like to keep me busy," she remarked.

"We aim to please, Ms Manning. Is there anything you can give us?"

"I've asked Deidre to join us if you don't mind. She'll be here shortly. I'm afraid this one is just as gruesome as Tony Leopold, if not worse."

"Is it true what I heard?"

"It looks that way. The genitals were removed again, but there were not stuffed down the throat until post-mortem, so he bled to death. I would say it was several minutes before he lost consciousness. Based on the horrific injuries on his body I'd say this man died in a lot of pain. The face was untouched, read into that what you will. After the victim died, he was then dumped where he was found. It was outside the Metropolitan Police jurisdiction which is why we've only just got him. I would have liked to have visited the crime scene personally, but I am meeting the lead forensic officer who attended tomorrow morning."

Deidre joined them. She looked down at the body without a flicker of being uncomfortable. Fenton wondered how many post-mortems she had been to in order to develop such a tolerance, but then remembered her work on serial killers and knew she had probably viewed some horrific crime scene photographs. She was probably immune to it by now.

"Did I miss much?" she asked.

"We were just talking through the different causes of death between the two victims," replied Manning.

"Yes, this was certainly a very personal kill," remarked Deidre.

"How do you mean?" asked Fenton.

"Well, Tony Leopold was probably a dress rehearsal, for want of a better term."

"You mean Tony wasn't a targeted victim?"

"Oh no he definitely was. It was just the killer made sure that this one died very slowly. I might be wrong. It could be that Tony was killed quicker for other reasons."

"Do you think they'll stop now?"

"With the men I am not sure, although I am certain the female victims are incomplete."

"What makes you say that?"

"Call it intuition, which I know won't help you in court. The first two were killed in quick succession and then there was a switch to men. Probably a different killer, but they are all linked. It's the killer of these men that will be harder to catch. The killer of the women shows signs that they are more erratic in the way they kill and are therefore more likely to make a mistake. If we are looking for a woman, I would almost certainly say they work at the club or have done recently. They will be that close. Your other killer is cleverer and will not be so easily detected. Your first killer will not give the other one up as they will be terrified of the consequences. That killer is immensely powerful and can dominate people with ease. It could be a man or a woman. These days it's getting harder to tell them apart."

Fenton thought she had managed to progress her theories quite rapidly from the last time she spoke with the team. A bit too rapidly for his liking. Did she know something he didn't? Had Manning shared some insights she hadn't yet told Fenton as her report wasn't ready? Deidre must have been able to read his mind as she added that since the briefing with the team, she had given a thorough review of all the evidence they had to date. She wasn't sure her theories fitted to the crimes until their latest victim had showed up.

"You think this victim knew our killer or killers?" asked Fenton

"Definitely," replied Deidre. "I would say him, and his killer were once remarkably close. It would be worth finding out what the man's orientation is, when he is identified, as that will certainly narrow the field down by half."

"What do you mean identified? It's Sid, the bloke who works on the door at Karen's Klub."

"Nice of someone to tell me," remarked Manning. "We could have had him formally identified by now."

"I'll get one of the team onto it now."

Fenton tried Jack's number. Still switched off. He then tried Brennan who answered and sounded like he was in a nightclub. After shouting down the phone trying to get Brennan to understand what he was talking about, he realised that Brennan was drunk and would be of no use in breaking the news. He thought of calling Shirkham, but she was a DC and given how hostile Karen could become, he would have to break the news himself when he finished. As if he wasn't tired enough!

"Is there anything else you want to share with me from your review of the evidence," Fenton added sarcastically.

Both women glared at him.

"No," came Deidre's reply. Her expression remaining one of fury.

Fenton had no idea why he had just said it that way. It was just that in a matter of minutes she had thrown his investigation up in the air. She also didn't follow her own rules, as she had told the team to be honest about what their intuition was telling them, when clearly, she had been holding back. He didn't believe for a second that this had all surfaced today.

He left the lab feeling irritated. With four victims in less than a week, his investigation was no closer to being solved. They didn't have a credible suspect if he was honest about it.

He realised that now was not the time to go and break the news about Sid. He wasn't in the right frame of mind to do that in a professional manner. He would use the excuse that he wanted to try and trace a family member first. He just needed to go home and rest, ready for the carnage tomorrow.

CHAPTER SEVENTEEN

Jack was sitting with Karen and Ryan in the office at Karen's Klub. He didn't like being there. He had wanted to meet somewhere neutral as he had no idea if his boss was going to show up. With it now being after midnight, he believed it was now unlikely, which is why he had insisted on meeting so late. He had checked his phone and there were several messages from Fenton asking him to get in touch urgently, apparently another body had been found – a man. He had decided not to say anything, until Karen burst into tears that she'd received a call from a woman, and she believed that Sid was dead. Jack hadn't heard that Sid was the victim and he didn't want to call Fenton to check.

"What do you want with us Jack? You know it is dangerous for us to be seen together," said Karen.

"I want to be straight with you both. I think I know who the killer is."

"Who?"

"I can't tell you that."

"Then you are not being, as you say, straight with us."

Jack couldn't tell them, as he believed the killer was in the club at that very moment and he knew Karen would immediately want to confront her, but he had to be certain before he told anyone.

"Jack, who is it? Even if you're not sure," asked Ryan. "This nutcase has possibly killed four people, all of them friends."

"That bitch Giselle was no friend of mine," added Karen.

"Be quiet, Karen. We know you didn't like Giselle, just drop it," retorted Ryan angrily.

"Who the fuck do you think you are talking to?"

"Let's stop this now before it escalates," shouted Jack. "I will not tell you who it is for two reasons. The first is that I'm not a hundred per cent sure and I don't want either of you kicking off and potentially letting on to the real killer if I am wrong. The second, and most important, is that I'm a police officer; a detective inspector and this must end now. I'll protect you all I can, but that won't be for much longer. I'm sorry but I can't keep doing this. I love my job, but the longer I keep this up the more I will love it and the harder it will be when it's taken away. I've decided to leave the police. I handed in my resignation this afternoon."

"Jack, your job meant everything to you. We would never have said anything to anyone," said Ryan.

"I know, but I can't have it hanging over my head for my entire career. It's fine, I'll find something else. I wanted you to know from me. Like I said, I will do all I can to stop the truth coming out. I need to go."

He could feel himself getting upset. He knew he would probably never see them once he left the police. It was too dangerous to go back to what they had. He'd thought about moving away as well, starting afresh somewhere and wondered if Emma would go with him. Then he dismissed that thought. She was dedicated to her career and he would have to accept that it was something else he was going to lose, but it was for the best if he just got away and started afresh. It had been the shame at his recklessness on this case, seeing Ryan and Karen again, and realising what he'd lost, and now his feelings for Emma, that had caused him to make such a drastic decision. It was his only option, as the longer he left it, the more hurt he would cause himself and others.

"Stay put Jack, I will get you a drink," Karen said, concern in her voice.

It wasn't a concern for herself. Despite her bravado, he knew that she genuinely cared for him. Her more than anyone carried the guilt the most.

———

Five years before, Jack had just been promoted to Detective Sergeant and was working in Vice. He had been tapped as one to watch. He had a great future, and his DCI, at the time, had suggested that he may want to consider the murder squad. He'd been clear that he didn't want to lose Jack, but it would be a good career move for him, if he wanted to get to the top. Jack stated that he was happy where he was and with the team; he wasn't going anywhere. Of course, Jack was ambitious, however he had other motivations for wanting to stay in Vice.

Jack idolised his mother and when she'd had to go into a home it broke his heart. She had slogged her guts out for years working in bars and clubs, being leered at by blokes and subjected to the obligatory grope from the friendly landlord. She had done this to ensure Jack and his sisters wanted for nothing. There was never a man on the scene. Jack's dad had done a disappearing act when his youngest sister was born, and they had never seen or heard from him since. Jack's mother had managed to buy her council house and had paid off her mortgage. She wanted something to leave her children and it devastated her when she was told she would have to sell her home in order to pay for her care. Jack wouldn't stand for it, so he offered to pay the fees himself. He wasn't expecting the home to cost four hundred pounds a week. He knew he should have checked the costs before making such a wild promise, but his mother had been so happy when he had made his promise that he couldn't go back on it.

He moved back into his mother's house to save money. He rented out his own flat, which covered most of the bills. He needed to top up the difference from his own wages and cover the running costs of his mother's house. That still left him short for the care home fees. That was when he met Karen Kowalski. Karen was firmly established on the sex industry circuit and her club was booming. He didn't like it at first, but he put the squeeze on her, with the promise that she wouldn't get busted. He knew that the Vice Squad weren't interested in Karen, as she was subtle and didn't tolerate drugs, or allow the street pimps anywhere near her place. However, Karen didn't know that, and she paid up five hundred pounds a week; well Jack liked to get his mother a few treats as well.

The arrangement worked well for a year. One night when Jack was doing his weekly collection, he saw his friend Ryan Killarney at the club. Ryan had set up his own gym and was struggling against the no frills chains that were popping up everywhere. He had wanted to offer something different, although he had no spare cash to advertise and bring in new revenue. He had resorted to working for Karen to boost his bank balance and get himself back in the black. Jack had been shocked to hear that Ryan had worked for Karen before, which was how he had raised the money to get the gym established in the first place.

Karen's Klub was doing phenomenally well, so Jack doubled his weekly pay off and used that to support Ryan, on the basis that he stopped whoring and make his gym a success. Karen had been fuming and at first refused, so Jack had instigated a raid. As a result, Jack seized her client list and arrested two of her girls for drugs – Becky and Giselle. He told her that he would hand over the client list and not bust her for prostituting a minor in Giselle if she paid up. She begrudgingly agreed to the extra payment, even though she insisted Giselle only lived there and Karen did not pimp out minors. The arrangement worked well for another two years. At this point Jack's mother deteriorated and it devastated him when she died. Within a week of the funeral he was back at work despite the protestations of his DCI. Jack became career obsessed and decided to take his DCI's advice and he applied for a transfer to the murder squad when he would then seek a promotion to inspector.

Jack went to see Ryan who had been incredibly supportive in the wake of his mother's death. The gym was doing well, so he understood when Jack told him that he was going to stop putting the squeeze on Karen. He was never in it for the money for himself, he just wanted to help two people he loved very much. This is when Ryan first told Jack about Gregory.

Gregory was a former doorman at Karen's Klub who had worked there when Ryan was initially establishing his gym. When Ryan had been working as a whore, Gregory had taken a shine to him and asked to buy his services. Karen had refused, as she had a strict rule that the staff were not to indulge in the merchandise themselves, whether they paid for it or not. Gregory was in his early forties and was still a very handsome man, who cut an incredible physique. He was obsessed with punishing gym routines, so he got round Karen's rule by using Ryan as a personal trainer instead. He paid double the normal rate, so he could see Ryan privately when the gym was closed. This had been before Jack was supporting Ryan financially, so when Gregory had offered Ryan a hefty tip for some extra services, Ryan had agreed, as he was desperate for money.

It was an arrangement they had both kept quiet as it was breaking so many of Karen's rules. Ryan had expected Gregory to be a brute as he had one of those, *I'll break your neck when I fuck you*, looks, although he had been surprised at how gentle the man had been and how emotional he was. He often burst into tears after sex. Not in a psychopathic way, he was genuinely a very emotional person who put on an outward confidence. Ryan should have realised that Gregory was falling for him and stepped away, yet every time he tried to put an end to it, he would offer more money. Ryan had no idea where it all came from and he never asked.

When Jack had made his offer, Ryan knew it was his excuse to get out and he ended that side of the relationship with Gregory, although he agreed to continue seeing him as his personal trainer. Gregory had been relentless in his pestering for Ryan to start their arrangement again, but Ryan kept things strictly professional for a long time, until in a moment of weakness, he slept with Gregory. However, because he had promised Jack that he wouldn't be a whore again, he had refused any money from Gregory. Unfortunately, Gregory had misread this as a sign that Ryan felt the same way about him. Ryan had made it clear that this was not the case, but Gregory would not let it go. Now Ryan was scared about what might happen, as Gregory had been following him everywhere. He had also beaten up one of Ryan's gym clients, who had made a move on Ryan. The move had been rejected; however, Gregory had seen the incident, as he used to sit in the gym watching Ryan for hours. Ryan ended their personal training sessions and terminated Gregory's gym membership, hoping that would be the end of it. Shortly after, Ryan noticed his male client list declining rapidly and despite the bullshit excuses they gave, he knew Gregory was scaring people off, so he'd become dependent for money again.

Karen and Ryan had remained friends ever since he had worked for her and she didn't begrudge him benefiting from Jack putting the hard word on her. In fact, she didn't begrudge Jack. It was going to come from somewhere and at least Jack wasn't like the arseholes some of her counterparts in other establishments had to put up with. She had also told Jack later that a grand a week hadn't been a problem for her; she earned twenty times that a night in her commissions. Business really was booming, and everyone was reaping the rewards. However, it all changed on one fateful night.

Jack had arrived when it was all over. He had walked into Karen's office unannounced, as he usually did, and was faced with Ryan in a state of undress. He had been beaten. Karen had blood splattered all over her. On the floor lay a motionless figure – Gregory.

From what Jack could piece together from Ryan and Karen, who were both in a state of shock, and from their subsequent conversations over the following days, was that Gregory had followed Ryan into Karen's office. Ryan had just stopped by to see Karen, unaware that Gregory was following him. Gregory had, once again, declared his love for Ryan. Unfortunately, Ryan had reached the end of his tether and launched into a rant at Gregory, telling him that nothing would ever happen between them, and that Gregory disgusted him.

Gregory had flown into a rage and severely beaten Ryan, before sexually assaulting him. Karen had walked in and been confronted with the full horror of what was happening and, in an impulse, had picked up something heavy and hit

Gregory hard over the head. It didn't have the desired effect, as Gregory shook it off and then flew at Karen. In her frantic attempts to fend him off, she had grabbed the first thing she saw, a pair of scissors and stabbed in the neck.

The scene was like something out of a horror film. Jack should have known then that perhaps the police wasn't the right place for him, as his first reaction wasn't to call them, it was how he was going to help his friends out of the mess. Jack had managed to calm them both, so they stopped crying and shouting. The last thing they needed was for someone to come in, so he had locked the office door.

"Karen, is there anyone here you can trust to help us with this?" Jack asked her urgently.

"Sid and Tony – I trust them with my life."

"Well you're about to. I'll go and get them. Lock the door behind me."

Jack located Sid and Tony, who were both very loyal to Karen. He briefed them on what to expect, which at first, they thought was a joke, until Jack gave them a look which made it clear that it wasn't. They handled it all remarkably well, which was good, as they were going to have be quick and efficient to hide the evidence.

Karen and Ryan both had signs they had been assaulted, but they could both have their own stories for that. If they weren't seen together until they had both healed, there should be no problems. Nobody suggested at any time that the police should be called. There was an unspoken agreement that it was not something they would even contemplate.

They worked quickly and methodically in stripping Gregory' body of all clothing and personal belongings. They were all bagged up to be burnt. The body was wrapped in multiple black plastic bags and heavy-duty duct tape. It was done so the body was sealed tightly; in effect mummifying it.

. . .

"What do we do now?" asked Karen.

They were all exhausted, but it was not over yet.

"You and Ryan will scrub this office from top to bottom. Over the next week or so, you will decorate this office, and everything will be replaced and burnt, including all the furniture," replied Jack. "Tony, Sid and I will take care of Gregory – the less you know about that, the better."

By this time, it was the early hours of the morning and Sid had washed himself up and closed the club, seeing the staff off for the night. He had made excuses for Karen, saying she wasn't feeling well. He entertained the staff with a drink, as that was the norm, and he didn't want to arouse any suspicion amongst them.

Jack, Tony and Sid had then left whilst it was still dark, using Sid's van which would be scrapped the next day. Karen would ensure Sid had a new van. They drove out of London to some chalk pits which Jack knew about. The drop on them was so huge, that even on a clear day you couldn't see the bottom. They would have to wait until daylight broke as the last thing, they wanted was the body landing on a ledge and being found before it had chance to decompose. Gregory had never spoken of family other than two younger sisters, who he never saw, and he hadn't spoken to them in years. Jack doubted he would be missed, and he knew that Gregory had no police record, so wouldn't be detected by fingerprints. Jack had checked him out when he had first heard about him harassing Ryan.

Daylight came and it was clear that it was a straight drop to the bottom. It was extremely dangerous being so close to the edge, as the side of the pit was crumbling. They managed to get the body to a part of the quarry that was sturdier and in a silent motion it was pushed off. They listened but never heard anything hitting the bottom; the pit was that deep. It was done. Next, they had to get back to London and get the place looking presentable before staff started arriving again.

In the following days, weeks and months, they barely spoke about what had happened. They made a rule that they would never all be seen together again. It was agreed that Tony would go and work for Ryan at the gym. Sid agreed to stay at the club as a doorman. He'd had enough of being a working boy, so this suited him well, and he'd always had a soft spot for Karen. Jack told Karen and Ryan that they could contact him if they needed him, however their social interactions were now at and end. Jack had never told anyone of the location of Gregory's body, and he believed Sid and Tony had stuck to their agreement.

———

She watched as Jack approached Sandra. She had known that if anyone would uncover it first, it would be him, and it looked like he was going for the glory alone, being his egotistical self. She saw him whisper in Sandra's ear and the realisation dawn on her face that perhaps the game was up. She just hoped that Sandra could hold it together long enough for her to get there.

This wasn't part of the plan, although plans change, and you had to be adaptable in these situations if you were going to survive. She saw them leave by the back entrance and knew that the best option was for her to go via the front, round the street and meet them there. As she approached the back of the club, she could hear their voices talking in a whisper.

She moved closer so she could hear them.

"Why did you do it? What did Giselle and Becky ever do to you?" asked Jack.

"I don't know what you're talking about," came the fearful reply.

"You killed them Sandra. I saw it on the CCTV. Giselle came back to Soho to see you. Why?"

"I haven't done anything Jack. I'm no killer."

"I've got the evidence Sandra and there are phone records. I just want to know why."

"Those fucking bitches were horrible to me."

It didn't take Sandra long to crack. She is pathetic.

"I know it wasn't you who killed Tony and Sid. So, who was it?"

"Sid is dead?" came Sandra's horrified response.

This is getting dangerous.

She raised the spanner and moved like lightening – slam, slam, slam!

Jack went down. She raised the spanner again, repeatedly smashing it into his skull. She had to be certain he was dead.

"Stop, just stop now," came Sandra's hysterical voice. "Oh my god, you've killed a copper, what the fuck are we gonna do?"

"I'll clean up the evidence and you go back in the club like nothing happened and wait for him to be found."

"But..."

"Just go."

"What if he told someone?"

"He won't have. Too many skeletons in the closet this one. He would have wanted to make sure you didn't know anything before he took you in."

"Know anything about what?"

"Exactly, now go back inside the club and clean yourself up. You've got blood on you, Take the backstairs, get changed, shower and then burn the clothes later."

"On my god, we can't just leave him here."

"We can and we will. We move him and we may as well

walk into the police station with the body ourselves. Now piss off before someone comes out the back."

"He said Sid was dead as well. Was that you?"

"Of course, it was me, who else would it be? Now piss off."

She watched Sandra disappear inside, hoping she could hold it together long enough for them to commit the final murder. She would need to remove what evidence she could from the scene, but she didn't have long. She could take the wrench with her. She would drop that down a grid a mile or so away once it had been cleaned.

Poor Jack. This hadn't been part of the plan, although perhaps this would escalate things nicely. Once she was clear of the scene, she had an important phone call to make.

CHAPTER EIGHTEEN

Fenton hung up the phone. He found it difficult to catch his breath. This couldn't be happening. In all his years of working on the murder squad he had never experienced something like this. His first instinct was that he had to tell the team himself as soon as possible, before they found out some other way. He had been assured that a press embargo was in force until they were ready. He'd had his ID on him, and Beeden had been and identified him. Fenton knew he was internalising his own shock to what had happened and that it would come and bite him in the arse soon, but right now his only priority was telling the team. He left without saying goodbye to his wife, something he had never done before and drove on automatic pilot to the station.

The team knew immediately that something was wrong as they had been called in so early. Fenton assembled them in the incident room and told everyone to ignore the phones. The constant ringing was making it hard for him to speak so he requested they all be silenced. He wasn't sure how he was going to tell them. He had delivered difficult messages like this to family members and friends of victims over the years. This was different. He tried to keep his voice controlled, although at times he knew it was cracking. All he could tell them was what he knew. Jack was dead and a murder investigation had been launched. It had been assigned to their investigation, as there were similarities between his death and that of Giselle Gorge and Becky Best. He had not suffered the same torturous death as Tony Leopold and Sid Verpa. Not that it changed anything; it might perhaps dull some of the shock. There would also be an internal investigation by the Independent Police Complaints Commission, as there was when any officer was killed.

There was a muttering throughout the incident room when Fenton explained that Jack's body was found at the back of Karen's Klub by Karen herself. She had been asked to provide DNA and fingerprints for elimination purposes and was said to be in a highly distressed state. Fenton was still not ruling out that she was in some way involved. He mentioned the police counselling service and encouraged them all to use it when they were ready to talk to someone, and that he wanted to see each of the team members individually throughout the morning. A full briefing would be given after lunch as the press were being held off until then. Once the news broke in the press, the pressure on the investigation would intensify. Beeden had agreed to additional officers being assigned to the case.

Fenton was sitting in his office, feeling exhausted. That had to be the hardest thing he had ever done in his life, not just his career. There was the question of informing Jack's sisters and Fenton was adamant that he do that himself, although had asked DCI Taylor if she would join him given her and

Jack had worked together for some time, and she had met his sisters, so would be a familiar face. Taylor had agreed straight away and then swiftly hung up the phone. Fenton wasn't surprised when she did that as he knew she didn't like to show any vulnerability in to others. Fenton had noticed Shirkham's face remain impassive when he had broken the news and when he looked out of his office window she was nowhere to be seen. He knew her and Jack had become close recently, although he wasn't sure how close people could become in such a short period of time. He made a mental note not to vocalise such thoughts – that would be a bad idea.

Fenton asked Brennan to find Shirkham and bring her to see him straight away. He also asked Brennan if he would be okay to accompany him to Manning's lab. She had agreed to prioritise Jack so they could have something for the press. Brennan hesitated for a second as he took in exactly what he could be faced with, then sombrely nodded his agreement.

———

Ryan still couldn't take it all in. He had been leaving the back way with Karen when they had found Jack. Karen had told Ryan to go, saying she would call the police. Seeing Jack that way was the worst thing he had ever seen, Gregory included. Not that Jack's death was more gruesome, it's just that it was Jack. Someone he had known since he was a boy and he would now never see again. He wondered if Jack's sisters knew yet and was contemplating calling them when the door opened behind, causing him to jump.

"Karen, what are you doing here?"

"The forensic people are still crawling all over the club. I cannot be alone Ryan."

She was close to tears. A side of her you rarely saw, yet lately it had been ever too frequent. Ryan was worried that she was close to the edge and may have a complete mental breakdown.

"Are they looking in the office as well?"

"They are looking everywhere. The club will not be open tonight. I have told everyone to have the night off. This could finish me, but I don't care anymore. That is how upset I am. Why would someone do this to Jack? Do you think someone knows what happened and they are taking everyone out? I mean, Tony, Sid and now Jack. The police confirmed that Sid is dead. This whole thing is so fucked up. I knew that Gregory was bad news the minute I saw him. Why I let him work at my club I will never know."

"This might have nothing to do with Gregory, and it was me who saw him behind your back. If this has anything to do with Gregory, then it's nobody's fault but mine."

"Jack would not want us to blame ourselves, or each other. We need to think. Could anyone else know about what happened?"

"I never told anyone."

"Neither did I."

"I don't think Jack would have told anyone."

"I agree, but what about Sid and Tony?"

———

ALPHABET KILLER STRIKES AGAIN
Daisy Dixon

A fourth victim has been claimed by the infamous Alphabet Killer who has stalked the streets of London for the last two weeks. The latest victim was Sid Verpa. It was been discovered that his real name was Ian Inglewright. Mr Inglewright was also a former prosti-tute, who still worked at Karen's Klub as a doorman. It is understood that his working name comes from Latin, and is the vulgar term used for penis. He was also a regular member of the gym Ryan's Retreat in Covent Garden. This is one of those trendy new gyms which claims to give their members an 'experience,' charging an astronomical fee of a hundred pounds a month. It appears that all the victims were members of this gym, with Becky Best working there, following her 'retirement' from prostitution.

New evidence has come to light for the police which shows that Becky Best was still an active prostitute and was 'working' on the night of her death. However, police have ruled this out and refuse to believe that their killer could be a client. A worker from Karen's Klub who wanted to remain anonymous tells us that there are several bisexual clients with a dark side. She says, "It's always the bisexual ones who are into the kinky stuff and like to push the boundaries."

It is understood the latest victim was mutilated in the same way as the previous male victim, Frances Fullerton, known as Tony Leopold, named so for his love of sadomasochistic practices. It appears Verpa was named in relation to his manhood, which was reportedly his only redeeming feature! "There wasn't much going upstairs for poor Sid," our source tells us. However, they add, "There was plenty going on downstairs, just ask Karen Kowalski, she used him like a sex toy." Miss Kowalski, the owner of Karen's Klub was unavailable for comment.

The police investigation seems to be going nowhere and even with a heavily boosted team the lead officer, DCI Eric Fenton, 49, has not been able to get the investigation focussed on identifying a suspect. A source close to the police reveals that although Fenton's reputation and track record are both impressive, he appears to have, "lost his mojo on," this investigation and he still refuses to have a focussed line of enquiry. He is determined to keep things open. This is despite continued assistance of top criminal psychologist, Dr Deidre Peters. She is believed to be working for the police on a pro bono basis as budget cuts show that the current Government feel that a serial killer, who has murdered four people, does not warrant every resource possible being thrown at it, to track the killer down before they strike again.

It is still believed that this killer is working through the alphabet with B (Becky Best), F (Frances Fullerton), G (Giselle Gorge) and I (Ian Inglewright). The letter E is still to be taken — perhaps now there will be a comment from Prime Minister, Edward Eves. One is assuming the twenty stone PM has no links to Karen's Klub or Ryan's Retreat, but that will be for him to comment on.

In the early hours of the morning it is believed a fifth victim was claimed by the serial killer. However, no details are yet available whilst the police wait to identify the victim and inform next of kin.

———

"Does press embargo mean nothing to that bitch?" Fenton asked Taylor, who was sitting in his office.

They had just had the unpleasant job of informing Jack's sisters of his murder. One sister had been so grief stricken she had had been taken to hospital. The other had hardly reacted at all, although they suspected it was delayed shock. They both had police liaison officers with them.

"She doesn't name anyone, so probably thinks that's okay," replied Taylor.

"No, she just has everyone thinking that the Prime Minister could be a target and that anyone who didn't come home last night who has the same initials is probably dead."

"Well it'll be all over the press about Jack this afternoon, so that will stop the agenda she is trying push. Did you get the extra officers?"

"Yes, but now with her article, how is it going to look. We bolster the ranks when one of our own is a victim. That's why she's sown the seed now. She knows about Jack, so she's just laying the groundwork ready for her next article."

"Fuck her!"

Fenton was surprised at her reaction. Taylor had never been one to hold back, although she had changed the way she openly expressed herself since she was promoted and had met her partner. He wondered which was the more calming influence; he suspected the latter.

"Are you still on leave?"

"Sort of. There are a few bits and pieces on some cases to wrap up and I need to prepare for the Superintendent exams."

"When are they?"

"In two weeks, so I doubt they'll give me anything that ain't open and shut before then."

"They're probably keeping you on standby to replace me," Fenton remarked.

Taylor flushed and then laughed, clearly trying to cover it.

"Lisa?"

"I'm in a really difficult position, Eric."

"No doubt." He couldn't believe it that he was being considered for replacement so soon. "How long do I have?"

"Now that's something I don't know."

"When was this first mentioned?"

"After Tony Leopold's murder. They felt as I was originally investigating that I was an obvious choice. Apparently, it wouldn't hurt my chances for Superintendent if I did something that was *professionally difficult*, as he put it."

"Who?"

She raised an eyebrow.

"Beeden?"

She nodded.

"There must be someone else pushing this. I've had cases drag on far longer and not been replaced. We're not even two weeks in."

"Well the body count keeps going up and now with a police officer as a victim there will be intense pressure from above. You know how the politics work Eric. It won't help that Pilkington has suggested the Prime Minister might be the next victim, especially now with Jack. The link to prostitution and that gym no longer apply in all cases."

"Jack probably found out something he shouldn't have and instead of telling the team, he ran off on his own to investigate."

"Perhaps there was something else he knew."

"Like what?"

"No idea, but he worked in Vice and dealt with Karen Kowalski a lot and I understand he was at school with Ryan Killarney, so he knew them both. The link is there, it's just not as obvious."

"Jack with to school with Killarney?"

"Yes. Didn't you know?"

"Clearly not and you found out this how?"

"Beeden, seemed to know about it."

"Nice of him to tell the investigating DCI."

"Where's Emma?" she asked, clearly trying to change the subject.

"Done a disappearing act."

"She's probably upset. Her and Jack were an item."

"It was just a one-night thing wasn't it?"

"It went deeper than that I believe."

"Well it's clear you know more about this investigation than I do. Should I just leave you to get on with it?"

"Eric?" she said, concerned.

He ignored her, stood up and stormed out of his office. He knew the powers that be were all about saving their own arse and would wait on the periphery, like vipers, ready to strike and take the credit and glory for themselves, but he never had Lisa Taylor in that box – not until today.

As he stormed out of the incident room, he hollered for Brennan to follow him. He was in a foul mood and needed to calm himself before he faced what he had to at Manning's lab.

———

Fenton and Brennan entered the lab to find Manning in a sombre mood. She didn't even mention robes, although they both took these off the peg and put them on, as if on automatic pilot. Fenton could also tell that she too had been affected by Jack's death. He didn't envy her job at the best of times. He braced himself as the sheet went back to reveal Jack. His face was barely recognisable, with Manning adding that she would do all she could before the sisters came to view him. This was something they had requested, despite there being no need as he had been formally identified by his fingerprints and by Chief Superintendent Beeden. Fenton looked to his left and saw Brennan doing all he could to hold it together. There was an urge to give him a gentle pat on the shoulder or something to show he empathised, although he knew that the slightest act of compassion might cause him to crack and Brennan was the type who would do that later – alone.

Manning asked them both to join her in her office, which Fenton quickly agreed to. She rarely let people in her office. Probably so they couldn't see the chaos and disarray, which was such a stark contrast to the spick and span laboratory. It gave an insight in to a person Fenton had known and worked with for about fifteen years, yet he knew so little about her outside of a work setting other than her relationship with Deidre Peters and her sister, Polly Pilkington. He understood from others that both their parents were dead and there was apparently a brother, although Manning had never mentioned him.

Manning confirmed that Jack had died from a severe blow

to the head with a blunt instrument, possibly a wrench or some-thing similar in structure due to the indentations in his skull. She would know more when she had completed all her tests. It appeared to have taken several blows to strike the fatal one, although it was likely he was knocked unconscious relatively quickly. Not much consolation, but at least his known suffering would have been minimal, unlike the other male victims. He was killed where he was found due to the blood distribution. The blood distribution had also revealed that more than one person was present at the time of the murder. They would have been splattered with blood. Whether they were involved in the attack or merely an observer was for the investigation to uncover. Manning just reported the facts. Additional blows to the skull happened after death and the frenzied nature of the attack indicated that Jack had probably been killed by the same person or persons as Giselle and Becky. The weapon was differ-ent, yet that may have been down to opportunity, as Jack had been killed close to the back entrance of the club, which had heavier foot flow than the locations of the other victims.

Manning told Fenton her full report would be ready by the following morning. She handed Fenton her preliminary findings on a sheet of paper. He was grateful for it, as although he was listening to what she was saying, he doubted if he would be able to recall it all to the team in the way he usually could. Manning informed Fenton that Deidre Peters was popping in as she knew Fenton was visiting and if he liked they could use her office. Fenton could really do with getting back to the team. He still had no idea where Emma was. He had received a text message from Taylor saying she had gone to try and find her, so he wasn't unduly worried. He knew he had to play the politics and Deidre Peters could be a useful ally if he was side-stepped. He thanked Manning and agreed to wait in her office until Deidre arrived. He'd told

Brennan to go back to the station knowing the guy needed some alone time. Manning went back to her work and Fenton was left alone.

He took the time to study Manning's office. The décor was plain although it was visibly different to the last time he was in here. There were more shelves than before, and they were either attached to or leaning against every available bit of wall space in the office. The shelves were overflowing with books, although unlike before they weren't all medical books. There were some historical books. There seemed to be a lot about the Henry VIII era. Perhaps she dreamed of beheading men with the frequency the former King did with his many wives? There were also some fiction novels, predominantly crime and suspense novels and a few of the more erotic kind. The books which had recently seen a boom in titillating the quiet and unassuming. Manning's desk was chaos, with trays overflowing with papers and he wondered how someone who was so meticulous and detail oriented could work like that. Well they say chaos brings about calm – he didn't know who *they* were, but he had heard it mentioned before. That he was sure of. Probably one of his daughters many phrases they'd picked up from Twitter or one of the other nonsensical social media outlets

Fenton thanked Deidre as she sat down and gave her condolences.

"I understand Jack liked to go off and investigate on his own?" Deidre asked.

"Yes, although we warned him about it enough times."

"Perhaps there is more to this than him being a police officer who got in the way."

"What do you mean?"

"Well I understand Jack was familiar with the proprietor, a Ms Karen Kowalski?"

"He knew her on a professional basis from when he worked in Vice."

"I see, and he didn't know her on any other level?"

"Not that I am aware of, but then clearly I didn't really know him."

"What makes you say that?"

"Well he also knew Ryan Killarney who owns the gym and they went to school together. I have only discovered this today."

"How does that make you feel?"

"Are you trying to psychoanalyse me?"

"Not at all Eric. It helps me to know how people tick when I work with them, so I can adapt my approach to suit them."

"You can just give it to me straight. Obviously, Jack's death has affected me, but that has to come later as we have two killers out there who now have nothing to lose as they know they are looking at a full life tariff."

"For killing an officer?"

"Of course. Jack will be regarded as a victim with higher value and unfortunately that is a view shared with society. Whores have always gotten a very raw deal. People think it's okay to treat them like shit – beat them, rape them and kill them. Then nobody will care about finding their attacker. Add in an officer and suddenly we have our team bolstered by twenty per cent. Try explaining that to the other victim's families, if they had any families who gave a shit about them."

Fenton had no idea why he was on a rant and Deidre appeared to be keeping quiet, which was no doubt deliberate. This wasn't supposed to be a therapy session for him though. It was supposed to give him some additional insight into finding the killers, so he could take something back to the team and ease their suffering a little.

"What do you think happened?" Fenton asked.

"He probably found out who the killer was and confronted them, not knowing the second killer would be waiting to pounce. Therefore, he was probably in the club before and may have been seen. More importantly he may have been seen with one of the people you are looking for. This means whoever he confronted left a clue which Jack found, so your team should look over whatever Jack was working on in the last day or so before his death."

"Or?"

"Or he knew something and was silenced, and he was always an intended victim. If I am honest, I think it is a blend of the two."

"How do you mean?"

"Jack must have known something, or he would never have gone to the club alone especially after the warnings you had given him. He was also, from what I gather, not a stupid man. This means he believed someone is involved that could be connected to him, which could be Karen Kowalski or Ryan Killarney or even both. He must have approached the person he believed to be the killer, unaware that the second killer was nearby."

It was an interesting theory and one Fenton had considered, although it was purely supposition. He would need to be straight with the team as she had been with him. He asked if she would be willing to come back with him to the station to brief the team together and she agreed straight away.

Back in his office, Fenton was informed, by Taylor, that she had found Shirkham and sent her home. Fenton had wanted to see her himself and check she was okay. Perhaps he would call in on his way home. He had a briefing to do and then there was the press conference. He had already had several calls from Pilkington. She clearly knew about Jack and wanted an exclusive. Well she would just have to wait for the press release like the rest of them. There would be no interview, despite what Beeden said. Although hopefully he was less persuadable than he was the last time Pilkington had focussed in one of Fenton's investigations.

The phone rang and Fenton picked it up without thinking.

"Eric, darlink we need to talk."

Bollocks!

"You'll need to wait for the press conference, there will be no interviews before then."

He was doing his best to sound calm and professional. There was something about this woman that just raised his hackles.

"I need to check a few facts, darlink. You know I only report the truth."

"Again, I can't comment until after the press release."

"Then we can speak after?"

"I have an investigation to run. I don't have time for interviews."

"Perhaps if you spoke to the press more darlink, you would have made some progress and not have five bodies stacked up in my sister's lab."

He knew she was trying to goad him. He wouldn't give her the satisfaction of him snapping.

"I see I am getting nowhere Eric, darlink so perhaps you can tell me just one thing. If we are to assume that DI Jack Jacobs was a victim of circumstance and opportunity from your killer, then why did he resign from the Metropolitan Police on the afternoon of his murder? Perhaps one to think about in advance of the press conference as I will be asking that question."

And with that, she hung up.

CHAPTER NINETEEN

ALPHABET KILLER MURDERS POLICE OFFICER
Daisy Dixon

The body of Detective Inspector Jack Jacobs was discovered at the back entrance to Karen's Klub in the early hours of yesterday morning. It is believed the police officer was the fifth victim of the Alphabet Killer, with the letter J now taken. In the wake of the latest murder, the investigating team have had their ranks boosted. It appears that the murder of four former prostitutes hadn't warranted extra resource initially.

The police investigation continues to meander along at a slow pace, led by DCI Eric Fenton, 49. Yesterday's press conference gave little insight into what, if any, progress had been made into the investigation. Many questions were avoided, and DCI Fenton appeared irritated at the thought of using the press to help solve this heinous crime.

It appears that all may not be as clear as it seems regarding the latest victim. The officer worked with the Vice Squad for several years and knew the Soho area well. It is also believed that he had a personal friendship with club's proprietor – Karen Kowalski. In addi-

tion, it is understood that DI Jacobs resigned from the Metropolitan Police just hours before he was killed. The investigating team are not pursuing this as a line of enquiry, which shows how woefully inept Fenton really is. In fact, sources close to the investigation have made it quite clear that it is only a matter of days until he is replaced, although by then Fenton would have probably racked up another half a dozen bodies...

———

"Emma will be off again today," Fenton told Brennan, putting down the latest article from Pilkington. He'd read enough.

"I'll re-assign her work."

He left Fenton's office looking subdued.

Fenton was worried about Brennan. The whole team had been affected, although Brennan and Shirkham were clearly affected the most. Probably as they had worked the closest with Jack. Fenton's wife had told him to take some time off as well and for the first time in their marriage he had yelled at her. It was hard to believe they had never had a row before, yet it was true. They bickered all the time, which was probably why they didn't have any big arguments. He would need to call her once he'd calmed down and apologise. He was still on edge – today was going to tough.

Fenton was also reeling for his conversation with Beeden earlier. He believed the latest Pilkington article to be libellous and wanted to raise a formal complaint to the Press Complaints Commission. Beeden had told him to let it go and to stay focussed on the investigation, to which Fenton had responded by asking Beeden if he was the high-ranking officer Pilkington was referring to. Beeden had told him to grow up and hung up the phone.

Fenton didn't know what it was about that woman that could rile him so much. Perhaps it was simply because this was now the third time, she had attempted to ruin his career by questioning his credibility as an investigating officer and she always did it openly and viciously via her newspaper articles. Therefore, his hatred of her was probably quite rational. She had disappeared to Australia when her last moral panic failed, yet here she was back again and terrifying the general public. A quarter of his team were constantly on the phones and even though most the calls were people wanting to rant at the police, confess to being the killer or to ask for the details of how they change their name by deed poll, all calls had to be recorded, logged and investigated, just on the off chance that they got a bite.

Fenton took out his notebook and tried to make sense of where they were in the investigation. The first two victims Giselle and Becky had both been killed by repeated blows to the head and the killer had used a brick. Both women were killed twenty-four hours apart and in Soho back alleys. They had both worked for Karen Kowalski and it was confirmed that Becky, despite her retirement stance would still occasionally work as a prostitute, in order to help Karen. Giselle and Becky both had links to Ryan's Retreat. Becky had worked there for the past month and Giselle was a regular client. It appeared that Giselle was not a popular person and had few, if any friends. She had spent her childhood in the care system and there had been no family to claim her body, although Andy had now come forward and formally taken over her funeral arrangements. Fenton decided that he wanted to talk to him as well.

Next, it appeared they were potentially dealing with a second killer. Someone far more sadistic and stronger as they were able to overpower Tony Leopold and Sid Verpa. No trace of drugs were found in their systems from early tests, so Fenton would ask Manning to run further checks. A puncture wound had been found in the neck of Sid, although those results could take weeks and that was something he didn't have.

The killer of the men had held them captive for a while, as their bodies showed signs of physical restraint and torture. It was possibly someone who had a hatred of men, as both victims had their genitals removed and shoved down their throats. Could both men have been in a relationship with the killer at one time? Fenton was aware that Tony had bisexual tendencies, yet Sid was only gay for pay, as in he never had sex with men unless he got paid for it. Fenton would need to speak with Karen Kowalski again to see if there was any history of them both having relationships with the same person, or possibly the same client. He knew Kowalski was hiding something, so the interview would be conducted at the station. He also wanted to speak to the men and women who worked at the club again, including those who had left once the murders started. It wasn't that he didn't trust Brennan's first enquiries, it was just that they hadn't spoken to any of them since the men had been murdered. Everyone had been interviewed to account for their whereabouts when Jack was killed of course, but Fenton had a lot more questions to ask them.

He moved on to Jack, who he believed had been murdered by both killers. It was also unplanned as they didn't use the brick or hold him somewhere first. It was obvious that Jack knew something or had identified the killer and confronted them. Why would he put himself in that sort of danger? Yes, he could be a bit maverick but surely, he wouldn't have been stupid enough to put himself at risk like that. He must have known the killer, possibly on a personal level and he either wanted to be sure before he said anything or give them a chance to hand themselves in. He also wouldn't have gone to the back of the club with just anyone. The second killer had obviously seen Jack with the first killer and then moved in from behind. Jack was a tall, strong man and his body showed no signs of a struggle, so he must have been caught unawares. The CCTV leading towards the back of the club on the street side would need to be checked. The camera at the back of the club was broken, which was convenient. They would also need to check how long it had been out of order and how close to the first murder that was.

He now moved back to the link with Ryan's Retreat, and the owner Mr Killarney, who would also need to be re-interviewed, and this time at the station as well. Getting Ryan and Karen out of their own environments could make them uneasy enough to give something away. Fenton was yanked out of his musings when the phone rang.

He yanked it up, annoyed at the intrusion, but he was then pleased he had taken the call. The missing personal trainer, Paul Johnson had walked in off the street as he had heard the police were looking for him. Fenton had forgotten about him with the chaos of the last forty-eight hours. The list of enquiries for the team was left incomplete on Fenton's desk as he made his way down to meet the unexpected visitor.

"Are you sure he doesn't want a solicitor?" Fenton whispered to Brennan outside the interview room.

"Says he hasn't done anything wrong, so why should he need one. Are you going to arrest him, Guv?"

"See what he says first. If we arrest him then he'll get no choice and we'll get him a solicitor. The charges will too be serious not to, although I've never known a serial killer just walk in off the street before."

"Good cover though innit, Guv?"

Fenton nodded and signalled for them to go in. Whilst they got themselves settled Fenton was able to take in Paul's appearance. The guy clearly looked after his body. He looked fit and tanned, albeit with an orange hue, so clearly a beach of the electric variety. His face looked haggard though, giving away a clear signal that the guy was suffering from lack of sleep. Fenton would have usually said drugs, however the guy's body defied that as a logical explanation for his appearance.

Fenton asked if he could record the interview, to which the eyes changed quickly to fear, and the chest puffed out. Paul asked if he was under arrest, to which Fenton assured him that he was just helping with enquiries, and by recording the interview they would save time, as they wouldn't need to make notes. Paul seemed to relax a little so Fenton cut to the chase and started the interview off with the right tonality – this was serious shit!

"So how was Gran Canaria?" Fenton asked, watching him closely for any reaction.

"I wasn't in Gran Canaria."

Bollocks!

"So, where have you been this past week?"

"I've been in Manchester with some friends who are helping me set up my own gym. I've got their names and phone numbers here," he said, passing over a piece of paper.

Double bollocks!

"So why did you tell everyone you were in Gran Canaria."

"It wasn't certain that I'd get the premises and I didn't want Ryan to know until it was finalised. We've worked together a long time and I felt like I was letting him down as I've got a lot of clients. It's why I chose not to set up in London, as I didn't want him to think I was taking his business away."

Triple bollocks – he's a nice guy as well!

"Did you not think to get in touch when you heard about the murders?" asked Brennan.

Good question!

"Honestly – I didn't know about them until a couple of days ago. I don't watch the news or read the paper and you know that most people outside of London don't really care what's going on in the city, so I never heard anyone talk about it."

Serial killer murders five people, one a police officer and nobody mentions it?

"I came back when I heard about Tony and then after that copper was murdered, I heard the police were looking for me so thought I'd better come in and sort all this out."

Big fat hairy bollocks!

They'd allowed Paul to leave, letting him know that they would need to check out his alibis. Fenton knew they would put him in the clear. The boxes still needed to be ticked, as the vultures were ready to attack the corpse that was Fenton's career – and he wasn't just thinking about the press. So, now what? How could so many people be killed in such a short space of time and there not be a single clue?

Deidre Peters had implied that the attacks had been frenzied and yet there was no evidence at the scenes, so the killer or killers had been methodical after their victims had been murdered. She also implied the killer who murdered the men, except for Jack, was someone who had a deep-seated hatred of men. Lesbians hated men, didn't they? He'd read it somewhere! Was he being ridiculous? It was a thought. She seemed certain that Jack was killed because he knew something, and it was done to silence him. Before Fenton had spoken to her he assumed Jack's murder had been linked to his role in Vice and perhaps he knew the killer or had stumbled across something accidentally. Deidre implied that it could be more than that and she seemed certain that there was more to it. How was she so certain unless she knew something she wasn't sharing? Why was she was so determined to get on the case that she had offered her services for free? The woman was at the top of her professional field and could command the highest fees, yet she wanted to be on this case. She was always at the lab whenever Fenton was as well. Did she want to ensure that all the evidence was gone? Was Manning in on it as well? No – that he was certain of. Manning was a lot of things but being a killer or destroying evidence was not her.

The more Fenton thought about it, the less bizarre it sounded. Should he discuss it with someone? That adrenalin rush, he had not had on this case so far, was back. He was sure there was something in it. Didn't she say that the second killer was pulling all the strings and would be extremely hard to find? It was her job to come up with theories, yet she seemed so sure of herself and that could only be because she knew that there was no evidence against her and there wouldn't be any. Fenton could prove that theory wrong, as he would find the evidence and keep it to himself until he was ready to use it. He wouldn't mentioned anything to his superiors, as they would warn him off.

He replayed the session she ran with the team in his head. Jack had been quiet in that meeting, which was unlike him. Had he picked up on something and confronted her? That could be it. The irritating thing was that it was all just supposition as well. There was not a shred of evidence to even support an arrest. He couldn't question her informally or it would tip her off. The only way he was going to find that evidence was to find the other killer and crack them in the interrogation, as the last murder had both killers present. The evidence supported that. There was a loud knock on the door, which caused Fenton to jump, given he was so deep in thought.

"Come in," he shouted.

"Guv, forensic evidence shows a partial footprint in the blood."

His pulse quickened.

"Can they identify anything?"

"It's a size thirteen."

"And?"

"Ryan Killarney is a size thirteen."

"Arrest him on suspicion of murder."

"All of them?"

"Just Jack's for now."

"Right, Guv." He left closing the door behind him.

It was all falling into place.

———

SUSPECT ARRESTED FOR ALPHABET KILLINGS
Daisy Dixon

Police made an arrest last night in relation to the five murders which have plagued the streets of London for the last fortnight. The suspect, Ryan Killarney, is the proprietor of Ryan's Retreat gym in Covent Garden. He charges over a hundred pounds per month for membership under the strapline – 'this is not a gym; it is a lifestyle.'

All victims, except for DI Jack Jacobs, were either members of the gym, or they worked there. It is known that the late police officer attended school with the suspect, and they had been friends for many years. In fact, sources close to the suspect confirm that in the early days of the gym it struggled financially, no doubt due to its exorbitant membership fees, and the club was financed by DI Jacobs. This is yet another twist to what is becoming a seedy investigation into these barbaric crimes.

The first four victims were all former prostitutes, with the women being murdered by a series of blows to the head, and then men being tortured and mutilated and left to die slow and agonising deaths. DI Jacobs is believed to have been murdered in the same manner as the female victims. His body was found at the back of Karen's Klub and it is widely known in the sex industry that Mr Killarney and Ms Kowalski are long-standing friends, with Mr Killarney once working for her as a prostitute himself.

Sources close to the police have made us aware of how the victims were all killed, and DCI Fenton still refuses to be interviewed. He refutes the belief that the links to the sex industry are merely a coincidence and that there is indeed a crazed killer on the streets of London, looking to claim twenty-six victims, one for each letter of the alphabet. The fact that police have remained silent on this, one can only assume is because there is some truth in it, and they don't want to be accused of scaremongering. It is understood that police want another victim, in the hope of uncovering some evidence, because right now, they have nothing!

Sources in the Vice Squad have revealed that DI Jacobs ran a protection racket and took over a thousand pounds a week from Karen Kowalski. It is believed that on the night of his murder he was visiting for his weekly pay out, something he still took, despite no longer being part of Vice. It is then believed that Killarney murdered DI Jack Jacobs with an accomplice – yes, the police are hunting for two killers, which means one of them is still out there!

———

"How long have we got left with Killarney?" snapped Fenton, putting the paper down, his hands shaking with anger.

"Until nine o'clock tonight, Guv," replied Brennan.

Fenton looked at his watch, it gave them thirteen hours.

"Where's Emma?" he asked.

"Still off, Guv."

"What did you want anyway?"

"Pilkington is here."

"Right, put her in one of the interview rooms and leave her there."

"I thought Chief Superintendent Beeden said you had to give her an interview."

"I know and I will. In fact, I am looking forward to it!"

"So, are we doing something else first, Guv?"

"Yes, we're going to arrest Karen Kowalski for murder."

CHAPTER TWENTY

Harriet was in the middle of a conversation yet felt totally alone. Sandra and Aerial were in full flow sitting in the club. It was the middle of the day. There was usually had a bit of passing trade; today the place was empty. Karen was stocking the bar herself as she had no bar staff left. Harriet had seen Karen attempt to move the new barman over to be a working boy. She usually did this in a slow and calculated way; a technique which had resulted in much success. He had fled, along with the other guys following Tony and Sid's murders, and who could blame them. The press banding around the word *mutilated* had done nothing to abate their fears or quell their overdramatic imaginations.

This was all Karen had left; these three girls. Karen had also lost her drive, her spunk – whatever that meant. It was a word Harriet had heard mentioned in relation to Karen. Nobody would have left Karen until recently. Now people were treating her like shit, and she was letting them get away with it, or she appeared to be. Harriet couldn't understand it. This was a woman she had admired for years. Yes, she was a ball-breaker, yet she stuck up for her staff and protected them in exchange for their loyalty. Everything had changed when Giselle was turned from the naïve girl she once was, to the horrible blood-sucking leech she became when the industry took hold of her. Harriet was worried that Karen was close to a nervous breakdown, and one of these bitches who were left would be only too happy to push her over the edge. They were clearly loving this weaker version of Karen.

Sandra and Aerial were in full flow and hadn't even noticed that Harriet had switched off from their conversation. Apparently, Mr Yatumoshi had seen them for the last few nights, and they were coining it in, whereas Harriet hadn't earned a penny. The girls also seem to have found a new best friend in the guy they had been working with. How had her life got to this? She was jealous of these little scrubbers. That was the problem with this business, you lost your soul to it and things that should be ridiculously funny suddenly weren't anymore. Harriet would describe it to people using a bathroom light switch analogy – the type with the pull cord. She would walk into the room with a client and pull the cord. Instead of turning a light off, she would turn off her emotions. On and off, repeatedly – usually more than once a night. It was initially a way of protecting herself, as she would be with the clients physically, but not emotionally. Her spirit would be somewhere else, although Harriet felt she no longer had a spirit to go to better place, it had been screwed out of her. Even if she got out now, she would never be the same again. Karen had been right in that she shouldn't stay in the business for so long, or she would never escape it in her own head. Was it too late for her? She had enough stashed away now. She had done for a while and simply kept increasing the target as the money kept coming in. This time she really wanted out and would talk to Karen. Business was bad, although Karen would hopefully understand. Sandra and Aerial may be making a fortune for the time being, but these murders had as good as killed the club. Harriet doubted Karen would ever be able to recover from this crisis, so there should be no reason for her to have an issue with Harriet walking away now.

"You okay Harriet?" Sandra asked. "You seem miles away."

"Yeah, wouldn't mind being on beach right now."

"I hear ya babes. I was just saying to Aerial that we should go on holiday with the money we made from Mr Yatumoshi."

"Will you be taking King Kong?"

"Who?"

"King Kong with the big dong. The deaf guy you were chatting about."

"Ha – oh dear Harriet, I'd give up trying to be funny babes." They both laughed at her.

"I'm going to the shop. I'll be back in a..."

Harriet stopped as she saw DCI Fenton and DS Brennan walk into the club with two uniformed officers, one of them female. It looked serious and they walked straight up to Karen. As the club was quiet, the music was low, so they could hear everything that was being said.

"What can I do for you officers?" Karen asked.

"Karen Kowalski I am arresting you for the murder of Detective Inspector Jack Jacobs, you do not have to say anything, but it may harm your defence if you do not mention when questioned something which you later rely on in court. Anything you do say may be given in evidence. Do you have anything to say?"

"Not until I have spoken with my lawyer," she spat back.

She looked angry, which escalated to boiling point with Fenton's next words, which he directed at the female officer.

"Cuff her!"

Karen was cuffed and marched out of the club. They didn't even stop to speak to anybody else. Karen shouted at them to close the club for the night and said nothing more.

"Mr Yatumoshi is coming later, what are we gonna do?" asked Aerial.

"Are you serious?" remarked Harriet. "Karen has just been arrested for murder. You can't see clients on these premises tonight. The police will probably come back later to tear the place apart again."

"We'll have to sort out a hotel. I'm not missing out on five hundred notes. Come on let's go Sandra."

Sandra was in her own world and clearly hadn't heard the instruction.

"Sandra," Aerial shouted poking her. "Let's go."

"Where?" she asked.

"I'll explain on the way. Harriet can you lock up?"

"Of course, be happy to."

She now had the perfect opportunity to put herself first.

———

Fenton was back in his office. Karen Kowalski was in consultation with her solicitor. Ryan Killarney had not requested one, however one had been appointed, given the seriousness of the offence and the fact that it involved the murder of a police officer. Fenton was taking no chances and was going by the book on this one. With Beeden and Pilkington gunning for him, he wasn't going to rush anything. He had requested a twelve-hour extension on Ryan Killarney so he could have them both in custody until the following morning. By then, he believed he would either have enough to charge them or enough to have them held in custody without charge for the maximum time."

"Who do want to interview first, Guv?" asked Brennan.

"Killarney, he'll be easier to crack."

"What about Pilkington?"

"Oh yes, I forgot about her. I'll see her first."

. . .

"Polly darling, sorry to keep you waiting," beamed Fenton, as he walked into the interview room where she had been left waiting for three hours.

"What the fuck is going on. I was told I would get an interview and I've been left waiting in this shithole all morning."

"You may have changed your name, but you've still got a potty mouth on you haven't you my girl. You're still Polly Pilkington of the gutter press," he replied, remaining cheerful.

"I don't like being pissed about Eric. If you weren't prepared to speak to me then that is fine, just don't fuck me around. Clearly this is part of you trying to assert yourself as dominant male, well bully for you. Why don't you just slap your dick on the table and growl in my face? Now if you don't mind, I have an article to write."

She made swiftly for the door, gathering up her belongings.

"So, you don't want to hear about the second person we have just arrested in connection with the murders? Okay, well off you trot then."

"Now you've got me interested." She sat down, taking out her notebook.

"We've arrested Karen Kowalski for Jack Jacob's murder."

"Just that murder. What about the others?"

"We'll be questioning her and Killarney in relation to all five murders, but at present they have both only been arrested for the murder of DI Jacobs."

"So, bugger the whores basically."

"Not at all Polly. The evidence in relation to the murder of Jack Jacobs was what prompted these arrests. You know how this works, so don't put words in my mouth."

"Will there be a full press release?"

"It will be limited until charges are brought"

"Or they are released."

"That too," he replied.

"Very well, I can see you have your hands full, so I will wait until you have made some progress. Perhaps we can talk then?"

"Yes, of course."

He was bewildered. It was like she'd had a personality transplant in front of his eyes.

"I can see myself out Eric. You do what you need to do."

And with that she was gone, leaving him flummoxed.

Fenton looked at Ryan Killarney. He looked like he'd been crying all night and hadn't had a wink of sleep. He needed a shave and you could smell his sweat, although not the type that made you gag. Ryan's solicitor looked she was about nineteen years old, yet her black wavy hair was pulled tight in a bun and her glasses aged her about ten years when she put them on. Her name was Laura Lindsay —Pilkington would have a field day with this. Fenton wondered if having the same initial for names was more common than people realised, or perhaps they were just sucked towards this case, as if it was the epicentre of chaos and doom. Ms Lindsay, as she had asked to be addressed, spoke in clear, clipped tones, like a machine gun firing. She immediately questioned the validity of the arrest. Why had a search warrant been issued, yet her client had not been offered the opportunity to witness the search. Why an extension had been granted for his being held, when the evidence presented in the disclosure was circumstantial, except for the footprint, for which her client had a perfectly legitimate explanation. She then demanded his immediate release and a retraction in the press from any infringement to his character. This would help mitigate any damage to his business. She did this all without drawing a breath and then took off her glasses and glared at Fenton and Brennan, daring them to challenge her. Fenton kept his face impassive.

"Those are all interesting points *Ms* Lindsay. We still have a number of questions to put to your client regarding five murders which have been committed in the last two weeks and he will remain in custody for as long as I see fit."

"Excuse me, DCI Fenton, my client has only been arrested for the murder of one individual, not five as you put it. He is here to answer questions on the murder of Jack Jacobs only, or have you withheld important information from your disclosure?"

"You mean the murder of *Detective Inspector*, Jack Jacobs."

He held his hand up to silence her when she tried to interrupt again.

"You are correct in that we have arrested your client for one murder. However, we believe that these murders are linked and once we ascertain your client's version of events and have had a chance to question the other suspect in relation to this case, we may have further questions to put to your client in relation to the other murders. If that is the case, then I will present you with further disclosures. Is that clear? Now let's move on, so we don't waste any more time."

"May I ask who the other suspect is you have arrested? And can you also clarify why you are continuing to hold my client if you believe someone else may have committed this murder?"

"We believe the murder of Detective Inspector Jack Jacobs was committed by two people and have arrested another suspect, Karen Kowalski, as we believe she was present with your client when the murder occurred. Which of them smashed Detective Inspector Jack Jacobs skull in, is something we intend to ascertain during this interview. Now, may we proceed, *Ms* Lindsay?"

The woman was getting right on his tits. She had been meek as a lamb during the disclosure. Fenton wondered if she was suddenly hyped up because she had taken something in the toilet when she realised the high-profile nature of the case she had landed, just by being the duty solicitor. He then dismissed this theory as lunacy. Would a solicitor really go and snort a quick line in the toilets before representing a client at interview?

"Did you say Karen had been arrested?" asked Ryan, concern in his voice.

"Yes, this morning. We'll come to that shortly Ryan. We have some other questions to put to you first, if your solicitor will permit us to begin?"

Fenton smiled, as did Ms Lindsay – with the same degree insincerity.

———

Karen Kowalski was sitting in the cell staring at the ceiling. She was scared. Someone had set her and Ryan up for Jack's murder and she had a horrible feeling that it had something to do with Gregory. Somebody knew and they had done a good job of dropping them right in the shit. Her solicitor had told her that they could prove Ryan was at the club and near the body. They must have some sort of DNA evidence, but how? They only thing he touched was the door handle and she had wiped that thoroughly and then made sure her own fingerprints were on it, so it didn't arouse suspicion if it was completely clean. She had called the police when she had found Jack. She had told Ryan to get out of there quickly. If they were seen together then they could be linked in the past. Now that link had been made. Would she now pay for what she did all those years ago? She had no idea who was doing this to her. It had to be someone close to her, but who had betrayed her? The only thing she could do was tell the truth about everything she knew about the murders. She was innocent. She would say nothing about Gregory, even with Jack dead, as she would not tarnish his memory, no matter how much they pushed her.

———

Ryan knew he had to tell the truth, everything except for Gregory. He felt a loyalty to Jack's memory and record. He also knew that Jack wouldn't want him to give himself up after all this time.

"Ryan, can you explain to me why your shoe print, which we have now been able to confirm, was found at the murder scene of Detective Inspector Jack Jacobs?" asked Fenton.

"I was with Karen when she found the body."

"Why didn't you wait for the police to arrive?"

"Karen and I agreed it could look bad if we were both there. These murders have been linked to both our businesses and it might look dodgy."

"How did you know Jack?"

"We went to school together and have been friends ever since."

"Why do you think Jack didn't tell us that he had a conflict of interest with you, yet he did with Karen Kowalski?"

"I don't know."

"So how do you know Karen Kowalski? Did you work for her?"

"Very briefly yes. It wasn't for me."

"Was this to set up your business?"

"Yes, that's correct."

"So, if you didn't do it for long then how did you get out of the financial mess you were in a few years ago. There are large sums of money going into your account, yet nothing to indicate where this came from. Where you earning this money by working as a prostitute?"

"No, it was a loan from a friend."

"Jack?"

"Yes."

"And where did he get the money from?"

"I don't know. He just said he didn't want me doing that job and that he'd give me the money. I don't know where it came from. I assumed he had savings or something."

"That doesn't make sense."

"I'm sorry."

"Well if someone gives you a loan and it's from savings then surely, they could give you this in one lump sum. This is five hundred pounds a week going into your account over two years and all cash deposits. So, where did the money come from?"

"My client has already answered the question, DCI Fenton, and I fail to see what relevance this has to the allegations you have levelled against my client. We are going around in circles, so if you have no new evidence, I suggest you release my client immediately."

Fenton wasn't perturbed. He held her gaze for a moment before turning back to eyeball Ryan. There was no need to repeat the question. Ryan knew Fenton wasn't going to give up and move on.

"Jack was an incredibly good friend for the last eighteen years and he was good man. I don't want to blight his memory."

"Where did he get the money Ryan?"

"Karen Kowalski."

———

Fenton was sitting in his office trying to assimilate all he had heard and piece it together. It was hard to hear that Pilkington was probably right about Jack being on the take. It would blight his record as an officer, and it would be unlikely that he would now be posthumously awarded for his death in service, as it would have to be reported. It was all done for fair reasons. He was helping his mother and best friend, yet it was still illegal, and it would have to go on record, especially as it had now been corroborated by Karen Kowalski. Fenton wondered if they were telling the truth and they had simply found Jack's body. It was too much of a coincidence though. There had to be more to it. Why would Jack be there? Jack had told them he was investigating the murders. None of it made much sense. Jack was clearly trying to hide something, as he had resigned from his job the day he was murdered. He had come across as an ambitious officer, so why the turnaround? Was he afraid he'd be found out for being on the take? Fenton was sure that if Jack was still alive, both Karen and Ryan wouldn't have said anything. They both seemed to genuinely care about Jack and were clearly upset by his death but wasn't letting them off the hook yet.

Fenton couldn't quite put it all together. Something was missing and his gut feeling told him that it was linked to the murders of Tony and Sid. It was late, almost ten o'clock at night and he needed some sleep. They would both be interviewed again in the morning; he would need to decide what he was going to do.

———

Sandra watched discreetly as Harriet packed up her belongings. She was clearly in a hurry. Why was she running? Did she know?

"What are you doing Harriet?" she asked, causing Harriet to spin round startled.

"What do you want Sandra? Can't you see I am busy?"

"Where are you going?"

"That is none of your business. I thought you were with Mr Yatumoshi?"

"He cancelled, so I came back and it's a good job I did. You can't leave."

"You cannot tell me what to do. You are not the boss of me. Now leave me be so I can finish what I am doing."

"You're not going anywhere," came another voice

It caused Sandra to jump, even though it was familiar to her. The coldness of the tone made her shudder.

"What are you doing here? What are you two up to?"

Harriet looked worried.

Sandra was excited.

"Sandra, what is going on? Why are you looking at me that way?"

"Grab her!"

Sandra moved quickly forcing Harriet's hands behind her back. She was frozen in fear. There might have been a chance she could shrug Sandra off, yet she didn't react quickly enough to defend herself.

"Hold her tightly Sandra. I'm going to enjoy this. I know you wanted this one for yourself, but I've got a taste for it now and I think this one deserves something a bit more dramatic than Giselle and Becky."

"It was you two? Why did you hurt Becky? She's done nothing to you."

"You see Sandra, it was like I said. Nobody gave a flying fuck about poor Giselle. Becky had to be done for the maximum effect."

"You will not get away with this."

"Oh, I think I will," she said smiling, as she pulled out a flick knife.

"What are you doing?" asked Sandra.

"Making a mess. This is the final act and it's time to get caught."

Sandra was scared. The eyes of her accomplice looked psychotic and spittle was forming at the corners of her mouth – she was literally foaming.

"I don't want to be caught," added Sandra.

"Don't be ridiculous, how can we be famous if we aren't caught?"

She moved quickly and with a very swift motion slit Harriet's throat. The amount of blood was astounding. Sandra let go and Harriet dropped on spot still gurgling. The blood spilling out of her as her heart desperately tried to pump the blood around the body. It continued to seep out onto the floor. Within seconds Sandra saw the light go out in Harriet's eyes. She didn't feel what she felt before. She was terrified – was she next?

"Sandra, if you want to run then run."

Sandra didn't wait to be told again; she fled without looking back.

―――――

Left alone she looked at Harriet's body – it was complete. If only Sandra had killed Harriet on the third night as planned, then perhaps Jack wouldn't have got so close and would still be alive. It was a shame, but necessary. Thankfully, that had not blown up the way it could have.

She looked around the room. There would be no clean up this time. It was over, and she wanted to be caught. First, she would make a phone call, effectively throwing her partner under the bus, in the hope that Sandra would crack under interrogation and give her up as well. She wanted to be caught in dramatic fashion. She was going to go down in history as the most brutal female serial killer of her generation. She would be spoken about in lecture halls in years to come and studied by students. The thought excited her. She left the room and walked down the stairs of the club. There was one more thing she had to do. She took out her phone and dialled. The number stored to memory and not in the phone.

"It's done," she said and hung up.

She brought up her call record and deleted the last number dialled. There could be no trace. The phone would now be destroyed. Her backer had served their purpose and now this was her moment. It was going to be magical. She would be famous – forever.

CHAPTER TWENTY-ONE

Fenton was sitting in his office preparing for the second round of interviews with Karen and Ryan. They were both adamant that they had nothing to do with any of the murders. What was clear, was the reputation of DI Jack Jacobs was potentially in tatters, if their revelations proved to be true. There would need to be an inquiry. It was a great shame, as it appeared it had not been done out of greed or corruption; it was to help his mother. When she had died the payments had stopped, yet Jack had given the impression that they continued to avoid anyone else putting the squeeze on Karen. Fenton knew intuitively that they were both hiding something else about Jack. It was looking more doubtful that it was his murder, yet until he was certain of that they would remain in the frame. Even if he had to release them.

Brennan was due back soon from the search of Karen's Klub. Karen had not wanted to be present for the search which would make things run a lot smoother. However, her solicitor had insisted that he was present. He was one of those overly efficient types, although he was not as eager and irritating as Ryan's solicitor. She had already phoned twice to remind Fenton that his thirty-six hours were almost up.

The search of Ryan's Retreat had elicited nothing other than the shoes which had left the print at the scene. They still had traces of blood, which made Fenton even more doubtful that this was their killer. For someone to be so methodical, to then become so sloppy didn't make any sense. However, it was believed that Jack's murder had not been planned like the others. It had been a spur of the moment decision; well according to Dr Deidre Peters that was the case. Fenton's phone rang and he could see it was Brennan. Hopefully, he was calling to say that he was on his way back...

They had searched the club area and found nothing, which included Karen's office. They had moved upstairs to the rooms the clients were entertained in, and this had also elicited nothing. It had been when they moved to the residential area where some of the staff lived that the horrific discovery had been made. A woman's body had been found with her throat cut. Her name, according to the ID found on the body was Harriet Harper. Another identical initial and a letter not yet covered off. Could Pilkington have been right? Fenton hoped she wasn't, as they already had six murders; another twenty was unimaginable.

Fenton went out to let the rest of the team know what had happened. He'd decided that based on this latest development he would have to release Ryan and Karen, yet he wanted them on police bail. He would need to clear it with the Chief Superintendent. First, he would need to inform Karen that another of her girls had been murdered.

. . .

The cell door was opened by a reluctant desk sergeant. Fenton suspected this was more about the yard of Jaffa Cakes she had left behind, rather than about permitting Fenton to bend the rules slightly.

Karen looked like shit. There was no other way to put it. The immaculate brothel madam, which is what she was, really needed sleep and makeup in order to maintain the glamorous demeanour she presented.

"Ms Kowalski, I'm afraid I have some bad news."

"Is it Harriet?" she asked, with pleading in her voice.

"We found the body of a woman at the club this morning. Her ID implies that it is Harriet, yes, but she hasn't been formally identified yet."

"I'll do it. She had nobody." Karen broke down.

Fenton hadn't planned for this response from such a hard-nosed woman. The duty sergeant looked around the corner, with four Jaffa Cakes in her hands. Fenton gave her a look which said *piss off.* He sat down on the bed next to Karen and gently rubbed her back. This made her cry more. He knew she had to get it all out if he had any hope of finding out how she knew something could have happened to Harriet. Could they finally be about to get the break in the case they so desperately needed?

Fenton arrived at Manning's lab to find Brennan was already waiting. He looked tired out. Manning waltzed in from her office snapping on her gloves. She was followed by Deidre.

"People are going to think I'm only assigned to your team, with this many bodies!" Manning said giving her girlish laugh.

"Well let's hope this is the last," he said smiling.

"I hope you don't mind Dr Peters being here for the examination. She was here when the call came in, so I asked her to wait. I thought it would save you some time, especially as she is assisting with your case."

"Not at all Ms Manning. Shall we crack on?"

Manning proceeded and walked over to the table where Harriet's body was already laid out.

"Did Karen Kowalski tell you anything, Guv?" asked Brennan.

"We'll talk later," said Fenton, eyeing Deidre with suspicion. He didn't want her hearing too much.

"How did your interviews with your suspects go DCI Fenton? I suspect this latest murder throws a spanner in the theory that they worked it together?" said Deidre.

"Perhaps, but they are still hiding something."

"What's that?" Deidre asked.

"Well if I knew then they wouldn't be hiding it would they?" he snapped.

She looked at him affronted. "Are you okay, Eric?"

"Fine, shall we proceed with the examination?"

Manning had already begun, oblivious to their conversation, or she simply didn't care and wanted to get on with her own work.

"This one is different to the other women, obviously, as she has had her throat cut, whether it is the same knife used on the male victims I am not sure, although based on the wounds they are certainly similar. Yes, Eric? You look like you have a burning question," she said eye-balling him. He knew only too well not to interrupt.

"Nothing, it can wait."

"Indeed... so, where was I? Ah, yes... she died from blood loss and it would have been quick, as in less than a minute before her heart stopped beating. There is bruising on her wrists which implies she was held roughly by one person, possibly whilst someone else slit her throat, as there are no injuries to imply she tried to defend herself, or that she touched the wound in any way. She was held so tightly that there's a potential thumb print, which we'll try to lift later."

Fenton looked down and felt dizzy. It appeared the killers had ramped things up and were now basically bat shit crazy and were just killing anyone who got in their way.

"Eric!"

He realised Manning had stopped and was trying to get his attention.

"I can see that brain of yours whirring into action. Just stay with me for a few more minutes, as the best is yet to come."

He was all ears now.

"Your killer has suddenly become very sloppy as it's not just the thumbprint. There is evidence everywhere this time. Get a suspect and I'll have no problem being able to match DNA. We'll run it through the database as soon as we've swabbed, but I won't have that for you until tomorrow and that is even if they are on there. There is so much blood it will take time and we'll have to be careful."

He paused waiting for her to continue.

"I'm done, Eric. Do you want a fanfare? Those are the facts I have to date. I'll leave you and Deidre to your supposition," she said, with a derisory snort.

"Ignore her," said Deidre, with a smile.

Fenton frequently did. He just smiled back in return. She was looking at him in a peculiar way, like she knew Fenton was distant from her. Bloody psychologists – far too intuitive, or was it a woman thing? Well here was a female psychologist who knew something was up. He needed to say something.

He summarised his thoughts about the killers, as they were now definitely looking at two and Deidre agreed with him. She had laughed at his term *bat shit crazy* and asked if she could steal it. Fenton wasn't sure how to read her, although agreed and smiled again. He felt like some inane politician, except that he hoped that when he smiled it didn't make your blood run cold in the same way it does with them. Deidre was keen to add her own take on the latest developments, so he sat down and braced himself for a long session. Brennan looked like a spare part, yet Fenton was keen that he remain with them.

"I think your killers have reached... how should I put it? They have reached their climax. This is certainly the case for the killer of Giselle and Becky, who I suspect is also Harriet's killer even if it is a different MO. They are all women working at the same club or did so until recently. Jack was not planned, but again it's the same killer. To make it easier let's call them Killer A."

Fenton felt this wasn't very appropriate given the alphabet theme Pilkington was pushing. It certainly wouldn't be the approach he used when briefing the rest of the team. Not very astute for a psychologist.

"I see the irony in using a letter instead of a number, given the press attention, but just humour me."

This woman is a mind reader!

"So killer A had a mission to kill Giselle, Becky and Harriet. They had another person involved, let's call them killer B, who was pulling the strings. I believe they were present for Harriet's murder as well as Jack's. They may have even been responsible for the fatal blow. I also wouldn't be surprised if killer B staged the scene so killer A could be caught."

"Why would they want to do that, as if we catch one, they will lead us to the other?"

"Eric, I think you are missing my point of just how powerful killer B is. Killer A will be too terrified to give the other killer up. That person has dominated all the killings even if they've not executed all of them personally. The male killings are the most sickening and brutal, involving torture and mutilation. This person killed them for very personal reasons. Have you looked into how Tony and Sid knew each other and for how long?"

"To a degree," he lied.

They hadn't even considered this and just assumed it's because they were all whores or gym freaks or both. Who the fuck was this nutcase?

"Well, I would suggest you target your team's attentions there, or you will never catch killer B."

Seems sure of herself. She also seems to doubt Fenton's interrogation skills.

"Do you think they have stopped now?" Fenton asked.

"I think killer A has completed their *mission.* Killer B remains unfulfilled. There will be others they want to see suffer. This is far more personal than for that of killer A. I'm not sure if this will mean more murders, or your killer will find other ways to enact their revenge. This is an extremely dangerous and very clever individual who will always remain one step ahead of the investigation. They genuinely believe they will never be brought justice and would probably rather die than permitting that to happen."

Fenton had heard enough and stood up just as Manning was walking back into the lab from her office carrying a tray of papers.

"Deidre Peters, I am arresting you for the murders of Tony Leopold and Sid Verpa." Now he knew what those names stood for it was almost laughable. "You don't have to say anything, however it may harm your defence when questioned if you do not mention something which you later rely on in court. Anything you do say may be taken down and given in evidence."

Stunned silence, broken only by the sound of a tray of papers hitting the floor.

CHAPTER TWENTY-TWO

ALPHABET KILLER STRIKES AGAIN - SENIOR POLICE
OFFICER SUSPENDED
Daisy Dixon

The case of the Alphabet Killer took some dramatic twists yesterday when a sixth victim was discovered. Two suspects were released without charge and the senior officer leading the investigation, DCI Eric Fenton, 49, was removed from the investigation and suspended from duty. He has been replaced by DCI Lisa Taylor, who once worked for DCI Fenton when she was of lower rank. Fenton is believed to feel "utterly betrayed" by someone he once arrogantly called his 'protégé.'

It has been reported that Fenton's replacement has been on standby for some time by Chief Superintendent Harry Beeden, who oversees all murder squads in London. Taylor had been deliberately kept off other cases ready to step in if needed, given Fenton was floundering. When Fenton arrested renowned criminal psychologist, Dr Deidre Peters for the murders, it was game over for the embattled detective. An officer assigned to the case, who wished to remain anonymous, remarked, 'The Guv has finally flipped.'

The latest victim claimed by the Alphabet Killer is Harriet Harper who was still an active prostitute. The victim was found in the staff quarters at Karen's Klub. At the time, the proprietor, Karen Kowalski was being held in police custody on suspicion of the murder of DI Jack Jacobs. Ryan Killarney of Ryan's Retreat was also being held on suspicion of the same crime. Both have subsequently been released without charge. However, there is grave concern that a third killer is involved, which has allowed the two suspects to have cast iron alibis. Only time will tell if a poor investigation has led to two brutal killers being released to claim more victims. The blood will be on DCI Fenton's hands, who will no doubt sleep soundly tonight, on his full pay suspension.

Dr Deidre Peters was released from police custody immediately and senior officials have been grovelling in the hope that they can retain her expertise on the investigation. She was unavailable for comment last night, although a close friend remarked that she was very shaken by the event and that it was obvious that Fenton needed psychological help, albeit not from Dr Peters!

The case continues to baffle police and it is understood that DCI Lisa Taylor will be expected to make arrests soon to calm the growing panic within the public of who the killer will claim next. Both Karen's Klub and Ryan's Retreat are closed for business, because all their staff have fled in terror.

———

DCI Taylor was sitting in Fenton's office, with DS Brennan reviewing the case to date. She hated stepping in. She knew Fenton would prefer it to be her if it had to be anybody. The Pilkington article was right in some sense in that she had been kept on standby as a potential replacement. For some reason multiple murders now demanded a suspect to be apprehended in a matter of hours, unlike the months and years it once took in a time long since passed. She had been given strict instructions to keep away from DCI Fenton and knew she would be being watched. She also knew Pilkington would give anything to get a scoop of them together, so she would have to avoid seeing or speaking to him for now. She was worried about him. Why had he arrested Deidre Peters? Was there something in it? She didn't believe he had *flipped his shit* as Chief Superintendent Beeden had put it.

"Do you know why Eric arrested Dr Peters?" she asked Brennan.

"No ma'am. The look on Manning's face was something pretty special though," he smiled. "She then flipped and went nuts at the Guv. He said he had evidence and would be taking her to the station immediately."

"What did Dr Peters do?"

"She was calm as anything and just asked if she could get her bag."

"What did you do?"

"Pulled me jaw off the floor and then went along with it, I mean he's the Guv."

"What happened when you got here?"

"Beeden was waiting at the desk. He ordered the Guv to follow him and told the duty sergeant to get Dr Peters a cup of tea and to take her to one of the victim suites whilst they sorted things out. Beeden kept apologising to her."

"What did Eric say?"

"That was it, he didn't argue, he just followed. I was told to go to the incident room and to keep my mouth shut."

"Then what?"

"Beeden came up about an hour later, told us all the boss was taking some personal time and that you would be taking over and we were to give you all the assistance you needed to get up to speed. He took me to one side, said Dr Peters had been released and I wasn't to mention it to anyone, although everyone knew and guessed the Guv had been forced out."

"Did you speak to Pilkington?"

"I wouldn't speak to that bitch. I know she's made out like she's quoted me but she's full of shit. I never said nothing."

She could see he was upset that she thought he would speak to the press. She didn't, yet she had to ask the question, before Beeden did.

"I know that Gary, let's hear no more of it. Can you get the team together for a briefing in about an hour? I just need to go through a few things and then I'll be ready. Has Jack's drawer been checked yet?"

"I don't think so. I think it's locked. You know how long office management take. You need to fill in about twenty fucking forms to get a paperclip."

"See if the lab has still got his property. His keys may have been on him. If not, break the bugger open. I want to make sure we've not missed anything. I also need someone to review the CCTV that Jack was looking at. Not all of it, just what was covered in the last twenty-four hours before he died. There was others working on it as well, so it should be logged somewhere. Can you get that moving? I'll see you with the rest of team at nine."

He nodded and left, leaving her to look over the case files.

She'd never led on a serial case before and this wasn't really her case, she was just the caretaker and if she could find something to justify the arrest of Dr Peters then she would. They had six victims and no clear suspect. Treating Dr Peters as the professional she was for a moment; Taylor considered her summation. They were looking for two killers. The first killer had started things by murdering Giselle and Becky within twenty-four hours of each other. The second killer had then murdered Tony and Sid a few days apart. Jack had clearly stumbled upon something or was involved in some other way, perhaps due to his past in Vice. Forensic evidence backed up the theory that he had probably met both killers, no doubt unintentionally, and paid the ultimate price. It then appeared that Harriet was attempting to flee as she had bags packed when she was found, and she had also been murdered at the hands of both killers.

They had ruled out Ryan Killarney and Karen Kowalski since they had both been in police custody when Harriet was murdered. The Pilkington article eluded to a third killer, although Taylor disregarded that as just scaremongering and a way for her to keep selling newspapers. The first suspect, Paul Johnson, the personal trainer had been in Manchester at the time of the first three killings and this had been verified by several alibis. As described in the Pilkington article, all the staff at both businesses had left. Tracing the whores would be tricky as most of them had lived in, so could now be anywhere. That was a top priority. She wanted to interview them herself. It was highly plausible that one of them was involved, potentially with a client. Getting a list of clients would be challenging, as most of them would have used an alias, and with the club closed, they would be virtually impossible to trace. They needed that DNA evidence from Manning who was still fuming over Deidre's arrest and was no longer prioritising their case. She had gone back to her, "I have to look at these in sequence," stance. She had tried to get Beeden to apply the pressure and had been told to lay off Manning. Based on the conversation with Manning earlier that morning, a night's rest had done nothing to improve her mood. Surprisingly, Deidre Peters had agreed to come in and visit Taylor. According to Beeden she was still assigned to the case if she so wanted to be. Taylor thought that after the Pilkington article had reported her arrest, she'd have told them to take a running jump, which would have been completely understandable, yet she was on her way in to discuss the case. Some people could surprise you. She had to keep an open mind and not risk getting into the same trouble as Eric!

———

Fenton sipped his cup of tea and sat back in the chair. He was visiting Emma Shirkham, so she didn't read had happened in the papers and think they whole world had gone mad around her. He was also worried that she was isolating herself too much and she would find it harder to get back to work. She had excused herself to go to the bathroom, which gave Fenton the opportunity to look around her flat. The place was different to what Fenton had imagined. Emma was always the dedicated, quiet type. Hard-working, yet not career obsessed like some of the others, which could be a good and bad thing. It was quite ugly on some – Beeden for one.

The flat was vibrantly decorated. The lounge had neutral colours except for the feature wall which was wallpapered with fuchsia pink and lime green parrots. They type you would see in a shop and wonder what lairy chav would buy that. Bizarrely it worked. There was neutral furniture with vibrant accessories. It reminded him a bit of Karen's Klub, except there was not a chandelier in sight. Emma came back in and sat down. He had never seen her out of a business suit and here she was in jogging bottoms and a baggy t-shirt, she was also devoid of any makeup, although she usually only wore a little. Her hair was pulled back in a ponytail. She was not her usual polished self.

"Sorry to hear about the suspension, sir."

"Don't worry, the rest will probably do me good."

The night before he had been fuming. Now he had calmed down, which had resulted in the best night's sleep he'd had in ages. He would just let things run their course and knew that if anyone could solve the case it'd be Lisa. He wasn't even rattled by Pilkington's latest article, in which she'd personally attacked him again. She had done this too many times now. He did wonder why her paper allowed her to print so much defamatory bullshit. Perhaps she did have sources close to the police and wondered if she had worked her way back into Beeden's pants.

"Stop worrying about me, Emma. How are you?"

"I'm okay?"

"I know it must be hard given you and Jack were seeing each other on a personal level. His death has affected the whole team, but for you I know it's so much more."

"It's not that, sir. I want to get back to work. I just need to get my head round a few things first."

"Like what?"

"Between you and me?"

"Of course," and he meant it.

"I think I'm pregnant."

Bollocks!

CHAPTER TWENTY-THREE

Shirkham had agreed to return to work and Fenton had promised to tell nobody else about her possible pregnancy. It was too early to be certain, but she was never late, and she knew it was too early to do a definitive test. She didn't know why she had been so reckless with Jack, but she couldn't think about that now.

Once she'd made the decision to go back to work, the professional in her reared its head and she remembered the CCTV footage Jack had been viewing. That would be her priority. She'd telephoned DCI Taylor to let her know she would be in later that morning, who was clearly delighted, despite doing the usual, "are you okay?" and, "if you need more time," when in reality she probably wanted to say – "thank fuck, we are literally drowning here." Although in the case of DCI Taylor, Emma knew the sentiment was genuine.

It was clear the whole team knew she'd had a fling with Jack. Is that what it was? It had certainly been brief, yet that was not the fault of either of them. However, you couldn't call it a relationship after such a short space of time. Her colleagues were welcoming, particularly Brennan who seemed delighted to see her; again, she knew this was genuine. Despite his Neanderthal nature, he did care. They had worked together a long time and he always had her back, as she did his.

She went to her desk and retrieved the CCTV footage she'd stashed away after she saw Jack last leave the office and signalled discreetly for Brennan for him to follow her into what was now Taylor's office.

"Ma'am, Jack was looking at this footage the day he died. For some reason he didn't want me to see it. I noted the number and retrieved it after he'd gone. I didn't get chance to look at it before..." she trailed off, not wanting to finish the sentence, yet knowing she didn't have to.

"Let's go and watch it," replied Taylor, standing up.

"I think he was also trying to trace Giselle's other mobile. Have we checked his desk?"

"Gary, forget office management, just break the bloody thing open and I'll take the heat. And if there are any phone records in there, do the checking straight away."

"Leave it with me ma'am."

He left looking like all his Christmas's had come at once. Men did like to break things.

Taylor excused the guys who were viewing the CCTV footage and told them to go and get a cup of coffee. She put the disc in and they both sat down. There was a sense of hope that this would give them the breakthrough they had been looking for.

The grainy footage had a time stamp of one thirty in the morning and they had to watch for a couple of minutes before they saw Giselle come into view. She was walking extremely fast towards Soho, not away from it as they had found on the other footage. They saw her meet with someone else, although their face was obscured, and they couldn't make them out.

"It's definitely a woman you can tell by the build," remarked Taylor, to which Shirkham agreed.

Was this their killer, or one of them at least? They continued to watch the footage and Giselle was gesticulating with her hands and looked like she was yelling at the other person. Suddenly Giselle moved out of the shot and you could see the other person. It was fleeting and then Giselle moved back in the way. They rewound the footage until the exact moment and then froze the screen. The image wasn't great, and it was useless them trying to identify who it was. Even if it was someone from the club, they had not met any of the girls, although someone had.

"Get Brennan in here," remarked Taylor, reading Emma's mind.

Emma made her way back to incident room and found Brennan had just managed to break into Jack's desk, although it looked like he had smashed the thing to bits. Did it really take all that to get in? There was a couple of young female officers watching with interest, so it was clear he was performing for an audience!

"Gary," he looked up. "We may have something on the CCTV. Is there anything in the drawer?"

Gary looked down and pulled out a blue file and quickly looked inside it.

"Shit, it's phone records."

They both looked at each other knowing the implications. If the phone records or CCTV footage provided a suspect, there would be serious repercussions regarding Harriet's murder, which could possibly have been avoided.

Emma and Brennan went back to the CCTV viewing station and mentioned what they had just discovered. Taylor gave a grave look and then asked Brennan to look closely at the image on screen.

"She does look familiar. She works at the club. I can't remember her name though."

"Shit, well let's get those phone records checked and if there are any incoming calls there get them straight away, as that's what I'm interested in. Emma can you do that?"

She nodded.

"Gary, we are going to play the elimination game. Go and get your notebook and bring your laptop. We'll start with the girls you interviewed that have a record."

———

The following morning, Taylor walked into the pub; not a usual activity at eight in the morning. The changes to the licensing laws had made breakfasts in a traditional pub, a popular choice. The venue didn't appear busy, which is no doubt why he'd chosen it. There was a couple of geriatrics having their early bird special for three quid and one member of staff looking incredibly bored. He looked at Taylor expectantly as she approached, scanning the pub. She saw Fenton in the corner holding up a cup and mouthing the word coffee, so she ordered two, and a bacon roll for herself before taking her seat.

"Thanks for seeing me Eric," she said as she sat down. "You look surprisingly well," and she meant it. She'd not seen him look so fresh and relaxed in a long time.

"Amazing what a couple of good night's sleep can do," he replied between mouthfuls. Clearly the suspension had not suppressed his appetite.

"I thought you'd have done your nut about the suspension, and then the latest from that bitch Pilkington. "

"Well there's little I can do about it until the powers that be decide what they want to do, and as for Pilkington I don't want to know. It will take all my restraint to do it, but I won't be reading anymore of her articles. She called the house. Unfortunately for her the wife answered, so I don't think she'll call again." He smiled, gave a faraway look, shook his head and chuckled. "What can I help you with?"

"Well I'm having second thoughts now, as I don't want to disrupt your good mood."

"I always said I'd be here to help Lisa, even when you're my boss, so spit it out, or perhaps wait until the waiter has brought the coffees. You know what you're like when the flow starts."

She still wasn't convinced by his manner. It was like he didn't care anymore and that was one of the things that made him so great, he cared about getting the right result. Now he didn't seem bothered that his career could be hanging by a thread.

They made small talk until the waiter arrived with the coffees and her bacon roll. Fenton had finished his full breakfast, so they waited whilst all that was cleared away. The waiter kept faffing about taking one thing at a time. Taylor was itching to get started and breathed an audible sigh of relief when he'd finally gone.

"Thank fuck for that, I know he's got nowt to do, but he was taking the piss a bit."

"What's happened then? Have you arrested someone?"

"Yes, we arrested Sandra Simpson in the early hours of the morning. She didn't half kick up a fuss. We got her at Gatwick. Says we've got it all wrong, demanded a solicitor and so we won't get to speak to her for a couple of hours yet."

"Sandra? She was one of the girls at the club?"

"Yeah, we found her on the CCTV meeting Giselle on the night she was killed, and Giselle's secret phone has been tracked and it was Sandra who called her and made her change direction on the night she died. Her size and body shape also are identical to whoever was stood behind Jack when he was killed. There's a lot of DNA evidence for Harriet's murder so we're hoping to get something that connects her to that one, although Manning is being difficult and says she can't prioritise us."

"Sorry about that," Fenton replied with a cheeky grin.

Something didn't seem right. She had hoped to get his interest with what she had told him, and he hadn't reacted to any of it in the way she believed he would. It was like he was now just Eric and not DCI Fenton.

"We also had two anonymous tip offs naming Sandra."

"Interesting – have you been able to identify them?"

"One was definitely a woman. They tried to disguise their voice, but the guys are still analysing the call. The other was disguised with a voice distorter, so we can't even pick out a gender.

"The other killer?"

"That's what we think, which means the other caller is someone who knew who the killer was. Anyway, Deidre is still helping with the case and has offered to help with an interview strategy."

"I'd take her up on that if I were you." He looked at her intently. "You seem surprised?"

"Well I assume you arrested her for a reason."

"Yeah because I'm going mad," he laughed. "This coffee is good don't you think?"

"Erm..."

"Lisa I'm just messing with you. The case was really getting to me and Deidre just seemed to know an awful lot. That's because she's good at what she does. Better than me, and you know what an egotistical twat I can be. The case was going nowhere, and I just snapped. Harry did the right thing. The doctor has signed me off, so I don't have to return to the case even if they change their mind, which I doubt they will. I just need a break. Maybe it's time to retire."

"You're not even fifty. You can't retire," she said incredu-
lously. "You'll be bored shitless within a month."

"Perhaps you're right," he laughed again.

She hadn't seen him laugh this much in a while and
perhaps he was right, he had simply burnt out.

"Right well, so how should I use Deidre?"

"There are two killers and it looks like you have one of
them. It all fits. They are close to the club and the other girls
and there must be a personal reason for her killing Giselle,
Becky and Harriet. It must be personal because of how they
were killed so play up to that, almost seeing Sandra as the
victim in all this, as it's the other one you want. She won't talk
if you go in on the attack. She may be too scared to give up
the other name. When you get to Jack, she may say that was
an accident, which it could have been. It was unplanned and
done on the spur of the moment. It doesn't take away what
she did. Just show her empathy and she might reveal who was
with her. Don't quiz Sandra on the men straight away, as she
will be likely to clam up. It's possible that she will have had
nothing to do with them. To accuse her of that straight away
will cause her to retreat and you won't get anything else off
her. Use the female victims to build rapport with her. Run
this all past Deidre though and see what she thinks. It helps
to have a heavy hitter behind you. Beeden will want to muscle
in, as he'll want the glory. Keep him sweet as you don't want
to fuck up your promotion. Don't let him interview any
suspects though, as he has this tendency to get people's
backs up."

"I've never seen him interview," she replied.

"No and you don't want to. Just find a way to deflect him
and using Deidre's interview strategy should help with that.
These are just a few seeds you can sow with her. She'll know
you've spoken to me as she's a shrewd woman. Tell her I'm
sorry and I'm sorting it out. Now I'm going to dash off before

someone sees us together. Don't call me again and don't worry about me."

He stood up, gently squeezed her shoulder and quickly left before she could speak. Her mouth was full of a very dry bacon roll and the only thing she had to wash it down with was her coffee which was about a million degrees, based on the amount of steam still coming off it.

She was still worried about Fenton. She knew that he was aware that he needed to get himself together. Whether that was a simple beach holiday with the wife, or some intense therapy in a Norwegian woodland, and everything in-between, she knew he would sort it out.

He had made some good suggestions and she would take his advice and talk them through with Deidre. She thought about trying to use Deidre's influence over Manning to push for a quick forensic result. Then she quickly dismissed it as a bad move. She hoped that Fenton was wrong about Beeden wanting to muscle in on the interrogation. It was for all the reasons Fenton had said, although she hadn't seen him interview first-hand, she had heard enough over the years to know there was some truth in what Fenton had said. Beeden was currently all over the case and calling for regular updates. Was it because he doubted her ability to wrap it up? He had given her an indication that she wouldn't get Superintendent first time round. Everyone she had spoken to had always failed the first time, yet this happened with a lot of DCIs as well, and she had been one of the few to sail straight through on her first try. This was why she had waited five years at this level, as she only wanted to go for it if it meant she would succeed. The thought of not getting it first time hadn't entered her mind. She needed to solve this case.

———

Ryan took in his surroundings of the secluded coffee shop. They had used old barrels as tables, which was very quirky and stylish, yet didn't work on a practical level, especially when you had two cups of coffee and then two plates of delicious salted caramel cake on them. There seemed to be more staff than was required, as the place could hold a maximum of twenty customers and yet there were five staff on duty. Despite this, they still seemed to take about three years to make a latte. The place had been decorated in warm colours, although dried herbs hung from the ceilings, for no obvious reason, and the barrel theme continued all over the walls with lids dotted around in various places. The seats were wonderfully comfortable, in fact too comfortable. You would have little hope of getting up if you were over a certain age without assistance. Perhaps that was why all the staff where there.

The place was virtually empty. There was a young South European couple in the corner. Ryan could make that assumption as they were very tactile with each other, in a natural way. It was subtle, yet clear that they were deeply in love, rather than the teenage couple next to them who believed that eating each other's face in public was acceptable social etiquette. Ryan found their behaviour abhorrent and felt it was just a way of the woman saying, "Someone thinks I am gorgeous – notice me people. NOTICE ME!" It worked, although for all the wrong reasons.

There was an elderly gent reading his paper who had an old-fashioned tobacco pipe on the table. A true English gentleman – a dying breed. Nobody under sixty seemed to have any concept of how a gentleman should present himself these days. It wasn't a skill which could be taught. It was a generational thing that was soon to be no more. There was a woman alone who was engrossed in her laptop and was wearing dark glasses. Why did people do that indoors? It was incredibly irritating, although having sunglasses on the tube was great for checking out trade in a subtle manner. Ryan always felt that people wearing dark glasses indoors were trying to hide something, or perhaps she was American, in which case her behaviour was completely normal. A tourist off the beaten track? And the final customer was Karen, who had chosen the place because it was away from their usual hangouts. She kept looking at the door every ten seconds in the belief that the police would suddenly burst in and arrest her again. In the end Ryan had insisted they swap seats so she could watch the door without turning around constantly, looking like an electrocuted whippet.

"Ryan, this is all a fucking mess. I have no business left."

"Join the club. It's easier for you to start up again. There are a million other gyms in London. There are less places to get your rocks off."

"No, it is over. No customer with the big money will come anywhere near me. There will always be whores looking for a quick buck in a safe place, but they will not be the ones I want, if I can't bring in the big spenders."

"Maybe it is time to retire?"

She burst into tears, yet nobody seemed to notice. It was London after all. You could be lying, bleeding on the street and people would walk around you and mutter under their breath, whilst absorbed in their smartphones.

"What is it?" he asked.

"There is no money. I made some bad investments. I wasn't worried, as I knew I could earn more. When I sell the lease for the club, I won't even be able to buy anywhere to live without a mortgage, which I will never get."

Ryan could sympathise. He was in the same boat. It hadn't been investments; he was just shit with money, which was why Jack had needed to bail him out. He told her this to try to ease some of her suffering, to show she wasn't alone, yet this just made her even more upset that they had both lost everything. Ryan had already considered trying again in another city. He had some friends in Sydney who might back him. He needed out of London and all its dark memories. The thought of being surrounded by pretty people with great weather all year would be a welcome distraction from the shit heap that was now his life.

"That bitch has a lot to answer for."

"Who?"

"That bitch who has been killing everyone."

"Do you know who it is?" he whispered.

"Yes. I have a fairly good idea."

"Who?" he asked urgently. He wanted to know who had ruined his life, whether intentional or not and murdered several of his friends.

"It was Sandra."

"She's a meek little lamb," said Ryan shocked.

"She is a hard-nosed bitch. You don't know her like I do."

"I still can't believe it. Could she do it all on her own? The police think there are two killers."

"I don't know who the other is, but I know that bitch is involved in this."

"How?"

"I don't want to get into the detail Ryan, especially in such a public place," she whispered.

"Are you going to tell the police?"

"I already have."

"What?"

"Don't worry. I didn't say it was me."

"And you don't think they'll recognise your voice?"

"I disguised it," she smiled.

He didn't say anything. He knew they would probably be able to do some new-fangled technology with the voice recording and work out it was her. He needed to put some distance between himself and Karen, but he couldn't go anywhere until his bail was rescinded, as the police were holding his passport.

Ryan looked at his watch, it was eleven o'clock in the morning, so he suggested they go and get something stronger to drink. They paid the twenty pounds for two coffees and two slices of cake and left for the nearest pub.

———

She watched Ryan and Karen leave and took off her glasses. Despite their whispers she had heard everything. They were right about Sandra. She had also tipped off the police but knew her voice would never be traced. Her role in all of this would remain undetected though, that she was certain of. All the loose ends were ready to be tied up and it was now just a waiting game. Karen and Ryan had lost their livelihoods, which was the revenge she wanted for Gregory. Sid and Tony were nothing, so had paid with their lives. Jack had been too nosey for his own good. She would have been happy at ending his career in the police, but he had caused that to change. Karen and Ryan could have their lives. There was no merit in killing them. Gregory may have been a bastard and probably had it coming; he was still her brother though and vengeance had been sweet.

CHAPTER TWENTY-FOUR

Taylor and Brennan were sitting in the interview room across from Sandra Simpson. Another double initial, Taylor thought. She had attitude seeping out of every pore, kissed her teeth and told Taylor she was *chatting shit* when told the potential charges. She spoke with what appeared to be a put-on accent which was a mix of cockney and Jamaican with some bizarre American twang mixed in as well. Sandra had been caught at the airport doing a runner, although she claimed to be going on holiday and was furious that she had missed her flight as she had been upgraded to first class. She wasn't aware that this was a ploy to ensure they could arrest her without causing too much of a scene. Beeden had wanted armed officers to handle the arrest, as this was someone who had potentially murdered six people. Taylor had managed to persuade him that a quiet approach would be better as the last thing they wanted was an armed raid in an airport. It wouldn't be good for politics. If he hadn't relented then she would have gone over his head, and to hell with her promotion. Beeden had called her twelve times to give his input into how the interview should be handled. She needed to keep him sweet so he didn't try to muscle in, as Taylor suspected that he would just get the suspects back up and they'd get nowhere.

Sandra had said little to the solicitor who sitting next to her. It was unfortunately the same one who had represented Ryan Killarney and insisted on butting in every five minutes as if to justify her Legal Aid salary. Taylor had remembered Fenton's description of her and had to suppress the urge to smile whenever she spoke or reacted to something.

Beeden had screamed down the phone at Taylor that Sandra had to have a solicitor present no matter what her views were. If they got a confession and then couldn't use it, Taylor would be back directing traffic. This was something she had never done, although felt it wasn't the time to correct him. Beeden said he wanted her charged with all six murders, even if some were circumstantial. They had to put the public's mind at rest. There was no question of them charging her with just the murders they believed she had committed, it had to be the lot and then he started muttering about the Home Secretary being a ball breaking she-bitch who wanted his testicles on a skewer if this arrest turned into another fuck up.

Taylor needed to focus on the job in hand, so had chosen to follow the strategy Fenton had suggested, which was later backed up by Deidre Peters. She seemed in good spirits and had asked after Fenton. This was unlike Manning who had made it quite clear that Fenton was banned from her lab for life and had started calling Taylor by her surname, which she never did with women. Still that wasn't necessarily a bad thing as the *purr* after Lisa no longer happened either.

Beeden had suggested they start on the attack and put the pictures of all the victims in front of Sandra and tell her she would be charged with all six murders unless she gave cause not to. That wasn't going to happen, and Deidre had done a fantastic job at placating Beeden for the time being. Taylor knew he was watching the interview in the viewing room, as was Deidre – thankfully! After all the ego stroking Taylor was exhausted and she hadn't even started the interrogation yet. If that was the stress at the top, she wondered if it was all worth it. Of course, it was men who just couldn't handle it very well. They internalised their emotions until they burst out like a volcano spewing out deadly and destructive vitriol making everyone else feel shit about their own inadequacies This was why women were still repressed from being at the top, as men knew they would handle the pressure far better and show them up.

"Sandra, why don't we start with you telling us about your relationship with Giselle," asked Taylor.

"What you tryin' t'say? I ain't no lezza."

It's going to be a long day!

Taylor was sitting in Fenton's office with Beeden pacing up and down in front of her. She had been interrogating Sandra for three hours and her solicitor had insisted on a break for lunch. Taylor needed a rest so willingly agreed. She could feel Beeden watching her through the camera and was dreading facing him.

"I'll replace Brennan when we go back in."

"I don't think that will be necessary, sir."

"It wasn't a request Taylor. You've got fuck all. She is running rings around you in there. Her solicitor is right, you have nothing but circumstantial evidence. You shouldn't have arrested her until you had more."

"Then she'd be clear out the country by now and we'd definitely have nothing. You authorised the arrest. As soon as forensics get back to us, we'll have some evidence to put to her."

"And when's is that going to be? Manning is fucking fuming and refuses to prioritise our case and trust me I have tried to persuade her otherwise. We need a more aggressive approach with this Sandra so we can crack her. We need a fucking confession!"

He continued to pace up and down. It was a small office, so this usually meant four steps and then turn – Taylor was feeling disorientated watching him, and she had a splitting headache.

Beeden was of average height yet had clearly been affected by the snacking aspect of a desk job and had put on a lot of weight over the last few years. He was the same age as Fenton, yet he looked a lot older. This bright red round man pacing up and down in front of her, all sweaty and irritable, could be quite comical if the situation wasn't dictating otherwise. She didn't really have a choice and would have to take him into the interrogation room, although she wanted some terms.

"Will you be leading the interview, sir?" she asked.

"Of course not, you are the lead officer in this case and therefore you will lead the interview. I am just there to support you and my rank, no doubt, will give greater emphasis to the seriousness of what has happened here."

Yeah, right! "What do we do with the interview strategy Dr Peters suggested to us?"

"Ditch it, as it isn't working. Thank fuck we don't have to pay her. Great use of taxpayers' money that would have been."

They'd hardly given it a chance Taylor thought. It remained just a thought; he stormed out of her office before she could respond. She could feel the case slipping away from them when they had made such a breakthrough. Why did people get to the top, then assume it was because they could do everything better than everyone else? There's got to be an assumption that you will have people who work for you who are better at parts of your responsibilities than you are. That was common sense, wasn't it?

Taylor introduced Chief Superintendent Harry Beeden which prompted Sandra's solicitor to start questioning why such a high-ranking office was interviewing her client when all they had was circumstantial evidence.

"I'd hardly call this circumstantial evidence," snapped Beeden, as he lay down mortuary shots of every victim.

The photo of Jack still brought a lump to Taylor's throat. Clearly Taylor wouldn't be leading on the interview; she'd sit back and let him fuck it up for himself. Either way her promotion was shot to shit. If she fought against him in the interview she'd be screwed and if she let him carry on and it all blew up in his face, she would be the one to cop the blame. That's just the way it goes. The police force was basically no different to a benign dictatorship.

"You will be charged with six counts of murder, Sandra."

"Excuse me, but I have not been informed that my client is to be charged with all these murders. DCI Taylor informed me that my client may be charged with four of the murders."

Beeden ignored her.

"Sandra, talk to me. You need to talk to someone. I will have to insist on a psychiatric evaluation of course. This isn't the behaviour of a rational person."

"Are you a qualified psychologist superintendent?" asked the solicitor.

"Chief," he spat, then turned back to the suspect ignoring her. "Sandra?"

"I ain't crazy?" she replied. She had turned the photos over. Beeden scooped them up and passed them to Taylor who stacked them back in order with Giselle on the top.

"Then talk to me, convince me, because this is some fucked up shit," Beeden said, pointing at the stack of photos.

"I ain't killed no one, I ain't done nothing and you is just trying to make me say I done something when I haven't."

"Why did you call Giselle at one thirty in the morning, which was just before she was murdered?"

"I didn't call her."

"We have your phone records that prove you did."

"I lost my phone."

"The same phone we took from you when you were arrested?"

"I found it again?"

"Well then can you explain the CCTV image DCI Taylor showed you earlier?"

"I already said that ain't me."

"We've had it matched by facial recognition technology and it is you. What were you doing with Giselle just before she was killed? There is no question it's you and your repeated denial can only suggest that you are trying to cover up the fact that you lured her into the alleyway and then murdered her. The question I want to know is why? What did she do to deserve that?"

"I didn't do nothing. Giselle was a bitch, and everyone hated her. That was why she had to leave the club cos everyone was well hating on her, and she was a slag who used to take everyone's punters. It was Karen who wanted to fuck her over. Talk to Karen, she was probably the one that done her."

"No Sandra, you done her, didn't you?"

"You is chatting shit man," she said, kissing her teeth.

"Well Becky was next, wasn't she? You were jealous of her because she was out of the business and you hated her for it. And to top it all Karen still had her come back now for the important clients. Becky had class you see. Karen didn't trust some scrubber like you to service the clients that mattered. Becky was in a different league and when she took that important punter that night, you were angry and caved her head in as well just like you did Giselle's, didn't you?"

"That Becky were a slag an all, but I ain't done nothing and you got no evidence. I want to leave now. I know my rights." She stood up.

Her solicitor told her to sit down.

"You're not going anywhere Sandra. This is six murders. You'll get a full life tariff for this. You'll never see the outside of a prison again."

"My client hasn't even been formally charged yet and you are making wild assumptions about the outcome of the trial, to which she will be pleading not guilty, and then you assume to know what sentence a judge will pass. I really must protest against this aggressive interview stance."

Ignored.

"Becky and Giselle were dead and then Harriet was your next target, but something went wrong didn't it? How does Tony fit into all this? Did he find out what you'd done? Did he have to die then? What sort of sick person cuts off a man's dick and chokes him with it?"

"I never done anything like that. That is some sick twisted shit, I had nothing to do with it and you can't prove that I did."

Taylor noticed her demeanour had changed since they had moved onto Tony. She had denied all the murders so far, yet in this instance there was something in her body language and demeanour that suggested she was possibly telling the truth. With the women her attitude was cocky and arrogant; with Tony it was fearful. Was it because she feared being charged with a murder she hadn't committed, or was it the person who had committed those murders that she was fearful of? Beeden's interview technique had fostered no confession so far, yet Sandra's non-verbal signs were giving away a lot more than before.

"What happened with Sid? Was it the same as Tony, knew too much? Or was it more personal. I see you chopped his dick off and let him bleed out instead. It must have taken him a long time to die and in absolute agonising pain. What sort of twisted pervert does something like that? What made you go that far Sandra? Did Sid reject you?"

"He was Karen's bitch. I wouldn't dirty myself on him."

"But you wanted to?"

"No babes, you're wrong there."

Taylor busied herself with the photos, having Jack's ready to bring out, if needed, as the next victim. This helped her to keep a straight face after Sandra had called Beeden *babes*.

"So, you tell me what really happened then."

"Nothing. I keep telling you, I killed nobody."

"But with Jack, it was different?"

He clicked his fingers at Taylor for the photo, much to her annoyance, and then slapped it down in front of Sandra.

She touched the photo and then Taylor was shocked to see tears in her eyes.

"Jack was a good man," Beeden said. "An officer that had a great career ahead of him."

"He was on the take," Sandra added. She had managed to pull herself back together after a minor wobble.

"I know," Beeden replied. "He still had a great career ahead of him Sandra. We all make mistakes. Jack would have bounced back from this one, no doubt. He had not had an easy life and then you took it away just when he had found some happiness."

Taylor realised that Beeden had clearly done his home-work in preparing for this interview. Just how long had he been scrutinising the case?

"We've got you at the scene of the crime Sandra, murdering a police officer in cold blood could get you a full life stretch on its own," Beeden added.

"I never did it?"

"Then who did?"

"I don't know."

"Stop lying. Who are you protecting?"

"I'm not protecting no one."

"Would it be the person who called the station to tell us you were the killer?"

Sandra was starting to crack. Taylor could feel it.

"Why wasn't I informed about this phone call?" said the solicitor, breaking the flow.

Beeden glared at her in such a way that she didn't say another word. She just started making notes.

"We had two different people call to say you were the killer. We know one was Karen Kowalski."

"That bitch don't know nothing. She was probably the one who done it."

"Well let's forget Karen's call shall we and why don't we listen to the other call. Then you can tell us what you think."

The solicitor went to speak and then decided against it, returning to her note taking. Beeden held up the recording for the video camera and then stated for the recording that he was introducing the evidence. The recording started and although Taylor had heard it dozens of times already, she was intrigued to watch Sandra's reaction again, now she was under pressure.

"I am calling about the recent murders of sex workers in London," started the distorted voice. "The person you are looking for is Sandra Simpson who works at Karen's Klub. She murdered them all, including the police officer who she smashed over the head with a spanner. She's planning more murders and she needs to be stopped."

Beeden stopped the recording. Sandra was visibly shaking. She had been fine at first, until the caller had mentioned the spanner.

"I didn't kill Jack," she muttered.

"Speak up for the tape."

"The men aren't connected."

"What do mean by that?"

"The men were killed by someone else, but I dunno who it is. I killed Giselle, Becky and Harriet."

Why is she suddenly confessing now?

"Why?"

"Harriet and I go back a long way and she fucked me over too many times. I knew when I killed the others that Harriet would be the last one and she would know who done it."

"Is that why you cut her throat instead?"

"She was doing a runner and I had to finish her. I just acted in the moment."

"And why did you kill Giselle and Becky?"

"Because they were bitches to me as well. They were always fucking horrible to me. Those bitches deserved what they got."

"What about this alphabet killer thing?"

"That's just some fucked up coincidence that journo said to sell her newspapers."

"And what about the men?" Beeden asked.

"I had nothing to do with that and I ain't saying anything else. I think I've said enough. I'd like to go to the toilet and speak with my solicitor now please."

She sat back and folded her arms making it clear that she would be saying anything else. Her solicitor looked pale; not relishing that she was about to be left alone by a woman who had just confessed to the brutal murder of three people. Taylor felt a small sense of pleasure when she left them alone in the room!

Taylor was in Fenton's office reflecting on what had happened that day. The case was now supposedly closed, yet the investigation had been run on the assumption of two killers for some time. Beeden had requested charges for Sandra on all six murders from the CPS and they had agreed. Beeden had then rushed off to deal with the press release. He had made a comment about Taylor not saying much in the interview, causing here to bite her tongue, almost in two!

There was another killer still out there and Beeden was just going to sweep it all away. Taylor didn't understand why Beeden was so eager to close the case. Surely, he wouldn't want there to be another killer walking the streets. There was a strong chance that Sandra wouldn't be convicted of all the murders at her trial, and then where would they be? Especially as it could be Jack's murder that she wasn't convicted of. Taylor thought about calling Fenton and then decided against it. This was something she'd have to work through on her own. The rest of the team had all gone home and it was almost nine at night. She'd watch the interview with Beeden and Sandra one last time. That would take her to almost midnight and then today definitely warranted a cab home.

CHAPTER TWENTY-FIVE

Aerial Adams entered the police station. It was ten o'clock at night, although she had been informed that DCI Taylor was still in the station. This was the end; her moment when fame would finally be hers. She just had to stick to the story. This was phase two of the plan; phase one was complete and had been an exhilarating journey. Taking someone else's life with your own hands was a feeling you couldn't top.

It was phase three which scared her the most; that was still to come, and she was resigned to that outcome, as that had been the agreement. That didn't stop her feeling utterly terrified. When she was asked what it was about, she calmly said she wanted to confess to the murders of Tony Leopold, Sid Verpa and Jack Jacobs. She also said she was an accessory to the murder of Harriet Harper. Sandra could be blamed for that one, as she should have killed Harriet long before and then perhaps Jack would have still been alive. The officer on the desk had looked at her like she was mad and then asked her to take a seat in the waiting area. Was that normal? She had just confessed to three murders and could quite easily have walked back out into the street. Perhaps they got a lot of this and just assumed she was a nutter. Hopefully, DCI Taylor would believe her. For Jack's murder it would be easy as she had done it herself, and Harriet of course, but she would blame that on Sandra – that way they each had three victims, so would both be classified as serial killers. Tony and Sid were quite different though. She thought she had all the information she needed to sound convincing; now it just needed to run as they'd rehearsed.

―――――

DCI Taylor was sitting at her desk when the call came through informing her that Aerial Adams was in the waiting room saying she wished to confess to three murders, one of which was DI Jack Jacobs. The duty sergeant knowing they had charged someone with all the murders assumed it was just a waste of time.

"Where is she now?"

"In the waiting room?"

"And where are you now?"

"I came into the back to make the call."

"Well you'd better hope she's still there when you go back. She's just confessed to three murders, whether you think she's a nutter or not, she should be in an interview room, so sort it and I'll be down shortly."

Should knew she had to call Beeden. The internal politics were a pain in the arse at the best of times, but she knew it was the right thing to do. Beeden was known for his early nights. Taylor held her breath as she called his mobile and was elated when the call went through to voicemail. She left a message and hoped he wouldn't pick it up until the morning. She called Brennan, who said he could be at the station in half an hour.

Taylor went to the bathroom to make sure she looked

presentable. The Sandra interrogation had been exhausting. Now, she was wide awake and ready to hear what Aerial had to say. She asked one of the uniformed officers to accompany her into the interview room, so she had a witness should Aerial say anything she later retracted.

"Miss Adams, I am Detective Chief Inspector Taylor. I understand from my colleague, that you would like to talk to me."

Aerial had stood up as Taylor and the officer walked in. She proffered her hand to Taylor, who instinctively shook it. Not usual behaviour with murder suspects. Aerial was well dressed. There was nothing spectacular about what she was wearing – jeans and a top. However, they were well fitted and styled with accessories and her makeup was flawless. She didn't look like a whore at all. She looked like someone who was going for a nice dinner with their friend, nothing too fancy, but not a burger either. Taylor wished she'd spent a bit more time in the bathroom before coming down.

Taylor asked Aerial to sit down and she sat opposite. The office stayed standing, close to the door.

"What would you like to tell me?"

"I would like to confess to the murders of Tony Leopold, Sid Verpa and Jack Jacobs. I was also an accessory to the murder of Harriet Harper."

"Do you have anything to back up your claim?"

"Shouldn't you be recording this?"

"Tell me something first that will convince me you're telling the truth and not wasting our time. Then we'll look at recording it."

"Will it be on video as well?"

Taylor noticed she looked excited at that prospect, and then knew in an instant what she was dealing with, but she still needed something from Aerial to prove she was telling the truth.

"Okay, so I cut Tony and Sid's dicks off and shoved them down their throats. I smashed Jack over the head with a spanner and I held Harriet's hands behind her back so Sandra could cut her throat. How's that for starters?"

Taylor had heard enough. She arrested Aerial for the crimes she had confessed to and said she would need to be formally booked into the station. Aerial was told her statement would be taken once her solicitor had arrived.

"I don't want a solicitor."

"Given the severity of your crimes, I must insist that you have a solicitor."

"Well as long as they hurry up. I need to do this confession tonight."

"What's the rush?"

"Get the solicitor and I'll tell you."

Taylor was also keen to wrap up the confession tonight, before Beeden could stick his nose in, so she asked the police officer to phone the duty solicitor whilst she booked Aerial into the station. She hoped by the time the solicitor arrived, Brennan would be here as well, so they could get started. She had no idea how long the confession would take.

Taylor had booked Aerial into the station and asked an officer to put her back in the interview room and get her a drink. Taylor didn't think throwing her in a cell would be helpful at this time. Once that was sorted, she was then informed that there would be no duty solicitor available until the next morning. Taylor decided to call them herself. She looked at the name. Thankfully, it was not one they had already had to deal with on this case.

"We have a suspect in custody who has confessed to three murders."

"I'm aware of that DCI Taylor, but it is eleven o'clock at night and surely you can wait until the morning so the suspect can seek proper counsel and then you can begin your interrogation."

"You do know the suspect has stated that they do not want a solicitor, don't you?"

"No, the officer did not inform me of that."

"I thought given the severity of the alleged crime it would be best if the suspect had a solicitor present."

"I completely agree."

"If I now tell the suspect that no solicitor is available and they repeat their assertion that they don't want one, then I would be quite within my right to interview the suspect."

"I'll be there in thirty minutes.

"Thought you might be!"

By the time the solicitor had arrived, spoken with his client and they were ready to start the interview, it was well after midnight.

Taylor and Brennan were sitting on one side of the table, with Aerial and her solicitor on the other. He looked like he was pushing fifty, so the fact that he was still doing legal aid cases as a duty solicitor did not say much for his credentials. He had requested again that the interview wait until the morning and that his client see a doctor first. However, Aerial had made it clear that the solicitor was there to act as a witness to her confession and it would be happening immediately. He was to say nothing and ask no questions or she would dismiss him without a second thought. This seemed to quieten him down, and he was no doubt keen for the notoriety that would come with representing her when she went to trial. Although Taylor knew that if Aerial stuck with the same solicitor's firm, a senior partner would take this case off the legal aid guy away.

Taylor began the interview by reading Aerial her rights and asked her to repeat what she had said when she arrived at the station.

"I killed Tony Leopold, Sid Verpa and Jack Jacobs."

"And?"

"I was there when Sandra killed Harriet Harper. Sandra did the others on her own."

"Why?"

"I dunno, ask Sandra."

"No, I mean why did you kill them?"

"Ah – I see. Right well I wanted to be famous and I ain't got no real talent other than screwing and being famous for that is few and far between," she laughed at her own joke. "Anyway, I thought why not become a famous serial killer. You don't get many female ones in the UK. So, I thought I'd need someone with me, and Sandra was so easy to convince. Not all there that one," she added, the last part with a whisper.

"So, these murders were just random then?"

"Please don't lead my client DCI Taylor."

"Excuse me, you were told to keep it zipped and just take notes. Don't be rude to the nice lady detective. Where was I? No, they weren't random, I thought why not kill two birds, or in this case three birds, with one stone and become famous whilst killing some people I didn't like."

Her eyes were wild with excitement and Taylor wondered if she was on something. Maye she should see a doctor. The last thing she needed was the confession to be deemed null and void, but the thought of Beeden hogging the glory again convinced her to press on.

"So, let's start with Tony. Why did you kill him?"

"Sid was the one I really wanted as I knew how much Karen would be devastated. Can't stand that fucking bitch. She was such an arsehole to me but killing her would have been too quick. I wanted to destroy her livelihood and take away the only man she ever loved. Tony was just for practice."

"Where did you kill him?"

"Some place out of the city."

"We'll need to examine it."

"You can't, I torched it."

"We'll still want to know where it is..."

"Let's move on, shall we?"

"Excuse me Miss Adams, but I am one leading this interview."

"Do you want your confession or not," she spat. "Look I killed Tony by cutting his dick off and sticking it down his throat and watched him choke. With Sid I did the same, but I realised that Tony had been too quick, so I let Sid bleed out instead. He took a long time to die, it got quite fucking boring actually."

Taylor couldn't believe how she was describing the murders, as if they were some inconvenience, she had to tolerate in order to become famous.

"Shall we move onto Jack?"

"I have further questions on the others first."

"Yeah, I'm getting a bit bored now. Can we move on to Jack or not? I need to get my beauty sleep before my court appearance tomorrow. I can't be looking like shit in front of all the cameras."

"You won't be going to court tomorrow."

"And why the fuck not?"

"The CPS have to agree to you being formally charged. That won't happen tonight."

"Oh, for fuck sake. Will I be in court the next day?"

"Almost certainly."

"Brilliant – now shall we talk about Jack. Sorry about that, I know he was your mate..."

Her tone didn't reply she was sorry. The woman was clearly unhinged, and Taylor thought it best to call it a night and continue the next day, so she could plan for the interview properly. This wouldn't be a straight-forward confession, so she had to do it right, no matter if Beeden got involved or not.

She was about to adjourn the interview when Brennan spoke.

"What did Jack ever do to you?" he asked Aerial.

"He was too nosey for his own good that was all. He was on to Sandra and we weren't ready. Harriet was still alive. If Sandra had stuck to the plan and killed her on day three then I'd have probably let Jack arrest her."

"No other reason?"

"Not at all, I mean it's no consolation I'm sure, but he was just in the wrong place at the wrong time. He had pulled Sandra into the alley at the back of the club, so I went out the front and walked round the back of the club. I heard them talking. He wanted to know why she had killed Giselle and Becky. Sandra couldn't really hold it together. She wasn't the best choice of accomplice, but she was nutty enough to do as she was told and believe that she was the one in control. I knew he was gonna take her in and I had this spanner with me in case any clients get a bit lairy. I just smashed him on the back of the head, and he dropped like a sack of shit. I had to keep hitting him to make sure he was dead. His skull made this crunching sound, I lost count of the amount of times I hit him, but I had to make sure he was dead. Stupid twat, should have kept his nose out of everyone's business."

Brennan looked like he wanted to dive across the table and throttle her. The solicitor looked like he wanted to be sick. Taylor just felt nothing but contempt for a woman who had destroyed so many lives, just to be famous. Unfortunately, she was going to get what she wanted. A prostitute being the murderer for a change, and one of her victims a copper – the press would love to hate her, meaning she would get her headlines.

Taylor had heard enough for one evening. There were a lot more questions to ask, as she knew she wasn't getting the full story, but she had enough to hold her and seek charges in the morning. It was almost two o'clock and she just wanted her bed.

The next day Beeden seemed irritated by the latest events. He wasn't interested in being part of any more interviews and said he felt Taylor was more than capable of taking a statement from someone who was confessing. Taylor said nothing, another moment of biting her tongue. She longed for the day when she would be his peer, or even better his boss, and she could tell him exactly what she thought of him.

Taylor spent six hours taking Aerial's confession. She still couldn't get any detail on the murder locations for Tony and Sid. In fact, for those murders, Aerial was not as detailed in her descriptions. It was like she was reading a script and there were times when Taylor wondered if she was responsible. Could there be someone else? A mastermind behind it all? Aerial implied she was the mastermind, but Taylor wasn't convinced that she had the intelligence to take that role. She acted on emotional triggers and was not rationale enough to have killed Tony and Sid, as that had required patience, something Aerial didn't have.

There was no doubt that Aerial had killed Jack, as she was much more detailed, and her description of the murder matched the forensic evidence. The same was said for Harriet's murder, although Taylor suspected it had been Aerial who had slit her throat and Sandra who had been the accessory. Hopefully, forensics would provide some clues when Manning got around to their case! Aerial kept repeating the same mantra: they had both killed three people each, so they were both famous serial killers. That's all she seemed to care about.

When Taylor had raised the prospect that there could be someone else involved, Beeden had told her to let it go, wrap up the confession and charge both Aerial and Sandra with all six murders. He said it was now up to the jury to work out the whole sordid mess.

Three weeks later Taylor got the call. Aerial Adams and Sandra Simpson had both been remanded into custody and were both awaiting trial at Holloway Prison. Why they were in the same prison, let alone on the same wing was a question that would need answering.

Aerial had taken a razor blade, from god knows where, and slit Sandra's throat killing her within seconds. She had then cut her own throat and was dead by the time the prions officers and medical staff had arrived. Before taking her own life, Aerial had used Sandra's blood to daub two words on the wall... *Social Justice*

EPILOGUE

ALPHABET KILLERS CLAIM THEIR FINAL VICTIMS
Polly Pilkington

Sandra Simpson and Aerial Adams died in a suicide pact in Holloway Prison putting an end to their murderous rampage and claiming two new letters as their final act of defiance. In the end the final piece of the puzzle was solved by Aerial Adams walking in off the street and confessing. The police were convinced that Sandra Simpson was enough to close the case, despite the investigation focussing on two killers for some time.

The suspension of DCI Eric Fenton, 49 was lifted once charges were made, although he is said to be taking some 'personal time'. It is understood that the suspension being rescinded was at the request of Dr Deidre Peters who has confirmed that she will not make a formal complaint against her wrongful arrest. However, it is expected that Dr Peters will benefit from her services being used by the police on future cases, charging her usual fees!

Detective Chief Superintendent Harry Beeden had to come to the rescue to save DCI Taylor from floundering in the interrogation of Sandra Simpson. When questioned about this DCS Beeden insisted it was a "team effort," whilst DCI Lisa Taylor responded with a string of obscenities followed by 'no comment.' It would appear she is channelling the same disrespect for the press as her former mentor, DCI Fenton.

The delayed funeral of murdered police officer DI Jack Jacobs takes place today, amidst tight security. It will be a private affair with family, close friends and colleagues the only ones in attendance. Perhaps his death may have been thwarted had the investigation been led by DCS Beeden from the start. DCS Beeden is understood to be under consideration for the position of Commander, with a decision due imminently. DCI Taylor is believed to have withdrawn her application for promotion to Superintendent, citing personal reasons. It appears that DCS Beeden has his work cut out for him with the personal problems of all his officers, although at least thanks to him our streets are now safe again.

———

Polly Pilkington read the article with a feeling of intense satisfaction, especially seeing her own name back in print. She had a large glass of Chablis in the other hand, as she walked around her Camden loft. The place had been gutted following her return as the tenants had left it as a complete shithole. Her other place out of the city had been okay as a stop gap; it had certainly served its purpose these last few weeks.

She stroked a photograph on the mantelpiece and then stood back, looking at the picture of the handsome man beaming at the camera. She raised her glass to toast.

"To you, my darling brother Gregory, may you now rest in peace!"

FREE BOOK!

NOTE FROM THE AUTHOR

Thank you for reading my book – I hope you enjoyed it!

I cannot thank the family, friends, peers, and professionals enough for helping to make the DCI Fenton Murder Trilogy a reality. However, the biggest thank you must go to all the readers of my books. Without your support, I would never have pushed through the procrastination and self-doubt to finish the series and make this dream of becoming a published author a reality.

If you enjoyed this book, then please consider leaving a review on the online bookstore you purchased it, or anywhere else that readers visit. The most important part of how well a book sells is how well it is endorsed by other readers. Even a line or two would be incredibly helpful. Thank you in advance to anyone who does.

If you would like to find out about my other books, and read my short stories then please visit my website:

www.nicklennonbarrett.com

ALSO BY NICK LENNON-BARRETT

Murder for Political Correctness

Murder for Social Media

Printed in Poland
by Amazon Fulfillment
Poland Sp. z o.o., Wrocław

61972267R00167